WELCOME TO THE DUNGEON

It is a fog where time twists minds and voices call out from a swallowing darkness.

It is a jungle in which finned creatures dwell and torment all that pass through its vines.

It is a maze whose tunnels trap the daring and whose creatures challenge the brave.

It is a chamber in which proportions are lost and fortitude is one's only weapon.

From the veldt of the dinosaurs to the gates of Tawn, this is the quest of Clive Folliot, explorer and hero.

Philip José Farmer's

The Dungeon

Book 3

The Valley of Thunder

Charles de Lint

iBooks
Habent Sua Fata Libelli

iBooks

THE VALLEY OF THUNDER

Special thanks to Lou Aronica, Shawna McCarthy, Richard Curtis, David M. Harris, and Mary Higgins.

Cover and interior art by Robert Gould.
Book and cover design by Alex Jay / Studio J.

THE DUNGEON is a trademark of Byron Preiss Visual Publications, Inc.

ISBN 978-1-59687-609-5

February 2017

iBooks are published by iBooks, an imprint of J. Boylston & Company, Publishers
Manhanset House, Dering Harbor, New York 11965 •www.ibooksinc.com•

for
Philip José Farmer

because
I can think of no better
opportunity than my work
on this project
to thank him for
all the years of reading pleasure
that he's given me

Table of Contents

Foreword

Nightmares . . .

The "nightmare" comes from the Middle English *nihtmare*, meaning *night demon*. When I was young, I thought that the word derived from female horses that galloped into your sleep with eyes flashing fire, with unhorselike teeth sharp as a tiger's, with flaring nostrils spurting poisonous gases and hooves ringed with spikes. Their monstrous whinnying was echoed in my fear-filled and desperate cries for help just as I awoke.

But even the Land of Nod has its pleasant beings, and these were the enjoyable dreams. Though I always awoke during a nightmare, I sometimes also awoke after the "good" dreams. Whether they were enjoyable or terrifying, if they were easily analyzable, I would go back to sleep soon. If the nightmares were not transparently understandable—nightmares and dreams are nocturnal semaphores—I would spend some time trying to probe their origins before going back to sleep. Most of the time, I was too tired to spend much effort on them, but would remind myself to think about them during the daytime.

Dreams and nightmares are many, but I think I've had at least one that I could remember in each week of my life. Of course, I've forgotten many of these. But, counting the period when I was an infant, at least three thousand six hundred forty dreams, interspersed with nightmares, have spurted out of my unconscious. I only logged a few, and only the most striking can be summoned up from that wild data file called the memory.

Dreams/nightmares have inspired me to write stories. One, for instance, was a short tale titled, "Sail On! Sail On!" This is about Columbus's first (and last) voyage in an alternate universe. In this, Earth is both flat and the center of the universe. And Roger Bacon, the thirteenth-century English Franciscan and proponent of experimental science, has not been persecuted by the Church as he was in our universe. Instead, he founded the Baconian order of monks. Thus, when Columbus sets out on the Atlantic to look for a new route to the Orient, his flagship has a radio shack on its poop deck and inside it is a friar operating a simple spark-gap radio.

This story was derived from a dream in which I saw a galleon sent out by Prince Henry the Navigator, of Portugal. The galleon had a shack and a friar as described above. His messages were in Latin.

The transition from the dream-Prince Henry to the otherworld Columbus was done, of course, by my conscious mind.

But the dream that inspired the short story, "The Sliced-Crosswise-Only-On-Tuesday-World," seems to have no rational connection with the story I developed from it. In the dream, I wandered through a tropical jungle (many of my dreams take place there) and came out into a clearing. This was occupied by bamboo and grass huts, in the doorways of which stood natives. Their skins were chalk white, and they had large dark rings of fatigue around their eyes. They were motionless, their faces were rigid, and their eyes seemed dead.

I've never figured out just how I went from that dream to the concept of the short story and the resulting *Dayworld* trilogy. But that came to me the next day as I was going over the dream.

In any event, I have, like some people, had serial dreams, or perhaps I should say a dream series. The adventures started in the first dream were continued in another dream, and then on to three to five dreams. There was no pattern in the time gap between the dreams. Sometimes, the sequel occurred the next day; sometimes, a week or even two weeks later. Unfortunately, I never completed any of the series. I was like the kid who watched Saturday afternoon serials in the movie theaters of my younger days and then was prevented from seeing the final chapter. I was frustrated.

Two stick in my memory, and I may use them as the bases for stories someday. One serial dream was about a band of Vikings who had invaded the underground kingdom of dwarfs or trolls to grab the gold of these subterranean beings. (The dwarf king had some resemblance to the Gnome King of Oz. In Baum's books, not in the second Oz movie.) The Vikings had to fight their way in and out and run a gauntlet of ingenious traps.

The other dream was really fever-inspired. I was in high school when I got one of those diseases so common in the 1930s. I don't remember what it was. But I was lying in bed and hot with fever, half out of my head. The Shadow, a.k.a. Lamont Cranston, was somehow in another world and was being pursued through a jungle by a large band of beings who seemed only partly human. He was not armed with his usual pair of .45 automatic handguns. He had only a bow and a quiverful of arrows. Finally, after shooting many of his hunters, he took refuge in a cave halfway up the face of a mountain. The enemy toiled up the steep slope. Thwang! Thwang! At least six of them were struck. Six enemies of The Shadow, a vicar of The Good, bit the hard rock and tumbled down into the poisonous green jungle below.

The above took place as a serial within three days. I don't remember how many episodes there were, but there must have been at least six or seven. Their rapidity in occurring was doubtless inspired by the fever.

The above leads into the *Dungeon* series and volume III, the book at hand, *The Valley of Thunder*. This title is evocative of the spirit of my writings. As I said in previous forewords, this series springs from the spirit, or one of the spirits, of my fiction. It does not derive from, nor is it a spinoff of, any specific story of mine. It embodies the Geist, the Psyche, incorporated in my fantasy and science fiction adventure tales.

Thus, it is a nightmare. And, at times, it certainly seems fever-inspired.

But, unlike the nightmares I've had, its mysteries, and there are many, will eventually be explained. Also unlike my terrifying dreams, it will have a satisfactory and definitive conclusion. No cliff-hangings in the sixth and final book of the *Dungeon* series. Richard Lupoff, who wrote volume I, will write volume VI. He will come up with the answers and rousing climax. I am sure of that, though I have no more idea than you of how the series will end.

At the moment our hero, Clive Folliot, and his grab-bag companions are fighting in another universe for survival. They hope they will be able to solve the mystery of the forces behind this sinister world. They are halfway through *their* ordeal (though they do not know this), and it seems that things cannot get worse. But they do.

In this respect, the Dungeon world resembles our Earth. We Terrestrials really do not know why we were born on this planet, or who made it, or toward what goal, if any, we are struggling. We have many theories (religions and philosophies) to explain the whys and hows and toward-whats. None is truly illuminating or truly satisfying. Not, at least, to many people. It's all opinion, without any facts to back up the opinions. Even those who reject the religions and philosophies do so on the basis of opinion, which derives from the personal set of mind and the conditioning of the individual.

Opinions are just so many firecrackers. They make a light and a noise in the darkness and then are gone. However, every day on Earth is the Fourth of July of opinions, and the unceasing supply of firecrackers makes a lot of light and noise on this world.

Firecrackers are real. Opinions are real. All thoughts are real, however momentary they may be. And fiction is as real as Reality. Fiction is part of Reality.

No one can successfully deny that fiction is just as real and as event-causing as politics and religion and hemorrhoids and headaches and stubbing your toe and slamming your car into a telephone pole. Fiction exists, and the thoughts and emotional reactions you have while reading it have an effect on you. It varies according to the story and the individual reader's reactions. Some of us are powerfully affected by a certain story, and it sticks like glue in us.

The effects are the results of electrochemical impulses, which are reactions to the fiction we read. These impulses are real because they do exist, and they bring into existence permanent things such as books, movies, buildings, paintings, music—all artifacts, in fact, and institutions and mores and changes in mores.

The thoughts you have while reading this series may result in something as real and hard as an Easter Island stone face.

The thoughts and speech of Bronze Age and Early Iron Age people were evanescent. But they made weapons and tools and buildings because of these thoughts and conversations. Some of these survive. They also, in Greece, resulted in the eventual writing down of Homer's *The Iliad* and *The Odyssey*. These have had a great impact. I know they did on me. They have influenced my writing more than my reading of pulp-magazine stories, though I am not disparaging *their* effect. As a result, my being influenced by Homer has influenced others, and they write stories which, you might say, come thousandth-hand from

Homer. Who got his stuff through centuries of sieving from many others.

Then there is the Bible. I read much of that when I was a child and a juvenile, and still read it now and then. That had a powerful impact on me, yet it originally was born from a series of electrochemical impulses in the minds of a series of men of the Bronze and Iron Ages. Finally, it became "real," a book. It, though partly fiction, has been tremendously influential for both good and evil. I am a student of history and biography, and deduce from these that the Bible has been, on the whole, used more for evil than good. But then, everything has its potentiality for evil or for good. Almost everything, I hasten to say.

Dante's *Inferno* derives from the Bible and his own hatred of certain people. It has not, I believe, influenced anybody in the religious sense, but it certainly has made concrete the vision of Hell. This vision has stirred electrochemical impulses in the brains of many, chiefly preachers and writers. Many, many sermons and much written fiction have resulted from this. In several senses, the *Dungeon* series owes some of its geography and population to Dante.

In a previous foreword, I likened the *Dungeon* world to Hell. The main difference between these two worlds, however, is very significant. In Dante, Hell was the be-all and end-all for its citizens. They will suffer forever, and their characters will not change for better or worse. In the *Dungeon* world, despite all its horrors, optimism flames brightly. Our hero and his colleagues will suffer, but their characters may change for the better.

In this respect (and, of course, in many others), the *Dungeon* world resembles my Riverworld. And our own Earth.

—Philip José Farmer

Chapter 1

The world was a flare of azure, riddled with sparks.

When Major Clive Folliot's party entered the gateway, the ground fell away underfoot as though it had never existed. A rushing sound filled their ears. Nausea struck, brought on by vertigo, but there was no sensation of falling. They simply floated in a limbo of blue, all the world a cloudless sky, so bright to view it hurt the eye. Every blink of an eyelid set up a new scattering of sparks and woke tears that burned the retina, momentarily clearing the vision until the blue glare struck again.

Have we died? Clive wondered.

His limbs flailed helplessly through the blue that felt too dense to be air. Breathing was a labored process. His stomach was in his throat. Shafts of neuralgic pain lanced through his head with each blink of his eyes.

Have we come so far only to die?

For this void seemed very much like death. Were Chambers and Darwin and those other atheist evolutionists correct? We came from nothing, climbing some damned evolutionary ladder, and we return to nothing. No God. No Heaven. Though perhaps this was Hell. Not fire and brimstone, nor the Purgatory that they had so recently quit on the last level, but a limbo of blue so painful it would drive a man insane.

Clive's hands clenched into fists, nails biting into his palms, knuckles whitening with the pressure.

Damn you, Neville. From the moment we shared the world I've been cursed to walk in your shadow. Must I now die in that same shadow?

The other members of his party were merely dark blots in his vision. He cried out to them, but the thick air wouldn't carry his voice. It rasped its way down his throat, leeching all moisture from its drying membrane. His chest ached, lungs hyperventilating as they tried to draw in sufficient oxygen, but succeeding only in creating an abnormal loss of carbon dioxide in his blood.

His vision began to cloud—not from the pain of the azure glare, but through lack of that simple substance upon which all men depend to survive.

Air.

Like a dark cloud, unconsciousness came roiling across the horizons of his pain. The glare was almost gone—pinprick sparks sprayed at the edge of the darkness.

So this is death, Clive thought.

It was not so bad. He could almost welcome the comfort it offered from the pain. It would be so easy to simply let go, to put away the responsibilities he had taken upon himself, to leave off the struggle, to let others beat their heads against the endless walls of the bloody Dungeon while he simply let go. . . .

But that wasn't his way.

Though he had to work harder than his twin at whatever he undertook, he wasn't one to quit, no matter what the odds against him were.

Not even if you were offered your heart's desire?

Clive frowned at the unfamiliar voice that interrupted his reverie—

And realized that the blue was gone.

He stood in a place devoid of color or light. He could breathe once more. There was a firm surface underfoot. A light breeze touched his cheek, tickling the hairs of his mustache. A faint scent of cloves was in the air. On his tongue lay the sharp bite of anise.

"Who spoke?" he asked.

He turned slowly, careful of his footing. Under his boots the floor was as smooth as polished marble.

The voice, he realized, had not spoken aloud. Rather, it had sounded only in his mind—a telepathic communication such as Shriek utilized. But it hadn't been Shriek's voice.

There came a whispering sound—like that of a curtain being lowered.

"Who's there?" he cried. "Where are you?"

To his right, he saw a lightening of the darkness. Where all around him was the black of a sealed tomb, there the air grayed with promise.

The scent of cloves faded. The sharp taste remained in his mouth, though it too was lessening with each passing moment.

He took a step toward the grayness. Another.

Like the last gateway, the air was thick here, but he could navigate through it. It was like walking through a thin gauze, the darkness clinging to his face like cobwebs, but he made his way through it, brushing at the dark with his hands until he came at last to the gray area.

At first, he could see nothing through its wash of fog. He put a hand out and touched a membranous wall that gave outward as he pressed against it. The fog began to clear, and Clive's eyes widened with astonishment.

He was looking into a very familiar apartment. Briefly, the voice he had heard earlier echoed again in his mind.

Your heart's desire.

The room he looked into was lit by an oil lamp. Standing at the window, overlooking Plantagenet Court, was a woman. The lamplight cast her in shadow, but not so much that Clive couldn't recognize the slope of her shoulders, the coils of her hair, the neat trimness of her figure.

Your heart's desire.

By all that was holy. Somehow, he had been given a window into the London quarters of his lover, Annabella Leighton. The leagues separating London from Africa, or from wherever this damnable Dungeon lay, had been set aside to gain him this momentary view.

He called out to her, but she made no response.

He pushed harder at the membrane that held him back. It stretched, but would not give way.

He cursed the Dungeonmasters for giving him this much—but no more—and pushed harder.

One moment his hand was filmed by the pressure of the invisible barrier holding him back, then it gave through. He stepped eagerly forward, pushing his face and chest against its clinging surface, tugging at it with his other hand. Slowly—so slowly—the wall gave way.

And he was inside.

He stood, disbelieving, in Annabella's room. Looking back, he could see no sign of where he'd entered. When he studied the room, it appeared no different from how it had been the night he'd taken his leave of her—too many months ago. It was as though all his time in the Dungeon had never been.

Lord help him, had it all been a dream?

Or was he being given a second chance? If he didn't take ship this time—if he remained in London instead and, poor though they'd be, married Annabella—could he undo all the pains he had left behind him when he'd taken the *Empress* and sailed away?

Clive frowned. But if his brother was still missing, his return to London did not negate his responsibilities. He would simply have to leave again. . . .

But how could he? Knowing what he knew now, how could he leave Annabella a second time? Surely it would be a worse crime to desert her when he *knew* what his leaving would mean to her?

And then there were his companions. Had they been left behind to carry on by themselves, or had each of them been given this opportunity as well?

He regarded Annabella. He could see no trace of her pregnancy from this perspective. Perhaps she didn't show yet. Perhaps she was still unaware that she carried their child. . . .

She turned then, that familiar smile on her features. But she wore no look of surprise at his sudden appearance, Clive noted. It was as though he'd never left.

She shook her head, a teasing look in her eyes.

"Are you ready to rise now, sleepyhead?" she asked.

"I . . ."

The sound of her voice tore at his heart. Her features, her smile, the cornflower blue of her eyes. . . .

He reached toward her, but she shook her head.

"Not again, my love. If you don't dress soon, we'll be late for the celebration—and that would never do. George would never forgive you."

Celebration? Clive thought. What in God's name was going on? How could she be so calm? She truly acted as though he'd never left— as though all he'd been through had been no more than some nightmarish dream.

He looked more closely at her, finally registering how she was clad. She wore an evening dress, the bodice cut low, the skirt wide. Her shoulders were powdered, her hair done up in coils that glistened in the light cast by the oil lamp on the dresser.

A celebration.

"But afterward," Annabella went on, "when we return, we will salute your new commission privately until neither of us has the strength left to move."

The promise in her eyes made Clive ache to hold her. But he concentrated on the odd things that she said. His new commission. A celebration.

Again, that echo came to him.

Your heart's desire.

Wasn't this what he had always wanted? To be able to take her for his wife, the two of them making their own life together, and to the devil with his father and twin, to the devil with her teaching?

He looked down at himself. He stood naked by her bed. Beside him, the bedclothes were rumpled.

You have just experienced a long and troubling dream, he told himself. There can be no other explanation.

He had never shipped on the *Empress* in search of Neville, never been trapped in that hellish Dungeon. . . . Of course. It made sense. The whole experience had held a nightmarish quality.

But it had seemed so real. And there was still . . .

He looked at Annabella. "My brother . . ." he began.

She laughed. "No need to worry about him—he hasn't been invited."

Clive sat down upon the bed and rubbed at his face. Immediately concerned, Annabella hurried to his side. She knelt by the bed where he sat. The hoops of her skirt made it difficult for her to embrace him, so she took his hands in hers.

"Clive—what is it?"

"I . . . I have had the strangest experience," he said slowly. "I . . ." He looked up to meet her steady gaze. "I can't remember anything about this celebration or a new commission. I dreamed I went to Africa in search of Neville and was trapped in an enormous mazelike Dungeon."

"Should we call the doctor?" Annabella asked.

Her worry was plain.

Clive shook his head. "No. Physically, I am well. I'm just . . . confused."

"We can cancel the party at the club. I'll send word to George that we won't be able to attend."

Clive gave her a rueful look. "You say he's organized the party for me?"

Annabella nodded.

"Then it's as you said a moment ago: He'd never forgive me if we didn't go."

The longer he spoke to her, the more easily he found himself slipping back into his old life. The Dungeon grew more and more like a bad dream.

"You said my brother wasn't invited," Clive said. "But, he's safe?"

Annabella blinked. "Of course he's safe! It's been over a month since his return and, by all your accounts, he's recovered enough to have returned to his old methods of dealing with you."

Anger flashed in her eyes as she spoke of his twin.

"And I never sailed to Africa?"

Her anger faded, replaced with laughter. "Oh, Clive! You're just teasing me—aren't you?"

Clive looked around the room, then settled his gaze on her. He squeezed her hands.

If the Dungeon had been a dream, then it was over and done with. He could put it from his mind. But if this was the dream, he'd be damned if he'd let it go.

"You've caught me out," he told her.

Shaking her head, Annabella rose gracefully to her feet. With quick, deft movements, she adjusted the fall of her skirt.

"Up!" she told him. "Your uniform's pressed and hanging on the door of the closet for you. I'll give you until the count of ten to be ready to leave. If you're not done by then, I'll find another escort." She gave him a broad wink. "One . . . two . . . three . . ."

Clive rose quickly from the bed. The uniform, the scarlet tunic and dark trousers of the Imperial Horse Guard—hung where Annabella had said it was, but it wasn't a major's. Rather, it was that of a leftenant-colonel.

He rose from the bed and crossed to where the uniform hung to finger the cloth of the tunic.

Lord help him. He no longer knew what was real and what wasn't.

"Seven . . . eight . . ." Annabella counted.

Shaking his head, Clive hurriedly began to dress.

Chapter 2

They took a cab from Plantagenet Court to du Maurier's club—a somewhat bohemian establishment, as George readily admitted, frequented by artists and writers, but at least it permitted ladies in its bar.

A London fog made the heavy traffic move even slower than was usual for this time of the evening, but Clive didn't mind it at all. He soaked in his surroundings, relishing everything he laid his gaze upon—the confusion of cabs and foot traffic, the vendors and hawkers still peddling their wares to the theater and restaurant crowds. From the squalor of the slums to the homes of the wealthy, Clive saw all the familiar sights as though through new eyes.

He had never thought to see London again, yet here he rode through her gaslit streets, Annabella at his side, a celebration in the offing.

Lord, could a man ask for more?

When they finally reached the club, Clive disembarked and handed his companion down to the cobble-stoned street. He paid the cab and, offering Annabella his arm, moved toward the entranceway, which was guarded by a uniformed footman. Before they could reach the steps, however, a tattered beggar shuffled quickly from the shadows, cap in hand.

"Here!" the footman cried. "Off with you!"

"Please, gov'nor," the beggar said, keeping his attention on Clive. "Won't you help me, good sir?"

Annabella shrank against Clive's side. Ordinarily, Clive would have sent the man off as quickly as the footman was attempting to, but something in the beggar's features caught his attention. There was a certain familiarity hidden behind the grime that streaked the man's face.

"A minute," Clive said.

He left Annabella standing with the footman and stepped closer to the beggar, peering more closely at him.

"Do I know you?" he asked.

The beggar shook his head. "I'm nobody, gov'nor. Nobody a fine gent such as your own self'd be knowing." Normally, this was true. Clive had never been one given to holding conversation with beggars and the like. But his time in the Dungeon had taught him that looks could very easily be deceiving. And there was that nagging sense of familiarity. . . .

"Just a shilling—if you can spare it, gov'nor," the beggar went on.

He held out a hand even dirtier than his face. A rank smell rose from the man—a combination of unwashed body and stale beer.

"What's your name, man?" Clive asked.

The fog was turning to a light drizzle as he spoke to the wretch.

"Clive!" Annabella called.

Clive nodded in her direction, but didn't turn.

"Your name?" he repeated.

The beggar took a step back, a frightened look crossing his features.

"I didn't mean you no harm, gov'nor," he said. "Don't be calling the law on poor Tom."

With that he turned and bolted. Clive took a step after him, then paused and let him go.

Tom. Those features. . . .

"Clive," Annabella said again.

She left the stairs and joined him on the street. When Clive turned his attention to her, he knew from the look in her eyes that she was worried about him again. He shrugged and gave her a quick smile.

"I had the oddest feeling that I knew that man," he said. "Absolute nonsense, of course."

Taking Annabella's arm, he led her up the stairs and past the footman, who kept his features carefully neutral. The footman opened the door for them and they stepped into the club.

"You're beginning to worry me," Annabella told him, once they were inside. "First, you play at losing your memory, and now, you seem set upon gallivanting about the streets with beggars."

"I thought it might be someone from the old regiment," Clive told her, "fallen upon hard times. All men aren't so fortunate as I am."

Obviously referring to her, that earned him a smile.

In the foyer a servant took her wrap and Clive's military cap, then, they went in to where George waited for them. A huge fire burned in the hearth, taking away the damp chill of the night air and fog outside. George rose from his chair with a welcoming smile and outstretched hand.

"I was about to give up on you," he said. "Our dinner reservations are for eight, but we still have time for a drink, if you like."

Clive glanced at Annabella. When she nodded, he ordered two glasses of sherry from the waiter, who stood nearby.

"George?" Clive asked.

His friend lifted his own glass, still half full, and shook his head.

"Just the two glasses, then," Clive told the waiter.

"So," George said once Clive and Annabella were seated, "have you set the date yet?"

Date?

Luckily, Clive thought the question rather than blurting it aloud as he'd been about to, for when he saw Annabella blush and lower her eyes, he realized immediately what George was referring to—their wedding. The real question now was, *had* they set a date? Annabella would think him a complete boor for not remembering, if they had.

He glanced at her, but found no answer in her features. He cleared his throat.

"Ah . . ." he began, and was rescued by the arrival of the waiter with their sherries.

"To your prosperity!" George cried, lifting his glass. "May you always be rich in health and know joy in each other's company." Before Clive and Annabella could clink their glasses against his, George added with a wink, "And a promotion certainly doesn't hurt, either, now does it?"

"To us," Clive said, touching his glass against the others, his gaze resting on Annabella.

"To us," Annabella said. She smiled warmly at him, then turned her gaze to George. "And to the best friend a young couple could have—bohemian or not!"

Laughing, they toasted each other and drank.

And then a cold thought knifed through Clive's mind.

The beggar.

Tom.

He had it now. The man bore an uncanny resemblance to the Portuguese sailor Tomàs, whom he had left behind in the Dungeon with his other companions. As a beggar here in London, he'd had a cockney accent, true enough, but the resemblance was so profound that Clive couldn't believe it mere coincidence.

Except the Dungeon was just a dream.

He was free from it now. He had awakened from the chains of sleep with the blessed relief of knowing it had all been but a dream—a nightmare, to put it mildly, but a fantasy nonetheless.

The Dungeon wasn't real. It was that simple.

But he remembered that voice again.

Your heart's desire.

If the whole thing had been but a delusion, then why did it *seem* so real?

"Clive?"

He blinked to find George and Annabella regarding him worriedly. He stood up from his chair.

"A . . . a momentary . . . dizziness," he said. "I need some air."

Before either could protest, he was walking away, back to the entrance. When he stepped outside, the footman turned to him. The man's smile took on a sudden wariness.

Clive had been about to ask after the beggar, but seeing that look on the footman's face, he realized just how foolish he was being.

"Did you . . . ah . . . happen to see a glove?" Clive asked.

The footman shook his head. "No, sir. Perhaps you left it in your cab?"

"My cab?" Clive repeated.

Get a grip on yourself, man, he told himself.

"Of course," he said with a quick smile that he was sure seemed as artificial as it felt. "The cab. Thank you."

He reentered the club before the footman had a chance to speak further. In the foyer, he smiled at the servant who came to collect his hat. The man appeared confused when he realized that he had already done so moments before.

"I just took a breath of air," Clive told him. "Lovely night."

To be sure, he thought. Fog and drizzle. Well, dammit, after months in the Dungeon—dream or not—it was a *wonderful* night.

He fled the servant's confusion to rejoin his companions. George arose immediately upon spotting him and met him halfway across the room. He took Clive by the arm and peered into his face, plainly concerned.

"Clive, are you ill?"

Clive shook his head.

"Only Annabella's been telling me you've seemed out of sorts ever since you woke from a nap earlier this evening."

"Nerves," Clive assured him. "It's not often a man gets promoted and engaged, all at once, as it were."

The reasonableness of the explanation was readily accepted. George studied him a moment longer, then gave his arm a squeeze and led him back to the hearth where Annabella waited.

"All's well, my love," Clive told her.

He was careful to control his hand as he took up his sherry. It felt as though it would shake free from his wrist.

"So," he said as he set his glass down again, "who all have you invited to the restaurant, George? Your theater crowd, no doubt?"

George laughed. "No, no. In honor of the occasion, we'll be a respectable company, barring myself, of course."

Clive gave an appropriate smile, but he couldn't shake the sensation that he was going mad. Which was real—this, or that bloody Dungeon?

With a great effort, he put the question from his mind and threw himself into the festive mood that the evening required. Yet, he couldn't help but feel as though he were not so much present and partaking of events as watching them unfold through a dark glass. He saw again the beggar's features, remembered Tomàs and his other companions—Shriek, Finnbogg, Smythe, and his many-times great-granddaughter, Annabelle. . . .

No, he told himself. Let it go.

He was successful for the rest of that evening as they left the club and went to dinner.

A few of his fellow officers were at the restaurant, along with their ladies, as well as some of George's friends that Clive and Annabella had grown to know over time. Congratulations—both for his promotion and their upcoming nuptials—raised many a toast. There was good food and better conversation, fine drink and dancing afterward. But throughout it all, a nagging concern remained in the back of Clive's mind, discoloring all that he experienced.

With all he had already experienced—or thought he'd experienced—in the Dungeon, what was to say that this wasn't simply one more move in the inexplicable game played by the Dungeonmasters? How could he know? If this was a lie. . . .

Your heart's desire.

If this was a lie and he was given a choice—return to the struggle, or live the lie—what would he choose? *How* could he choose?

Chapter 3

It was late when they finally returned to Annabella's rooms. The drizzle had continued throughout the evening, fog thickening in the alleyways, making their return in the cab a damp and miserable ride— or it would have, if they had not had each other's company. Annabella's cheeks glowed from both the evening's dancing and the wine, and Clive realized yet again how empty the world would be without her.

As it had been in the Dungeon.

His dream.

Her rooms were cozy once they had the oil lamps lit and a fire burning in the grate to take away the chill. While Annabella took a bath, Clive stood at the window and stared down at the wet streets. His mind was a turmoil of confusion. He should have enjoyed himself this evening, and on most levels, he had. Everything had been perfect—the company and setting both—yet he had been unable to shake a sense of foreboding throughout it all.

Glancing at the windowsill, he noticed the tiny length of a fennel seed lying on the wood, its pale green and white stripes appearing bright against the dark mahogany. He licked a finger and touched it to the seed, snaring it with his saliva, then brought it up to his eye.

Like the errant memory he'd tried to snag when approached by the beggar outside George's club, the seed reminded him of something . . .

Absently, he put it in his mouth and bit down. The sharp tang of anise filled his mouth. A scent of cloves touched the air. When he looked out the window, the fog thickened suddenly and approached the glass panes, making it impossible to see the street.

And he remembered once again.

The gateway. Falling through the blue. That same taste; that same scent. How he'd put into words one of the basic tenets of his life: that he wouldn't quit a struggle, no matter what odds stood against him. He hadn't spoken aloud, but then, that voice had replied all the same.

Not even if you were offered your heart's desire?

God help him—was this madness?

He had listened to George and his friends discuss odd philosophies before, one of which was that this world which they all inhabited was but a dream. When the dreamer woke, all would vanish. Foolishness, of course—mere intellectual diversion. For none of them—neither those arguing for or against the conceit—truly believed it.

But what if this world *was* a dream?

Your heart's desire.

Impossible. And yet, had his time in the Dungeon seemed less real?

He pressed his forehead against the glass, closing his eyes. The glass was cool against his skin. Soothing. The scent of cloves was fading, the sharp taste on his tongue almost a memory now.

"Clive?"

He opened his eyes at the sound of Annabella's voice. Outside he could see the street once more, the gaslights reflected in wet pools on the cobblestones, the light fog haloing each lamp post.

"Clive?"

He turned to see Annabella standing near the bath, her cheeks still ruddy and glowing. She was wrapped in a towel, and wore nothing else except for her hair combs.

"Clive, tell me," she said. "What's wrong?"

He ached to look at her, hated to lie.

"Nothing."

"If it's something I've done . . ."

He shook his head emphatically. "Never."

She came to him and laid her hands on his shoulders. Looking down at her, Clive could only wonder at how the most splendid creature on God's own Earth could bear such love for him. What had he ever done to deserve her?

"You can't hide it from me," Annabella said. "I know you're troubled."

Clive led her to the bed and sat her down.

"I'm troubled by dreams," he wanted to say as he sat down beside her. "Dreams so real that they leave me questioning which is more real—this life, or the dreams."

Or, "I fear I'm going mad."

But instead of speaking, he took her in his arms and kissed her. Gently, gently. They lay back on the bed, and for a time, Clive could forget his fears and worries.

Their lovemaking was slow and languorous. It swallowed Clive's sense of desperation, balmed his troubled heart. Afterward, while Annabella slept, he leaned up on an elbow and looked at her, marveling at the slight swell of her belly. He laid his hand upon it, caressing the smooth skin, imagining he could feel their daughter move below the skin, for all that it was too early for such movement.

Did Annabella know? he wondered. Or was it still too soon for her?

Then the realization came to him that the only reason he thought her pregnant was because he'd learned of it from the lips of his descendant.

In the impossible Dungeon.

Madness.

"I would never knowingly desert you," he told his sleeping lover. "I would always return. If I didn't, it would not be through want of any effort on my part."

Annabella stirred as he spoke, but didn't wake. Sighing, Clive rose from the bed.

The wet night beyond the room called to him. He stood naked at the window for a long time, staring out at the darkness, then dressed. He closed the door to Annabella's rooms softly behind him and went out into the night streets, searching. But for what, he couldn't have told.

Clive wore a cloak against the damp chill that rode the night air, but it crept over him all the same. His boot steps echoed wetly on the cobblestones. He'd forgone a hat, so his hair was plastered, lank and dripping, against his scalp. But he paid no attention to physical discomfort. His mind was far away—sifting through memories of an impossible place that it seemed, by now, he knew better than he knew London. That he had many months' worth of these memories only bewildered him the more.

At first he had the streets to himself, but the farther he walked from Plantagenet Court, the rougher his surroundings became. Now there were doxies in the alleyways—weary women, bullied on by their fancy men to earn a last few shillings before they called it a night.

Disreputable men stood leaning against the sides of buildings, watching him pass, their gazes measuring him. Beggars accosted him. Street urchins tugged at his cloak.

He ignored them all.

He ignored them with a finality that made even the cutpurses consider other options and let him pass by unmolested.

It wasn't so much the set of his shoulders, nor the military mark to his step. It was his eyes, which regarded them without seeing them. Not because they were below his station, and therefore unworthy of his attention, but because he seemed to them to walk in another world altogether, a world where even they would not tread.

Physically, he walked the London streets, but his mind walked in Bedlam.

Though the fine cut of his clothes tempted them sorely, even the criminals of Seven Dials, Spitalfields, and the like were wary of dealing with a madman. There were easier ways to turn a shilling. So they let him pass unmolested, watching him from the peekholes of their labyrinthine maze of secret apertures, manholes, tunnels, concealed passages, and hidden exits. A tall, well-dressed though hatless gent, wandering their dangerous streets without care, muttering to himself, his own gaze focused on that other world that only Bedlamites could see.

But one inmate of the criminal slums wasn't leery of him. She staggered from an alleyway to accost him under the dim light of a gas lamp. Her hair was wet and tangled, her cheap dress clinging to her body like a second skin. She gazed at him blearily, putting a hand against his chest to stop him from running her down. The impact of his weight against her arm made her weave dizzily before she caught her balance.

It took Clive a moment to escape the trap of his reveries and focus upon her. When he looked into her grimed features, he wasn't surprised at their familiarity.

She could have been Annabella.

Annabella, if fate had treated her worse than it had, reducing her to eking out a wretched existence on the streets, as this poor moll must. Her unsteadiness was due to either alcohol or opium. Plying her trade in the alleyways gave her her dirty skin and clothes.

She could have been Annabella.

Or their descendant, Annabelle.

Except Annabelle was only a part of the delusion he carried about inside himself. She wasn't real, any more than the Dungeon was.

"You look like a sporting gent," the prostitute said, slurring her words. "What say we have a bit of fun?"

She began to hike up her skirt as she spoke, exposing thighs as grimed as her hands and face.

"Get away from me," Clive told her.

But there was no force behind his words. It wasn't that he desired her. It was only the resemblance—that terribly uncanny resemblance.

"Now, don't be talking like that, sport," she said. "You don't want to send Annie back to her bully-boy empty-handed, now, do you? Wouldn't be right."

She let the hem of her skirt fall, but wet as it was, it still rode high on her thigh. Her hand lifted unsteadily to the neckline of her dress, which she pulled away from her shoulder to reveal a large, discolored bruise.

"Jack gets mean, y'see, sport. Hurts me, he does, when I don't bring home enough."

"I don't want—"

"You all want it," the woman said, cutting him off. "Or why'd you be walking these streets?"

She caught his arm and began to pull him toward the mouth of the alleyway. Clive shook her hand free.

"You say your name's Annie?" he asked.

"Didn't I say it was?"

"Annabella Leighton, I suppose?"

She blinked, momentarily confused, then grinned.

"I'll be anybody you like, sport."

Again she reached for him.

"Get away," Clive said.

This time he put a hand to her shoulder and gave her a push. She staggered back, losing her balance until she was brought up against a wall. The woman's eyes went hard.

"You don't want to be treating me rough, sport."

"You disgust me," Clive told her.

Lord help him. He knew what was what now.

The Dungeon had been no dream.

Your heart's desire.

This was the dream. As sweet as he wished, with Annabella and a promotion, or as foul as seeing his lover depicted as some wretched bawdy woman, stooped to making her living as a prostitute.

Had he stayed in Annabella's rooms, would the dream have maintained itself? Was it by faring abroad, by questioning its validity, that it was unraveling?

What matter when it was all a lie? Better the torment of the Dungeon—better reality, no matter how painful—than to live his life sedated like some opium smoker, cut adrift from the world as it was by his dreams.

He sent his gaze skyward. "Do you hear me? She disgusts me! I see through your lies!"

The woman shook her head. "You're not all there, are you, sport?"

"Go away."

Clive wouldn't even look at her. He was waiting for the Dungeonmasters to reveal themselves. For the dream to end. For a gateway to open and send him plunging down to some new level, some new torment.

The woman put fingers to her lips and whistled shrilly.

"Deny me a fair wage, will you?" she said as Clive looked to her once more.

Before he could reply, there was more movement in the alleyway. A broad-shouldered man stepped out into the arc of light cast by the gas lamp. His hair was slicked to his head, from both the drizzle and grease. He wore a tattered mockery of a gentleman's suit. His feet were bare.

"Bit of trouble, is it?" he said softly.

And this will be Jack, Clive thought. Her fancy man. The bully-boy who sent her out to peddle her body on the streets, while he collected the money afterward. And if she wasn't quick enough, or didn't earn enough, he'd beat her.

"Denying my girl a living wage, are you?" the man went on.

Clive shook his head.

So this was the way it was to be. The dream played out; the game continued until it ceased to amuse the Dungeonmasters and they cleaned the board to begin anew with a new set of playing pieces. And new stakes.

"You mistake me," Clive told the man as he took a step toward him.

"No mistake, mate. There's money owed and you'll pay—one way or another."

Clive shook his head. "I meant, you mistake me for a fool and a coward. I am neither."

Two quick steps brought him face to face with Jack. As the man started to raise his hands, Clive struck aside his defenses and hit him. The smack of his fist against the man's jaw sent pain shooting up his hand. But it was a satisfying pain.

Perhaps he'd been manipulated into this situation, but he was damned if he'd fall victim to it.

He let loose with a flurry of blows, and a moment later, the prostitute's Jack lay on the cobblestones, curled into a ball. Blood leaked from his mouth. He had at least one or two broken ribs.

"Do you see what I meant about your mistake?" Clive asked him, conversationally.

The woman threw herself at him then, but all it required was a shove to throw her off balance and she, too, fell to the cobblestones beside her fancy man.

Again he turned his attention from them and gazed skyward.

"Well?" he cried. "What have you in store for me now?"

There was no reply.

What if he was wrong? he thought. What if there was no Dungeon—if this was the real world?

What if he *were* mad?

No. He knew it to be a lie.

Your heart's desire.

The dream offered him his heart's desire—there was no denying that—but it was still a lie.

Forgive me, Annabella, he thought. But I can't live the lie.

"Answer me!" he shouted.

Ignored by him, the prostitute and her fancy man dragged themselves away, into the alleyway, where they were lost in the darkness.

"Damn you!" Clive cried. "I will not live this lie!"

And then it came to him—a wavering of his vision, the scent of cloves, the sharp taste of anise in his mouth.

The London slum surrounding him tore apart, as paper might be shredded in a storm. The fog came roiling up at his feet, swallowing him. He lost the sense of cobblestones underfoot, and once again he floated in a dark limbo.

His mind's eye filled with an image of Annabella as she had been when he'd left her, asleep in her bed—the perfection of her limbs, the angelic sweetness of her features, smooth and worry-free as she slept.

Lost again.

Stolen from him.

"Damn you!" he cried once more. "Show yourselves to me!"

Chapter 4

There was no way for Clive to judge how long he floated in the darkness. It might only have been a few moments, it might have been as long as an hour, but without reference points—with only the darkness that surrounded him and the confused turmoil that ruled his mind by which to gauge the passage of time—he couldn't even begin to make an educated guess.

It felt like forever.

He had cursed his unseen tormentors long and hard, and with surprising innovation, but received no reply. He had attempted to propel himself through the darkness, but while he could move his limbs, the air was thick about him, and his hands and feet could find no purchase. Finally, voice still, floating in the dark like one dead, he lay passively and waited.

And more time passed.

Interminable minutes ticked away, each lengthened far beyond any reasonable proportion. Clive felt himself begin to drift away—away from his present situation, away from the womblike dark, out of himself.

It was as though, freed of the sensory input normally provided by his body, his spirit was determined to go traveling of its own accord, like some witch's fetch riding the midnight winds when its mistress lies sleeping; as though his spirit had decided that, if its physical shell could not be shifted, it would simply leave the body behind.

So Clive drifted past his anger and frustration, past memory, away into a quiet, hidden place where peacefulness wrapped him in a dark shawl of comfort and he could simply be. Slowly, sight returned, but whether what he viewed came from external stimuli or was drawn up from his own mind, he no longer cared.

He was an invisible presence in an intricately laid out garden, flower beds and hedgerows all forming complex patterns about him. He floated like pollen, his vision encompassing a full three hundred and sixty degrees about him. As his sense of smell returned, the scents of the garden's blossoms arose about him, sweet and heady. A fruity taste came to him. The air was filled with quiet sounds—the soughing of a soft breeze and the murmur of insects.

But all was not well in his haven. He could sense, just beyond the periphery of his vision, an invisible blight. Pain lay there, and desolation.

The world he'd left behind.

The message was plain.

This acreage was his. Here he could remain in safety, freed from the madness that had taken charge of his life beyond this garden's borders. But if he strayed, if he allowed himself to explore beyond these confines, then it would all return once more.

The pain.

The madness.

No need for that warning, Clive thought dreamily. He was done with struggling. Done with it all. With the bedlamite Dungeon. With the lies that infested it like some cancerous disease. He would remain here, where he could be content.

Go back.

The voice didn't really register at first.

Clive. You must return.

He could see in all directions at once in this garden of his, but could spy no source for that voice.

It must be a ghost, he thought. Some errant presence, imperceptible to the eye.

Leave me, he told it, shaping the words in his mind, for he was only an invisible presence himself in this place. *I'm done with their games.*

You must go back, came the voice's monotonous response.

Clive recognized it now. Looking at the maze of this garden, at its patterned network of flower beds and hedges, he wondered how it could have taken him so long to do so. It was the secret voice from his childhood.

Are you a part of the conspiracy? Clive asked. *Do its roots stretch so deeply into my past?*

The tone of his voice was conversational, as though he were only mildly curious.

They have drugged you, the voice responded, *while they decide your fate. How can you allow them to treat you in this manner?*

If he'd had a body, Clive would have shrugged.

I have no choice, he replied. *They do with me as they will—whether I protest or not.*

You are a Folliot, the voice said, *and a Folliot never gives in. You've said as much yourself.*

But they change the rules each time I turn about, Clive said, beginning to show some interest in the argument, despite himself. *They wield godlike powers, while all I can do is stumble through their damned Dungeon like some bug.*

Is it really so different in the world from which they stole you? the voice asked. *Isn't it the measure of how a man struggles that marks his worth?*

Yes, but—

Shall this be your epitaph: "He tried hard, until the struggle grew too difficult, then he simply gave up"?

Easily said, but—

True worth is never easily gained.

Who are you?

There was a long pause, then once again, the voice repeated its initial command.

Go back.

The words cut through Clive's peace, echoing on and on inside him until his haven began to unravel. The garden surrounding him wavered in his sight. The hidden voice drowned out the soothing breeze and the hum of the insects. The scents of the blossoms became spoiled and the fruity taste lost its sweetness, grew tart, then bitter.

Go back.

To what? Clive demanded. *To more of the same? To the endless spin of their damned games?*

No. Return instead to be the man that they cannot bow—the man who will not give in, no matter what they do to him. Return as a Folliot.

And go mad.

Madness is relative.

It's madness or death—that's all that lies in wait for me in their damned Dungeon.

You are too strong to fall prey to madness.

And if I die? What use was it all then?

At least you'll die a man.

There was that, Clive realized. Put in such terms, it could not be denied. For he truly believed that it wasn't so much what a man accomplished, as what—in all good faith, and to the best of his abilities—he attempted.

He felt a fog lifting from his mind.

They have drugged you, the voice had said earlier. *While they decide your fate.*

A man should decide his own fate. A man should stand against monsters such as the Dungeonmasters, no matter what the consequences were to himself. It was only that which separated him from his tormentors.

Lord help him, what was he doing *here*, when he should be with his companions, striking back at the blackguards?

Go back, the voice said once more.

I will, Clive replied.

His return was instantaneous.

One minute he hovered in the fading ruin of the garden, the next he was inhabiting his body once more, cloaked in darkness. He had a brief sense of claustrophobia, brought on by the close measure of his flesh. After the freedom of floating free, his spirit felt trapped and heavy inside his skin. But that passed quickly as he tested his limbs, one by one, growing quickly used to their familiar fit.

Are you still there? he asked the voice.

There was no response. His mysterious benefactor was gone again, as inexplicably as it had come.

Unable to thank him, Clive turned his attention to his present situation.

He could sense no real change in his surroundings. The thick air still held him in its grip and he was still unable to make any real progress through it. But turning his head, he could see two pale smudges of dim light behind him. Though he could make out nothing of their features, the two shapes were indeed recognizably human.

He swam slowly through the air, trying to reach them, pausing when he could at least hear their voices.

They decide your fate.

They belonged to two men—one with a deep, gruff voice, while that of the other was smoother—not quite effeminate, but somewhat womanly all the same.

And they were indeed discussing his fate.

They have drugged you.

He tried to call out to them, not to vent his rage this time, but merely to let them know that they had not bowed him yet. The heads turned toward him.

"You see?" said the one with the gruff voice. "He's as bad as the other. He'll never give in."

The other? Clive thought. Did the man mean his brother, Neville?

"That's precisely his value," the second man said, slightly lisping his soft C's and S's.

"And when the weapon turns in your hand?" the first asked.

The second laughed. "But that's the challenge, isn't it? Without personal risk, we become no better than the others. When we realize our victory, it will be because *we*, at least, were willing to risk all."

It was no more than he'd supposed, Clive realized. It *was* all just some damnable game to them.

"I'll show you risk!" he shouted at them.

"So, you mean to send him back?" the first asked, as though Clive had never spoken.

"There was never any question. I allowed you this experiment, precisely because I knew he would prevail."

Experiment, is it? Clive thought.

"Damn you!" he cried. "I won't rest until you're defeated—each and every one of you."

He might as well have been shouting at the wind, for all the attention they paid him.

"You were that sure of yourself?" the first said.

The second shook his head. "I was sure of him," he said, indicating Clive.

"Don't toy with me," the first said, his voice deepening with anger. "I'm not one of the bugs, to be moved about the board."

"Of course not," the second replied. "But will you listen to reason now?"

"*Your* reason."

"Plain reason," the second said. "If we bicker among ourselves, we stand to lose it all."

"The others agree with you? *All* of them?"

Others? Clive thought. Speak on. Tell me all.

"After this? Yes."

The first sighed. "Then, return him. But the suits must go—his, and those of his companions. I don't know why Green allowed them to have them in the first place."

"The suits are gone," the second agreed amiably.

"And he must remember nothing of this."

Remember nothing? Clive thought. Lord in heaven, how did they expect him to forget?

"Absolutely," the second said.

"See how he drinks in every word? If he remembers, he'll be insufferable."

"I agree."

"I will forget *nothing*!" Clive cried. "Do you hear me? I will remember every foul moment of what you've done to me."

The two heads finally turned to face him.

"Not likely," the second said. "I'll admit the process hasn't been perfected to a preciseness we'd elect—given time—but it will do the job it must. If you lose a few other memories in the procedure"—the figure shrugged—"well, so be it. I can guarantee it will be nothing you'd miss."

The first laughed at that.

Clive renewed his effort to get to them, but the dull glow that gave them shape was fading, until the darkness swallowed them and he was alone once more. Laboriously, he turned a full circle, seeking something, anything, but the black void continued on all sides.

There came a sudden sharp pain in his left upper arm—a hornet's sting, magnified a dozen times—and then an inner darkness began to swallow him, as black as that which surrounded him. He fought the loss of consciousness.

He *would* remember.

He heard voices around him. He felt hands on him, but he could not move a limb.

Then the black took him away.

Chapter 5

When next Clive was conscious, he was falling through the bright flaring azure once more. He could see the pinpoint specks that were his companions on all sides of him—each of them falling as helplessly as he was himself.

He sensed a gap in his memory, as though time had sped by while he stood still. It was an odd sensation—a feeling of loss—but he couldn't define what it was that he had left behind.

He must have lost consciousness for a moment, he thought, and little wonder. If he could only breathe . . .

He remembered nothing of what he had experienced in the black void.

Vertigo made his head spin. His stomach heaved with nausea. He had a raw ache in his head, as though he'd suffered a concussion. His upper left arm felt swollen, and was painful whenever he moved it. He fought for breath in the thick blue air, but the oxygen simply wasn't there to draw into his lungs.

He peered downward, then realized he was no longer certain what was up, and what was down. He had the sense of falling, it was true, but in this place they could be falling sideways for all he knew.

He needed air.

Desperately.

If he didn't breathe soon, he'd—

There was a sudden jarring underfoot as his boots came into contact with something solid. His knees buckled and he collapsed like a puppet with its strings cut. He put out his hands to break his fall, and they sank into what felt like deep grass. His eyes seemed welded shut, but he was too busy keeping down the contents of his stomach to pay any attention to his surroundings.

His arms gave way then, and his face pressed up against the grass. Before he could even try to sit up, the blackness took him away.

Clive was among the first to recover. He opened his eyes, feeling wretched, and cautiously sat up. The world did a slow spin, then settled around him.

He and his companions appeared to have landed on a grassy plateau of some sort. Higher plateaus rose up behind them to meet a craggy sweep of tors; behind them, an immense mountain range almost blocked the sky. In front and below, the land gave way to a dense jungle of forest on the left, a wide sweeping expanse of veldt dotted with trees and shrubs to the right. Cutting between the two was a broad river that meandered off into the distance to where an outstretched peninsula of jungle cut it off from view.

It still bewildered him that such vast lands could exist under the earth. Turning, he took stock of his companions and then realized that the white suit he had been wearing was gone and he was dressed once more as he had been when he had first entered the jungle.

The Dungeonmasters must have taken the suits that Green had given them while they were falling through the last gateway. But at least they had all survived the crossing from the Dungeon's previous level to this one—Lord help them, it was the fifth now.

As Clive regarded them, one by one, he realized again just what a motley assortment of companions they made.

Obviously unaffected by his transition through the gateway, the cyborg Chang Guafe stood resolutely at the edge of the plateau, staring across the landscape of this new level. The metal workings of his skull plate and visage gleamed in the sunlight. His metallic eyes glowed slightly as they fed input into his brain, which was more computer than human flesh and blood.

He reminded Clive of the clockwork toys that were so much the rage in his native London—a walking, talking simulacrum—but Clive didn't make the mistake of considering the cyborg to be any child's plaything. He'd proven himself far too dangerously capable to be underestimated in such a fashion. And at least he had the shape of a human.

Not like Shriek.

She was a four-armed, four-legged monster. Her huge body was covered with spikelike hair that she could pull out and throw as a weapon, the hair apparently carrying some sort of chemical that she could vary at will, depending on the desired effect she wished to produce on the creature she was dealing with. But she was little more than a creature herself—a humanoid spider.

Her face was the most disturbing, with its vestigial mandibles on either side of her lipless mouth, and her six multifaceted, ruby-colored eyes, scattered on the top half of her head like a child's cast-off marbles thrown hither-skither, coming to rest where they would. And, like a spider, she had a pair of spinnerets just below the base of her back.

But under that alien visage was a being that Clive had come to realize had more heart than most men he knew.

Finnbogg was easier to look upon, if only in comparison to Shriek. He was a dwarflike humanoid who seemed more closely related to the canine family than to humanity, with a volatile temperament that could have him fall in love, burst into tears, or fly into a towering rage—all at a moment's notice. Squat, shaggy, and immensely strong, he claimed to be a native of a heavy planet where the biochemistry was enough like Earth's to allow him to breathe the same air and eat the same food as humans did. But he was still a monster.

The rest of Clive's companions were human—though not necessarily fit company for a good Englishman.

The Portuguese, Tomàs, was akin to the worst mags-man or garroter to be found in a London slum. He was swarthy and small, with dark, greasy hair. A wharf rat: alcoholic, dirty, and undoubtedly treacherous. His arrival in the Dungeon had rescued him as he walked the plank of the *Pinta* in the western Atlantic in 1492.

The Indian, Sidi Bombay, had joined Clive's party on the first stages of their search for his brother—before they were foolish enough to investigate the shimmering gateway in the Sudd, and plunged from it into the madness of the Dungeon. Sidi was small in stature, too, but there his similarities with Tomàs ended. His skin was a dark mocha, his hair a midnight black. Experienced and clever, there was an enigmatic mystery about the small Indian that belied his apparently unguarded and cheerful manner.

Disturbing for an entirely different reason was the presence of Annabelle Leigh. As Tomàs came from the past, she had arrived in the Dungeon from the year 1999, when her music-and-theater group, the Crackbelles, were performing in Piccadilly Circus on

Halloween Eve. She was a gamine creature, brazenly showing off her feminine charms in her tight-fitting men's garb. Her black hair was shorn in jagged layers, with absolutely no consideration for fashion or style. Implanted in her forearm—giving her a disquieting kinship to the cyborg—was her Baalbec A-9, a kind of mechanical device powered by her own body heat. The controls for it lay under the bodice of her shirt.

She was also Clive's descendant—his own many-times great-granddaughter, by way of the lover Clive had left behind in England when he first left in search of his brother—Miss Annabella Leighton.

It was disturbing enough to know that this gamine was related to him—that good English morals and mores could change so drastically in merely a century and a half—but what troubled Clive more was how, day by day, she came to look ever more like his own Annabella. For she had the same startling cornflower-blue eyes, the same pale skin suffused with a healthy pink flush, the same trim figure.

It was too easy for him to look at her and see Annabella. He could imagine this descendant of theirs in a high-necked and -waisted bustle dress, with a light mantle overtop following the contours of the dress. Her hair would be long, tied up in a bun under a close-fitting hat. She would be carrying a parasol. . . .

When he let his mind travel so, ungentlemanly thoughts arose—immoral thoughts. For the love of God, she was of his own blood! he had to remind himself. And yet that resemblance . . . and to know that he would never return to his own Annabella. . . .

The only truly familiar face in the party—though by now, Clive was growing accustomed to them all, even the most alien—was that of his one-time batman, Quartermaster Sergeant Horace Hamilton Smythe.

"Batman?" Annabelle had asked when she was made aware of Smythe's earlier position. "What's that make you, Clive-o? Robin?" That was only the first of many obscure references to fall from her lips that simply could not be translated satisfactorily to a man who had left the world a hundred and ten years before her birth.

Clive and Smythe had been together for years, and Clive had reacted with great relief the morning that the *Empress Philippe* had left England's shores and Smythe had turned up aboard ship—disguised as a Mandarin.

Smythe's gift was for makeup and mimicry. He had the ability to switch from a drawling fop to a rhyming slang-spouting cockney to a country bumpkin to a fast-talking pitchman—all at a moment's notice. Odder still, when he wasn't in character, Smythe was the most nondescript of individuals, virtually disappearing into the nearest background, be it a crowd, a jungle, or a drawing room.

"Christ. Talk about your acid flashbacks."

Annabelle regained Clive's attention as he tried to puzzle out what she meant.

Guafe turned from where he stood, overlooking the view below their perch. "Yes," he said in his slightly metallic voice. "The disruption did have the hallucinogenic quality of a drug experience."

Ah, Clive thought. Opiates.

He glanced at Annabelle, looking quickly away when she stood and stretched, the unself-conscious movement accentuating every curve of her trim figure. She gazed thoughtfully around them.

"I figure it was some kinda spatial portal," she said. "Like teleportation." At the mostly blank stares that drew, she added, "You know—not really connected physically?"

"Again, I concur," the cyborg said.

The others were slowly finding their way to their feet. Smythe joined Clive, tugging thoughtfully at his new beard.

"Sir Neville appears to have eluded us again," he said.

It was true, Clive realized. He'd been so disoriented by the experience in the gateway that the reason they had come here had been driven from his mind. He looked out now across the vast panorama of forest and veldt. Somewhere out there, his older twin Neville had made his escape. It was a disheartening view. An army could be hidden below and never seen.

"Where will we begin to look?" he murmured.

"Finnbogg thinks he could be anywhere," Finnbogg said. The dwarf had followed Clive's gaze with his own, absently brushing grass from his chest hair as he did. "Gate could drop littermate anywhere."

"Look," Annabelle said. "I hate to rain on your parade, but don'tcha think it's about time we stopped running around after that asshole and just tried to get outta this place? I mean, enough's enough already. We're never gonna catch up to him. He's playing us for a bunch of no-minds."

"There is no way back," Sidi said. The Indian gave her one of his quirky smiles. "The only way out is ahead."

Annabelle shook her head. "Maybe. I say we put it to a vote." More blank looks. "You know—everybody decides what they want to do, and whatever gig gets the most hands, that's the way we go."

"*I'm* the leader of this company," Clive began when he understood what she was driving at.

"Annabelle is right," Tomàs interrupted. "*Anos.* Whenever we follow you there is only more trouble."

"At this point, I am content to follow," Guafe said.

As am I, Shriek added. Her voice rang directly to their minds.

"Finnbogg will . . ."

The dwarf glanced at Annabelle and caught her frown. It was because of Finnbogg that she had lost her chance of leaving the Dungeon with Wrecked Fred and L'Claar. If he hadn't held her back for that last moment. . . .

"I think we should just split up," Annabelle said.

"I can't leave you here alone," Clive said.

"Oh, lighten up. You think I can't take care of myself?"

How a woman of her obvious good blood could be so crass was beyond Clive's understanding.

"I am responsible for you," he tried. "So long as—"

"Screw that. I'm a big girl now, Clive-o, and the only person responsible for me's me—got that? So back off."

A flush rose up Clive's neck and he took a step toward her, but then Smythe laid a hand on his arm.

"What does your brother's journal say about this level, sah?" he asked.

Sidi nodded. "That would be the wisest course. We must see what lies around us before choosing a destination." He smiled at both Clive and Annabelle. "Who knows? Our roads might well travel together for some distance farther."

Annabelle sighed. "Okay. Check out the bloody Bible."

"It is *not* a Bible," Clive replied.

Every time he thought he was coming to turns with her brashness, she managed to shock him again.

Do you even have the journal anymore? Shriek asked.

Clive hadn't thought of that. With the switch in their clothing . . . But he patted his pocket and found the familiar outline of his brother's diary.

"C'mon," Annabelle said. "Let's get to it. Read the book already."

What I wouldn't give for some good, sturdy Englishmen who know their station, in exchange for this motley crew, Clive thought. But he took the journal from his jacket pocket and sat down with it, spreading it open on his lap. His companions gathered closer.

Chapter 6

Annabelle lay on her back, staring up at the sky, while Clive looked for another of the mysterious, newly appearing entries in the journal. With its salmon-colored sun, the sky here ran more toward a greenish hue than the blue of the world she'd left behind. The odd tones this lent her vision gave her a creepy feeling, but right now she wasn't much missing her own world's skies. Just thinking of their deep blues reminded her too much of the last gateway—talk about your Big Sick.

She'd thought she was going to die in that blue limbo, and was almost ready to welcome the relief from the cramps and nausea that death promised when they'd finally landed on this new level and she'd blacked out. Wouldn't that've been a laugh for the guys in the band if they could've seen her. Tough old Annie B., passing out like some front-and-center groupie swooning at the shake of Tripper's Spandexed buttocks.

It was the height—always the heights. . . .

Thinking of her lead guitarist brought on a different attack of the blues. All that was gone now. Wasn't much chance of her seeing any of them again. Not her friends, not London, not that New Year's gig where they were sharing the bill with the legendary Prince and the Revolution, partying in the next thousand years to the tune of the aging rock star's twenty-some-year-old hit, 1999.

Instead, all she had to look forward to was dying here in the Dungeon, or growing old with this bunch of rejects from a Lucasfilm production and still dying here.

They were misfits all. Not to mention her many-times great-grandfather, who was suffering from a bad attack of a daddy complex.

If Finnbogg hadn't grabbed her, hanging on to her just long enough so that the bloody gate went and closed, trapping her. . . .

She was only half listening to the others talking as Clive leafed through his twin's journal.

Misfits.

She had the feeling that that was the key to this place. It gathered up the people who didn't quite fit in where they came from, and dumped them here. And what happened to them then? Who the hell knew. All she knew was that everybody here was either a misfit, or one of the hero types, like Clive and Finnbogg, who were too true blue to think about anything except chasing after previous victims.

She had to smile at the thought of someone chasing in here after her. Not bloody likely. Tripper, or her bass player, Dan the Man, or little Chrissie Nunn. . . . They'd all just think she'd pulled another one of her no-shows, and they'd be expecting her to turn up again in a week or so, like she always did. Of course, when she didn't, they might worry, but what were they gonna do? It wasn't like there were signposts or maps showing the way into this place or anything.

Maybe she should be keeping a journal herself, or a sketchbook, like Clive did, so that whoever it was that was running this place could sneak it back to the real world to lure in some more suckers, like Clive's brother had done, leading them around by the nose like the bunch of losers that they were.

She sat up suddenly. "What was that you just said?" she asked. "About that other gate on this level?"

Clive gave her one of his resigned looks. "Weren't you listening?"

"'Course I was listening. I just want to get the thrill of hearing it again, that's all. So give."

"It is in a village named Quan," Clive said after consulting the journal once more. "A place guarded by 'blue people' who should be avoided at all costs."

"And where is it?"

"It's not quite clear. Somewhere along the river."

Annabelle nodded. "That's where we should be going. If there's a gateway there, I want to see it. It'll probably just take us down to a deeper level, but maybe it could take us out. Either way, we're moving on—under our own steam."

Clive put his finger on a line of writing. "It says 'avoid at all cost.'"

"Of course it does. And that's why we should go there. Don't you see, Clive-o? When we go where your brother wants us to, all we do is get into deeper shit."

That is not entirely true, Being Annabelle, Shriek said. *We have put ourselves into as much danger as Neville's journal has led us into.*

"Okay. But I still think it's time we stopped playing the game by his rules and made some of our own."

Clive shook his head. "My brother will be heading for the lost city beyond the veldt."

Annabelle hadn't been paying much attention when he was reading that part, either. But before she could ask him to reread it as well, and earn herself another of Clive's reproving looks, Finnbogg spoke up.

"Finnbogg know story about Quan," the dwarf said. "Quanians worship a white stone that is the repository of all the souls of those who have died in their lands."

"Died how?" the cyborg asked. "At the hands of the Quanians?"

"There's also a story," Annabelle interrupted, "about how dwarves are these cute little guys who take care of princesses in trouble and whistle while they work, but that doesn't mean it's true, either."

That gave the group pause. They all knew by now that, for all his time in the Dungeon and the tales he could tell of it, Finnbogg had trouble distinguishing between reality and imagination, which made sorting out the fact from his fantasies a hopeless cause. That Annabelle had just cause to be angry with Finnbogg in no way lessened her warning. Listening to him, one needed a spoonful, rather than a grain of salt.

"Yet in his journal," Smythe said, "Sir Neville warns of danger, as well."

Annabelle nodded. "And we all know how much old Neville's looking out for us."

"He's still my brother," Clive said. "And I still have to find him." His tone was conciliatory, but firm. "I will not shirk that duty."

"I know, I know. And no one's asking you to. We just do like I said before: You go to that ruined city with whoever wants to go with you, while I go to the next gateway with whoever wants to go with me. It's simple, right?"

Clive looked as though he was ready to argue, but then he just sighed and nodded his agreement. One by one, the others made their own decisions. Smythe was going with Clive—no surprise there. Also going with him was the cyborg Guafe and Finnbogg, who had looked hopefully at Annabelle, then unhappily chosen Clive's party when all she gave him was a hard stare.

Shriek opted to join Annabelle, as did Tomàs. Annabelle was pleased with the former's decision, but not at all thrilled about having the Portuguese traveling with her. The only one who remained undecided was Sidi Bombay.

"What about you?" Clive asked the Indian.

"Well, now. I signed up to guide you, and I'm not a man who goes back on his word, but I don't know this land, so I'll be of little use as a guide."

"I release you from any obligations you feel you still owe me," Clive said.

Annabelle frowned. Like he owned Sidi. What Clive-o needed was a good shaking to loosen him up.

"Then I will go with Annabelle," Sidi said.

Well, thank Christ for that, Annabelle thought. Somebody sane to talk to and help her and Shriek keep an eye on Tomàs.

It took them most of the day to work their way down from the top of the plateau, to where they made a group camp at the base of the heights. The descent was made that much harder because of Annabelle's uncomfortable feeling with heights. After resting, they set about providing themselves with some supper.

Smythe fished in the river, using sturdy thread pulled from the bottom hem of his jacket and one of Annabelle's many earrings, bent into a hook. Grubs dug out of the mud served for bait. Finnbogg and Sidi foraged along the river bank for this world's variations on tubers and cress. By the time they returned, Smythe had caught three good-sized fish. They were bluish in color, but once they were gutted and scaled, and roasted over a fire, they proved to make good eating. They had the cress on the side, as a salad. The tubers, roasted in the coals, had a texture like sweet potatoes, and a nutty taste.

They took turns keeping watch through the night, unfamiliar constellations wheeling across the dark skies above. The stars seemed much too close—more like the special effects from the light show of one of her gigs, Annabelle thought, than real stars—and looked like winking chips of sapphire.

She and Clive shared the third watch. The air was warm and humid, so they'd let the fire die down. Annabelle had taken off her jacket and was wearing just her red leather jeans and an armless T-shirt.

"Guess you're kinda disappointed in me, aren't you?" she said as the silence between them grew too long for her.

She was a little surprised that what he thought of her made any difference at all. It was probably, she realized, that, for all her criticism of him, and his of her, he was still family. And that was more than most people seemed to get in this place. When she thought of what it'd been like when she was alone in that prison, before Clive and his party had joined her. . . .

Clive's face was just a shadow when he turned to look at her. "You carry yourself much . . . differently from the women of my own time," he said finally.

"Yeah, well, things change. The world's different."

"Too much so, I think."

"I don't know about that, Clive." She dropped the "O" that she usually tacked on just to get a rise out of him. "Seems to me freedom's a good thing."

"Freedom, yes. But when one forgets one's station . . . I find it disconcerting."

"Like a woman doing what she wants to do? C'mon. You can't tell me you really believe all that."

"Well, not exactly. But, still. Women aren't the same as men. In England—"

"Oh, gimme a break. You want to know what's happening in your merry old England right now? It's a pissant little country, up to its ass in debt, that brownnoses every major world power. Half its work force is on the dole, while the other half's running around with a pickle up its ass.

"And as for your macho attitude to women—where the hell do you come off thinking we're no better'n you?"

"Women are the weaker sex," Clive began. "It's a gentleman's duty to look after them."

"Right. The way you looked after my ancestor, Annabella. Knocking her up and then taking off on a little world tour for your asshole brother who doesn't even *want* to be found. Wake up, Clive."

"I had no idea that Annabella was with child."

"So tell me, was she just some tramp, as far as you were concerned?"

"I won't listen to you speak of her in such a manner."

Annabelle sighed. She reached out and added some fuel to the dying coals of the fire. Flames licked up, lighting both their faces. Shadows ran off beyond the periphery of the fire's glow.

"Look," she said. "I'm trying to make a point. You think I'm cheap—too brassy, too loose . . . a soiled woman, right? I speak my mind just like you do, I'm capable of standing up to the same shit you are, and I've slept around. I got my own kid, floating out there in the real world somewhere. What makes us so different? I'm here, aren't I—your descendant? But you never married. Are you trying to tell me that you never slept with a woman?"

"No, but—"

"Oh, yeah. I know. It's okay, because you're a man. Well, bullshit, Clive-o."

And then she grinned. By the rueful expression on his face, she knew that she had him.

"This is not fit conversation for mixed company," he tried to argue, but she knew his heart wasn't really in it.

Score one for enlightenment, she thought. Maybe there's hope for him yet.

"That's just the point I'm trying to make," she said. "We're not mixed. You're male and I'm female—right—but otherwise, we're just people. Under our skin, never mind our sex, we're the same. Do you understand what I'm trying to tell you? You're an intelligent man, for God's sake, so pay attention. Watch my lips. Under their skin, people are all the same."

Clive sat quietly, making no answer.

"That doesn't mean that every woman's gotta be hard," Annabelle went on. "There's still room for romance. People like being babied sometimes—men *and* women. Cared for, you know? But they want to be respected, too. It's a tough old world out there, Clive. We've gotta fight a lot of fights—but we shouldn't be fighting with each other."

There was another long silence.

"I . . . understand," Clive said finally.

Annabelle nodded. Yeah, she thought. At least you think you do. But it was a start. You couldn't expect miracles, but if he just stopped to think about it from time to time, it'd be worth it.

"So who do you figure for the World Series?" she asked.

"What?"

"Just a joke. Changing the subject, you know?"

"You are a very strange woman, Annabelle Leigh," he said.

She grinned. "Yeah. Real *Twilight Zone* material. What do you say we wake up the next watch and get some sleep?"

The two companies went their separate ways in the morning. As they made their farewells, Annabelle gave Clive a solid hug and a quick kiss on the lips that made him blush. She touched the red flush on his neck with a feathery brush of her fingers.

"Never met a man who blushed before," she said. "You take good care of yourself now, okay?"

Though he looked as though he had more to say, he contented himself with a simple, "Fare you well."

Annabelle watched them set off through the tall grass of the veldt until they were lost from sight, then looked in the direction that their own trail would take them.

The jungle hung heavily over the west side of the river. Although the east bank was treed as well, the undergrowth wasn't nearly as dense. While she didn't have the best of knowledge when it came to geography, it didn't seem quite right to her that the jungle would end so abruptly at the river, and become grasslands almost immediately after leaving the water. But then, there wasn't a whole lot about this place that made much sense—not when the veldt had a mauve tint to its yellowy grass and the jungle ran more to blue-green and burgundy, with splashes of pure purple that weren't fruit. The only really green—familiar green— things she could see were the blooms on a nearby flowering vine.

She turned to look at her own companions. Shriek returned her gaze impassively, while Tomàs wouldn't meet hers at all. Only Sidi flashed her a grin, white teeth gleaming against his dark skin.

"Well, kids," she said. "Looks like it's time for us to go play Tarzan."

"Tarzan?" Tomàs asked.

"Yeah. Hit the jungle trail, and all that. Knowing our luck, we'll run into our own Opar and all get sacrificed to some monkey god or something, but what the hell. Nobody said it was gonna be a picnic, right?" Blank looks all around. "Right. Let's go."

When Shriek took the lead, Annabelle indicated to Tomàs that he should go next. No way she wanted that weasel behind her. She and Sidi took up the rear. As they entered the less dense forest of the east bank, taking a game trail that followed the river, the oddly colored foliage closed in above them.

Why do I get a bad feeling about this? Annabelle wondered as she glanced back at the sunlit field they were leaving behind.

Chapter 7

The veldt was a vast, trackless sea of grass, dotted with small islands of bushes and trees. The grass swept off in endless leagues of yellowish mauve under the pale green skies, rising up to the shoulders of Clive, Smythe, and the cyborg, while swallowing the bulky but smaller Finnbogg with its height. The blades of the grass were thick and sharp at the edges, springing back up behind them after they had passed. By midmorning, the jungle was no longer visible. All they could see of their backtrail was the immense heights of the mountain range, pushing up at the cloudless sky.

It was dull trudging with so little to see in the way of landmarks. The islands of bushes and trees gave some relief, but the trees were so immense—the smallest was many times the size of the largest English oak, while the bushes were as tall as the trees the Englishmen were readily familiar with—that their presence left the company with a sense of disquiet whenever they passed through their shadows.

"She is a fine woman, is young Annabelle," Smythe remarked to Clive. "She will do you proud, sah."

The cyborg Guafe was walking well ahead of them—his tireless march was enough to make Clive weary just watching him—while Finnbogg lagged behind, so the two Englishmen were walking abreast. Clive had been relating his previous night's conversation with Annabelle to his companion—an edited version that didn't cover Clive's more personal relationship with his lover in England.

"Do you think so?" Clive asked. "She has some rather curious notions concerning class structure and a woman's place."

"If you'll pardon my candor," Smythe said, "I believe there's much to what she has to say. Take Sidi—he's more than simply clever. Give him white skin and drop him into London, and I'll wager that in a month or so, you would be hard put to pick him out from another

43

Englishman. He's adaptable, is Sidi Bombay. A good man, no matter what color his skin."

"Oh, I'll grant you that. But he's still . . . well, common."

"And so am I. Yet we eat at the same table, you and I, and you respect me, as I do you. It isn't merely the uniform we share that allows us our friendship—at least, I would hope not."

"A man never had a truer friend than I have in you, Horace," Clive said.

"It warms my heart to hear you speak so, sah."

"But all this talk of Annabelle's . . . I must admit I find it disturbing."

Smythe nodded. "A new idea is often disturbing—warrant the furor back home over the evolutionists—but if it speaks a truth, then the wise man would do well to listen. We are in a new world now, sah—one from which we may never escape. By such reckoning, we would do well to set aside some of our beliefs and be willing to accept the strangers that we meet here on their own terms, no matter how alien or 'common' we might perceive them to be."

"But damn it, Horace, we're Englishmen. We must set an example."

"You're beginning to sound like your brother, sah," Smythe said with a smile.

"You know what I mean."

Smythe shrugged. "Perhaps it comes easier for me, sah, being common and all—"

"You know I didn't mean—"

"But you'd do well to think about what Annabelle had to say. Even if we do escape this Dungeon, who's to say in what time we would find ourselves? If the world has changed as much as Annabelle has told us it has, then we'd do well to learn to adapt to changes *now*."

"It irks me," Clive said.

"As no doubt your own reactions irked Annabelle. There's a good deal of the Folliot in her—I doubt you'd deny that."

Clive smiled. "She certainly speaks her mind." "Headstrong—like every Folliot I've ever known."

"And not without her own charm—though, Lord knows, I don't claim that for myself."

"I wouldn't be so quick to deny it," Smythe said. "I've seen the ladies' eyes on you, sah, and it wasn't simply your uniform they were admiring."

"Yes, well . . ."

For the second time that day Clive felt his cheeks and neck burn. He cleared his throat and quickly changed the subject.

"Did we do the right thing, do you suppose—splitting the company in two as we have?"

"I worry for Annabelle, as well," Smythe replied, "but she seems a most capable young woman, and Sidi and Shriek will look after her, even if the Portuguese is of no help. Besides, I doubt we had much choice. To bring her with us would have required our binding and gagging her, I'll wager."

Clive nodded. "And as Finnbogg has pointed out, in this place there is no turning back, only faring onward. So I'll look to meet her again in the days to come. And if she promises to ease the sharpness of her tongue—why, then, I'll promise to keep a more open mind."

"No harm in practicing that now," Smythe murmured.

Clive gave him a sharp glance, then sighed. "If it's not the one of you, then it's the other."

"We're both looking out for you, sah. One can be an Englishman and still keep an open mind. It's never harmed me."

Clive smiled. "Why, then, here's my hand on it, Horace, and if you find me failing to uphold my side of this bargain, I give you permission to shape me quickly back into line—howsoever you see fit."

Smythe clasped Clive's hand and grinned back at him. "Watch what you promise, gov'nor," he said, "as there's some as'll take you at your word."

As he spoke, Smythe's features and stance shifted into that of a quick-stepping London cockney to match his thick accent, and for a moment, Clive was transported away from this bizarre world that familial loyalty had forced him into, back to the cobblestoned streets of home. A pang of loss touched him, but he kept his smile.

"I expect no less from you, Horace," he said.

Come the late afternoon, there was a new mystery for them to unravel. The grassland suddenly broke off, and they were confronted with a vast plain, pitted and scored with round indentations that measured some ten feet across. They were scattered everywhere, overlapping often. There were also indications of huge logs or something similar having been dragged about the area. The grass was reduced to stubble; the nearest copse of trees stood out like an island, and had not a leaf upon any of its branches.

"Now, this is curious," Clive said. "What are we to make of this?"

The cyborg had paused at the edge of the grassline, waiting for them to catch up to him.

"Could it have been caused by a shower of meteorites?" Smythe asked. "The heat from their descent would be enough to set fire to the grasslands—wouldn't it?"

"Unlikely," Guafe said. "The indentations left by meteorites would be explosive—these are compressive."

"Then what caused these holes?" Clive asked.

The cyborg shrugged—a very human gesture that he'd undoubtedly picked up from associating with them. "In the Dungeon? It could be anything."

Smythe was investigating one of the indentations. It was some two feet deep, and the earth was crumbly about its edges.

"Chang's right," he said as he straightened up. "If these had been caused by meteorites, then we should be able to see some part of them at the bottom of these holes. There's no trace of them." Shading his eyes, he studied the surrounding terrain and added, "But I do see supper."

They all looked in the direction he was pointing. Near the huge trees of the nearest copse, a small group of creatures was feeding on the short, grassy stubble. They had the heads and ears of hare, elongated necks like giraffes, and the body of deer. Their coloring was dun, touched with the same mauve of the grass, dotted with white spots. Their underbellies were white. In size, they were no taller than a good-sized hound.

"What are they?" Clive asked.

"Mammals of some sort," Guafe replied.

Smythe nodded. "They appear to be a cross between a hare and a deer."

"Dares?" Clive offered with a smile.

"A dare does sound more appetizing than a heer," Smythe said. As Guafe began to move in their direction, he added quickly, "Don't frighten them."

Sitting at the edge of the indentation he'd been investigating, he took off his boots and removed the laces from one of them. He tied a stone to either end of the lace, then rose to his feet.

"A Spanish trick," he said with a smile as he whirled the bola experimentally over his head.

While the others watched, he crept forward, moving at a snail's pace, freezing every time one of the longeared heads lifted. The wind made it easier for him, blowing toward him from his quarry, but from the prickling alertness of their ears, he was sure that they depended mostly on their sense of hearing to alert them to danger.

When he judged that he was finally close enough, he started the bola whirling again. Heads lifted among the herd at the whistling sound of the weapon, one after the other. Then one creature broke off and began to run. Smythe loosed the bola as the rest of the herd bolted, moving in a curious gait that combined a hop with a run.

They were as quick as an English hare or deer, but Smythe had been prepared for that. He gave his quarry plenty of lead before loosing his weapon. As the bulk of the herd raced away, the leather thong of the bola struck his target's neck, and the stones wrapped around it with such force that it broke.

"As I've provided supper," he said as he drew his knife and ran lightly to where his prey still kicked its feet, "I'll let someone else see to building a fire."

They had the dare meat for supper, and again for breakfast, and yet once more for supper the following night. It had a coarse texture and a slightly gamy flavor, but, considering their circumstances, they all pronounced it a rousing success.

They left the meteor field behind late on that following day, and pushed through the tall grasses of the veldt for the remainder of the afternoon before they finally made camp. The evening passed uneventfully, with Finnbogg regaling them with more improbable stories of the Dungeon and its curiosities. Smythe particularly enjoyed the dwarf's tales, matching them with ones just as preposterous from his own store whenever Finnbogg grew tired. The cyborg seemed to pay attention to neither of them—it was as though he simply shut himself off when they weren't moving or it wasn't his turn to take watch.

Clive listened with half an ear. Sometimes he sketched with bits of charcoal on the blank pages in his brother's journal, in the poor light thrown from their fire. Mostly, he worried about the other half of their company, following the river, worrying especially about Annabelle.

He had the dawn watch that morning. He was sitting with his back against a tree, the fire nothing more than dead ash, when he heard the grumble of thunder. The salmon-colored sun was already rising in the east, so the sky was clear enough that he could see it was cloudless.

Thunder without clouds? he thought.

Then the ground shook underfoot—a tremor at first, that grew until it was impossible to stand. By now, the rest of the company was awake as well.

"Earthquake!" Clive cried.

A strange expression touched Finnbogg's features. He crawled to the nearest tree and slowly hoisted himself up its trunk, clinging like a limpet to its rough bark. He scouted the horizon, then pointed off toward the north, losing his balance as he did so. He half fell, half slid down the trunk, landing on the ground hard enough to knock the air from him.

"What was it?" Clive demanded. "Speak up."

"Give him a moment to catch his breath," Smythe said as he knelt by the dwarf and helped him sit up.

The ground shook constantly now.

Finnbogg sat up weakly. "Now . . . Finnbogg remember," he said.

"Remember what?" Clive asked.

"The danger on this veldt—the Walking Mountains."

"The walking—?"

Guafe called to them then from where he stood holding on to the trunk of the tree. He pointed north as Finnbogg had. The thunder was all around them, the ground reverberating so that it was difficult to merely sit on it.

"That was no meteor field we crossed earlier," the cyborg said. "It was the feeding ground of brontosaurs."

Clive and Smythe joined him where he stood, hanging on to the tree for support. The cyborg kept his balance now without need of similar support, riding the shock waves. In the far distance, the two Englishmen could spy an enormous herd approaching them.

"What do you mean it was a feeding ground?" Clive asked.

"Their distance makes their size deceptive," Guafe replied. "Those indentations we discovered were not made by meteorites—they were the footprints of those monsters."

"Footprints?" Smythe asked.

The disbelief in his voice was obvious to Clive. He found it difficult to believe himself, but the shaking ground and the thunder of the creatures' monstrous tread brought the truth home with a harsh resonance. He clung to the tree trunk and stared at the distant herd.

The cyborg was nodding. "They reach lengths of up to twenty-five meters and weights ranging between forty and eighty ton. It will be most interesting to observe them at close hand."

"Walking Mountains," Finnbogg muttered.

"They're coming our way?" Clive asked.

"There's no need for alarm," Guafe told him. "They are herbivores. We need only keep out from underfoot."

"What if they think we are plants?" Smythe asked.

"Unlikely. Of more concern to us will be the scavengers accompanying the herd—coelurosaurs and the like."

Clive regarded the cyborg. "And how . . . how big are they?"

"Not large—perhaps the size of an ostrich."

Clive studied the approaching herd once more, then turned his attention to their surroundings. The nearest branches above them were some seventy feet from the ground. There was no other cover. The most they could hope for was to hug the side of the tree and hope the monsters didn't notice them. But then he remembered the feeding ground they had traveled through, how all the vegetation—from grasses to the topmost leaves—had been razed.

The ground tremors were so severe now that it took all their strength to hold on to the rough bark of the trees. Of the four, only the cyborg remained standing, still riding the tremors. The rest of them knelt beside the tree, hanging on as best they could.

"What I wouldn't give for a cannon," Smythe said.

"Or a few good horses to take us out of here," Clive added.

The sky was darkening now, but there were still no clouds. It was the vast bulks of the brontosaurs, shadowing the sun.

"At least Annabelle is safe," Clive said.

Chapter 8

The thing you forget, Annabelle thought, when you're watching all those old Johnny Weissmuller flicks, is that it's hot in a jungle. Hot and sticky.

She wore her jacket tied around her waist as she trudged along behind Shriek and Tomàs, her T-shirt sticking to her back. Her red leather jeans were uncomfortably heavy and chafed her legs. Her short hair hung limply against her scalp, and one hand was in constant motion, brushing mosquitoes and other bugs away from her face. The heat and humidity was draining her vitality with each drop of perspiration it sucked from her. She couldn't even spare the energy her Baalbec A-9 would need to vaporize the ever-attacking insects.

She wasn't sure how the trek was affecting Shriek, but directly ahead of her, Tomàs walked with his head bent, the heat sucking away his energy, too. His dirty shirt had sweat stains under its arms and all down its back, and his greasy hair hung even more limply than her own. Only Sidi appeared to be unaffected. He walked cheerfully at her side, not even breaking a sweat. By now, Annabelle was too hot and tired to try to imagine any more ways she could wipe that grin from his face.

What she wouldn't give for an ice-cold can of beer.

The game trail they were on continued to follow the contour of the river, under low-hanging boughs heavy with strange fruit, choked with blue and purple leaves and blossoming vines. Insects clouded around them, offering little respite. Beyond their vision, the jungle rang with odd animal cries. The few creatures they spied were uniformly bizarre.

Twice they'd seen troops of flying monkeys in the trees overhead—little wizen-faced creatures with pointed ears and white beards. They leapt from bough to bough, crossing wider expanses by utilizing the outstretched webs of skin between their fore and rear limbs. There was also a shrewlike creature, about the size of her hand, with a long, tusked snout and tiny red eyes, that she caught glimpses of in among the leaves.

They disturbed small herds of tapirlike beasts, striped like zebras, only the striping was reversed—white on black. In the river they saw swimming monkeys, with webbed feet and streamlined bodies, and a creature like a hippo that had flippers and a tail in place of limbs. It reminded Annabelle of a manatee, but was far larger. Once, they spotted what looked like a cross between a leopard and a monkey—an obviously feline creature that swung between tree boughs, its body slender to the point of anorexia. There were lizards and snakes, possumlike creatures with lupine features, and a hopping kind of rodent that appeared to be a cross between a rabbit and a squirrel.

The only things that appeared at least vaguely familiar to her were the birds. Though there was still something alien about them, they at least resembled the birds she knew from her own world, ranging from flocks of brightly colored parrots to long-legged wading birds, skimming kingfishers that fed on insects on the river's surface, and busy little hummingbirds the size of Annabelle's thumb. But they were still none of them quite right. The hummingbirds flew in flocks. The kingfishers had wide bills and a peaked fan of head feathers. The wading birds were like blue flamingos crossed with storks. The parrots chittered and scolded each other like monkeys.

"Can you believe this place?" she said, glancing at Sidi.

The Indian grinned. "We're here, aren't we? Hard not to believe what the eyes see."

"Cute. You know what I mean."

"Yes. Very strange, yet very familiar. Do you find the heat bothering you?"

"Every frigging thing is bothering me. I can't believe we've got a week of this to go through before we reach the village. Maybe we should Huck Finn it, you know? Build a raft and pole our way down the river?"

Sidi shook his head regretfully. "We've nothing to cut the trees down with, Annabelle. Nothing to lash the logs together with."

"I know. I'm just whining—don't pay any attention to me."

"Hard not to—you're the boss now."

The boss. Right. Well, the boss was beginning to regret taking the low road through the jungle. At least, out on the veldt, there'd probably be a breeze.

"Stop fighting the heat," Sidi said. "Accept it and let it flow through you—you'll feel much better."

"Easy for you to say."

"*Keh.*" He made a single, sharp clicking noise at the back of his throat that Annabelle was beginning to recognize as an indication of amusement. "Most discomforts are in the mind," he added. "Defeat them with your stronger will."

"Right now my mind's kinda turned to mush—like somebody's making a brain stew inside my head and they've got the heat turned way up."

"It will pass, Annabelle. You'll adapt."

She managed to find him a grin. "Sure. Just don't hold your breath waiting for it."

They made camp that night under a sheltering net of tree boughs that overhung the river, leaving a hut-sized space inside. When a troop of the flying monkeys passed by, high overhead, Shriek pulled loose one of her hair spikes and threw into the chattering cluster. One of the creatures came tumbling down; the rest fled.

As Shriek set about gutting and skinning the monkey, Annabelle turned away, feeling sick to her stomach. Tomàs smacked his lips.

"Did you never eat monkey?" he asked.

He added something in Portuguese that Annabelle found incomprehensible. He shrugged when she asked him to clarify.

"*Muito gôsto, sim?*" he said.

"Not for me, pal," she said. "It's too much like eating a relative."

While the other three feasted on the roast monkey, she settled for a vegetarian meal of tubers and cress, supplementing their blandness with a handful of greenish fruit that looked like grapes, but tasted like a blend of pear and lime, with a texture like a peach.

She planned to take the first watch—she doubted she could sleep anyway, with this heat—but before anyone turned in, a sudden silence from the jungle all around them stilled their own conversation. The hairs at the nape of Annabelle's neck prickled as she got the sudden sense that something was watching them from beyond the light cast by their small fire. Something sentient.

Chica-chic.

The sound came from their backtrail, as though someone had given a maraca a single shake. Not one of their small party even seemed to breathe. The only movement was Shriek's hand edging toward one of her hair spikes.

Chica-chic.

Now it came from the direction they'd be taking in the morning.

"What is it?" Annabelle breathed. "Some kinda animal?"

"It sounds to me," Sidi whispered back, "like the sound of a gourd rattle, filled with dry seeds."

Annabelle nodded. "Me, too. Do you think it's a person?"

The Indian shrugged, but he sat warily, his gaze roving restlessly as he studied the darkness beyond the campfire's glow.

Chica. . . .

The noise was farther away now. Muffled and incomplete. They sat in absolute silence, waiting, but it wasn't repeated. Instead, the normal sounds of the jungle arose

once more. Insects. The cough of a cat-monkey. The distant cries of night birds.

Annabelle let out a breath that she hadn't been aware of holding. "That was creepy."

"This path is much too dangerous," Tomàs muttered.

Annabelle frowned at him. "Hey, nobody's keeping you. Anytime you want to take off, you got my blessing."

The Portuguese made no reply, but something ugly flickered in the back of his eyes before he gave her one of his ingratiating, thin smiles.

I smell something, Shriek said suddenly. *An odd, unpleasant smell— like a fish, but it walks on the land.*

"Like something rotting?" Annabelle asked. She lifted her head and tried to catch a sense of whatever it was that the arachnid had smelled, but her own sense of smell wasn't as highly developed.

Shriek shook her head. *No, Being Annabelle. Whatever it is, it is alive.*

"How close is it?" Annabelle asked.

I can't tell. I . . . She shook her head. *It is gone now.*

Annabelle sighed. Perfect. Now they had to watch out for some kind of walking fish that played maracas?

"I'll take the first watch," she told Shriek. "You go ahead and rest— I'll be waking you all too soon."

The arachnid nodded. As she stretched out, carefully smoothing down her hair spikes where she lay on them, Annabelle turned to the other two. Tomàs was laughing.

"Walking fish?" he said. "*Bom*. Walk them into my belly, then."

Still chuckling, he turned in, leaving Annabelle and Sidi alone by the dying fire. Annabelle fed some more wood to the coals.

"What do you think it was, Sidi?"

"I don't know, Annabelle, but we'd better keep a close watch. If Shriek thinks it's dangerous . . ." The Indian shrugged. "I trust her."

"Me, too. She's good people. You'd better turn in."

Sidi reached out and touched the back of her hand.

"We'll be fine, Annabelle—you'll see."

She turned her hand to clasp his for a moment, and gave his fingers a squeeze. His skin was dry, the palms thick with callouses.

"I hope so," she said.

She watched him curl up by the trunk of the tree, head pillowed on a root, and envied the way he immediately fell asleep. Then she sat up, feeding more wood to the fire, and listened to the jungle night. She started at every sudden noise, but the weird shaking sound wasn't repeated during her watch, nor during that of any of the others, she found out in the morning.

Tomàs had the last watch, but when Annabelle woke, she noticed that Shriek was awake as well, though still lying down, two of her six eyes focused on the Portuguese.

I shoulda thought of that, she realized. Some leader I'm turning out to be. The bloody little weasel could slit all our throats while we're sleeping.

The following day passed uneventfully. That evening, Shriek brought down one of the tapirlike creatures and this time, Annabelle ate with them. Although she was still squeamish about watching the thing be butchered, she could handle eating it. But not the monkey—that was too much like eating a cousin, or a baby. Shriek was apparently aware of that, for she'd passed up a number of monkeys in favor of the tapir, and for that, Annabelle was grateful.

Annabelle had the dawn watch that night. She built up the fire, sitting back from its heat, but wanting the comfort of its glow no matter if it made the already stifling night hotter. Light was just creeping in through the overhanging boughs when she heard the sound again.

Chica-chic.

She looked quickly around, trying to sense the place from which it was originating. To her left?

Chica-chic.

Chica-chic.

Right and left.

She nudged Sidi with her foot and picked up a length of wood that she'd been planning to add to the fire.

Chica-chic.

Shriek was awake and sitting up. She plucked hair spikes from her hide, one for each of her four hands.

Chica-chica-chica-chica . . .

The sound came from all around them. In the growing light, Annabelle could make out humanoid shapes moving toward them through the trees. Except for the strange maraca sound, the jungle was silent. Then, the first of the approaching creatures stepped into clear view.

Shriek drew back an arm, but there was a *whufting* sound and she clapped a hand to her neck where a small dart had stung her. Her arms flailed and then she toppled over.

"Ah, Jesus . . ." Annabelle murmured.

She was on her feet, Sidi and Tomàs flanking her on either side, both armed, as she was, with lengths of firewood. Another pair of the creatures joined the first one, then two more, another three, until there were a dozen or so of them surrounding the small company. Looking at them, Annabelle remembered what Clive had read from Neville's journal—"blue people"—and Shriek's warning last night.

An odd, unpleasant smell—like a fish, but it walks on the land.

No kidding, for they did reek, and they looked like fish. And they were definitely blue-skinned.

They were no taller than four feet, but broad-shouldered and stocky. Their faces had the streamlined look of fish about them, with eyes set widely apart, almost to the sides of their heads. Their noses were only vestigial, their mouths wide, lipless slits that almost cut their heads in two. Instead of ears, they had holes in the sides of their head. Their hair was black and slick on the top of their heads, but there was none on their bodies. Loincloths covered their genitals. Each had a blowgun, and a number of darts sticking up between his knuckles, obviously ready for instant use.

It was when she caught sight of the back of one of them that she realized what they reminded her of—sharks. They had stiff fins sticking up along their spines, and when a few opened their mouths, she saw rows of sharp teeth. Mouths open wide, they tilted their heads back, and Annabelle saw their uvulas shake.

Chica-chic.

Mystery number one solved, she thought. Now, how the hell do we get out of this?

One who appeared to be a leader stepped closer to them. "Folly, folly," he said.

His voice was a wheezing rasp, and Annabelle wasn't sure what she was hearing. Was it English? Was he telling them they were stupid? No marks for brilliance there, pal. Or was it an alien word? And if so, what did it mean?

She thought of Clive and his party wandering happily across the veldt, and wished she'd been smart enough to stick with them.

"You know, kids," she told her companions, "I think the smart move now's to drop these sticks."

At the sound of her voice, blowguns lifted to the mouths of those who weren't making the weird maraca sound, each weapon fixed on Annabelle, Sidi, or Tomàs.

Chica-chica-chica.

Annabelle let her stick fall from her hand. "Take it easy," she said, in the most placating tone she could muster. "You win."

On either side, her companions let their own makeshift weapons drop.

"Did you ever get the feeling it's gonna be just one of those days?" she said to Sidi.

"Folly, folly!" the leader cried.

"You said it, pal."

A number of the creatures came up to them and forced them to lie on the ground, hands behind their backs. Their wrists were tied, and then they were forced back to their feet and pushed on down the game trail, blue hands prodding them with stiff fingers whenever they lagged. Behind, Shriek was tied to two long poles. Their captors then hoisted her bulk onto their shoulders and took up the rear.

Face it, Annie B., Annabelle told herself. You screwed up again.

Chapter 9

The ground tremors grew worse as the enormous herd of brontosaurs drew nearer. It was now possible for Clive's party to see the scavenging coelurosaurs as well, though they were still dwarfed by the monstrous herbivores where they ranged in the shadow of the herd. They appeared to be a kind of lizard and were, indeed, the size of ostriches. Their rear legs were far larger than the fore, though they appeared equally comfortable running on all fours or upright like a man, their long tails thrust out straight behind them for balance.

The scavengers would be his party's principle danger, Clive realized, but it was difficult to drag his gaze away from the behemoths that made up the herd. The Walking Mountains. Finnbogg's description of them was all too apt.

It was next to impossible for Clive to calculate the sheer bulk of the creatures. It was as though the glass dome of the Great Exhibition's Crystal Palace had become flesh, sprouted enormous legs, tail, and elongated neck, and begun to march across Hyde Park. But not just one dome become monster. Hundreds of them. For as far as the eye could see.

Clinging to the tree to keep his balance, Clive could only marvel that such creatures could even exist. The cyborg's estimates of the creatures' lengths and weights seemed inadequate.

"Well," Smythe drawled at his side. "We can't complain of this being a dull sort of a place."

Clive nodded. Mopish, it certainly wasn't.

"I could do with a little boredom," he said.

"Finnbogg would settle for merely surviving to remember," the dwarf muttered.

"My circuits will preserve the memory," the cyborg said, "even if we do not survive."

Smythe rolled his eyes. "Isn't that bloody reassuring."

"We should have gone with Annabelle's party," Clive said. "As soon as we saw that feeding ground, we should have turned back. Meteorites and grass fires, indeed."

"That's it!" Smythe cried. "Finnbogg, Major—each of you take a grip of my shoulders and hold me hard."

Clive gave his comrade a puzzled glance, then braced himself as best he could and took a grip on Smythe's left shoulder. On the other side of Smythe, Finnbogg did the same. Clive glanced back at the herd. Their approach remained steady, the sound of their tread like one continuous roll of thunder. The scavengers were closer still. Any moment they would be investigating this island of trees where his small party was hiding.

He turned back to see Smythe striking flint against steel.

"What are you doing?" he cried.

"Setting a grass fire," Smythe replied. "Don't you see? We'll start a fire and fan it in their direction to chase the bloody things away."

Capital, Clive thought. And if the fire chose to burn in their direction instead? But the wind was blowing toward the behemoths, and it was obvious that no one else had a better plan.

With a bunch of dried grass between his knees, Smythe worked the flint and steel, cursing with great imagination as he attempted to set it alight. Twice he dropped the flint as the reverberations grew too severe and both Clive and Finnbogg momentarily lost their grip on him. The cyborg had turned from the view of the herd to watch them with what Clive swore was amusement in his cold features.

Then a spark flew to the grass, and the grass smoldered. Smythe blew gently until it caught fire. With his makeshift torch in hand, he closed himself from the grip of his companions and crawled unsteadily away from the tree, where he started a line of fire in the tall grass.

"Help me now!" he cried over his shoulder.

Flint and steel returned to their pouch at his belt. He removed his coat, and began to fan it at the flames. The dried grass caught fire quickly, and soon the three of them were beating the sparks that leapt back toward them while simultaneously fanning the flames in the direction of the herd.

The wind at their backs gusted, and suddenly there was a wall of fire rushing away from them. Through the smoke they could see the monstrous heads of the brontosaurs lifting on their extended necks, turning in the direction of the flames.

"That's done it!" Smythe cried as the closest of the creatures lumbered away in panic.

But now they were busy beating out the flames that threatened to engulf their hiding place. Coughing and choking, they built a fire barrier of charred ground on three sides, but they need no longer have worried. The wind drove the fire away from them, and soon there was a sea of flames bearing down on the herd; their island copse was safe.

The earth tremors increased dramatically as the herd lumbered into a panicked half-trot, the behemoths pounding the plain with their immense weight, the scavengers darting among them, quick as lizards. Dust and smoke choked the air. Clive, Smythe, and Finnbogg clung to the ground as it rocked and buckled under them. Even Guafe lost his balance and assumed a similar undignified position. The air rang with the thunder of the herd's flight.

By the time the tremors had been reduced to mere vibrations, the party was so shaken that they could barely stand. Their sense of balance was all awry, and they lurched to their feet like East End drunks, grinning at each other.

"Hurroo!" Smythe cried. "That's foxed the bastards!"

Clive clapped him on the back. "There's the man!"

The cyborg suffered none of their loss of balance. Standing stiffly to one side of them, he brushed at his clothes.

"I see no cause for celebration," he said, his metallic voice sharper than ever. "All you have accomplished is the ruin of a perfect observational opportunity."

"Don't be such a wet goose," Smythe told him. "Would you rather be dead?"

"That is not the point. I believe it would have been far more interesting to gather data on such obscure fauna—not to stampede them."

Smythe didn't bother to reply. He spat on the ground and turned to look at where the fire was dying out as it came up against the tramped and cropped area of the behemoths' trail.

"I don't understand you," Clive said. "We might have died if Horace hadn't thought of turning the herd back with his fire."

Guafe studied the Englishman for a long moment. "Knowledge is a precious commodity," the cyborg said finally. "More important than a few lives."

"Died you would have, too," Finnbogg said. "What good's saved up *thinks* then?"

The cyborg touched his chest. "My memory circuits are stored in a casing that would survive the detonation of a nuclear bomb." At their baffled looks, he added, "By which I mean a great deal of destructive force."

"But *you* wouldn't survive," Clive said.

"That is not important."

Smythe turned to look at Guafe. "Sounds to me like a case of a wet arse and no fish."

Now it was the cyborg's turn to appear confused.

"A fruitless quest," Clive explained.

Smythe nodded. "A man's a man, for a' that," he said, quoting Burns. "For what he is, my clockwork man, for what he does. If a man's heart is true, he is more important than any cause. Better to be remembered for the good deeds you've done than for what bits of knowledge you carry around in your brain. You may have some indestructible memory chest inside you, but it'll do no one any good if you're to die here. Who's to find it?"

"My people would—"

"If your people knew where you are, they'd come looking for you, now, wouldn't they?"

"This is a pointless discussion," Guafe said, effectively ending the conversation. "We have the better part of the day ahead of us, and a long journey still to complete. I suggest we get on with it."

Without waiting for them, he set off.

It was easier traveling, following in the trail of the brontosaur herd. Without having to fight through the grass, even dodging the crater-like footprints, they made much better time, doubling the distance that they had covered the previous day.

"We're beginning to look like a pair of heavy swells," Smythe remarked to Clive as they followed the cyborg, who walked ahead of them with a stiff-backed gait.

Clive nodded, fingering his beard. A few decades ago—at least, in English years, and counting back from when they'd left London—the officers returning from the Crimea had started a new fashion of full beards, or opulent side-whiskers, that the heavy swells took as their own. They spoke in languid drawls to indicate their social superiority, turning all their r's into w's. Specimens of their kind survived well into the 1860s.

"At least we haven't descended to that wather weawi-some style of speech."

"Oh, Howace. How you do go on!"

Both men broke into laughter, garnering a puzzled look from Finnbogg.

"Don't worry, Finn," Smythe assured him. "We haven't both gone knackers."

"I needed that laugh," Clive said when he'd recovered his breath.

Smythe nodded. "It's a grim world," he said. "And, speaking of grimness, are there any other dangers on this level that you haven't warned us of, Finn?"

Clive patted the pocket that held his twin's journal.

"We need all the warning we can get. Neville said nothing about those creatures."

"I wouldn't count on too much help from your brother, sah," Smythe said. "That's one thing Annabelle had right—we're more liable to run headlong into danger following his directions, than going our own way. It's what he doesn't tell us that worries me."

Clive was in complete agreement. "More surprises, we don't need."

"Finnbogg heard story of Walking Mountains and their herdsmen a long time ago," the dwarf said. "Finnbogg doesn't remember much of it. But when they came and ground shook, then Finnbogg—"

"Herdsmen?" Smythe cried. "What herdsmen?"

"Perhaps he's referring to those scavenger creatures," Clive said hopefully.

The dwarf's brow wrinkled as he searched for the memory. "Finnbogg thinks they're a kind of bird. A low-flying bird."

Clive and Smythe worriedly scanned the sky.

"Silver in color," Finnbogg went on, "and they nest in the mountains." He waved a hand in the general direction of the mountain range that, for all their traveling away from it, appeared as close today as it had two days previous.

Smythe said, "It's at least a week's march across this plain. If luck is with us, for once, perhaps we'll miss meeting up with them."

Clive frowned. "Neville wrote nothing of these herdsmen."

"He wrote nothing of the herd, either," Smythe replied.

The remainder of that day, they watched the skies, getting cricks in their necks, but there was no sign of any bird, silver or otherwise. Smythe brought down another of the curious dares in the late afternoon, so once again they had fresh meat for their supper. The dares had been congregated about a small fresh-water seep, so while Smythe cleaned his kill, Clive and Finnbogg filled their watersacks, which had been growing steadily emptier since leaving the river.

That evening, as they smoked strips of the meat for the next day's meals, the two Englishmen kept after Finnbogg, wanting more information about this level of the Dungeon. The dwarf fended off their queries, growing more upset, until he flew into a sudden, towering rage.

"Don't know, don't know!" he shouted. "Finnbogg only ever remember bits and pieces. Finnbogg would tell you if he knew more, but he doesn't! He doesn't!"

He stood over the two sitting men, glowering with rage, then suddenly burst into tears. Clive and Smythe exchanged awkward glances. They'd been through the dwarf's sudden mood swings before, but that didn't make them feel any less like heels at the moment.

"By his behavior patterns," Guafe remarked conversationally, "I don't doubt that he's a schizophrenic." That drew blank stares from both Englishmen.

"By which I mean," the cyborg explained, "he has an abnormally high number of dopamine receptors in his brain, so these sudden shifts in mood aren't really his fault. Neurosurgery could correct the problem, though I doubt we'd find facilities advanced enough on this level for me to help him—if, in fact, that is what he is suffering from. Being unfamiliar with his physiology, I would need to do some exploratory—"

"Why don't you shut your gob for a change," Smythe told Guafe as he knelt beside the weeping dwarf. He put an arm around Finnbogg's broad shoulders.

"We're sorry," he said, giving Finnbogg a squeeze, "the Major and I. We didn't mean to have at you as we did."

"Finnbogg . . . just doesn't know any more," the dwarf said in a small voice. "It comes and goes and he can never remember sometimes."

"And we know that now, Finn—don't we, sah? You've been a great help to us many's the time already. Don't you worry now."

Finnbogg rubbed his knuckles against his eyes. Clive sat on his haunches in front of the dwarf.

"I'm truly sorry, Finn," he said.

The dwarf blinked, then suddenly appeared self-conscious under all the attention.

"Friends?" Clive asked.

He offered his hand. After a moment, Finnbogg nodded and shook. Smythe gave the dwarf's shoulders a final squeeze.

"There's the lad," he said. Then he gave Guafe a cold look. "Why don't you take first watch—seeing how you like to observe things so much and all?"

"I'll be glad to," Guafe said.

"One day," Smythe muttered, smacking his right fist into his left palm. Then he tugged Finnbogg over to where he and Clive were sitting by the fire and regaled the dwarf with a few preposterous tales, until Finnbogg was clutching his stomach with laughter.

It was on the following day, just as the salmon-colored sun was reaching its zenith, that they spied what looked to be a low hill a mile or so away on the plain before them. It was Smythe who first realized that it was a dead brontosaur, but it was Finnbogg who spotted the small silver airships that were parked around the carcass, their silver-suited drivers harvesting the behemoth's flesh. Guafe called the airships one-man hovercraft.

"The herdsmen," Finnbogg said.

Clive's throat felt suddenly dry.

"Best we don't play the jack this time," Smythe said. "Time to hide ourselves."

He jumped into the nearest brontosaur footprint, Clive and Finnbogg following suit, but it was too late. The herdsmen had already spied them. A number of the silver hovercraft left the carcass and sped across the plain toward them, riding the air a foot or so above the ground.

The flyers closed the distance between them with such speed, they realized that they had no hope of outrunning the machines.

Chapter 10

The village of the blue shark people was a half-day's march farther down the trail they'd been taking. It was a cluster of small, one-room huts, the walls and roofs constructed of reeds tied to wooden frames. Cookfires burned at the doorways. Domestic cousins of the lupine-faced possums hung by their tails from poles, heads slowly turning to watch the progress of Annabelle's party and their captors.

They were herded unceremoniously into the center of the village, where they were immediately surrounded by a crowd of the blue-skinned beings. Shark-toothed grins leered at them. Children with half-grown fins following the ridges of their spines poked at them with sticks. From all sides rose that maraca sound, as though Annabelle and her party had been dumped into the middle of a rattlesnake's nest.

Chica-chica-chica-chica . . .

Though she tried, Annabelle could discern no real variations in the sound, so she doubted it was a language. An expression of excitement, maybe? Or, how about amusement?

Prodded and pushed, they stood in a small, huddled group, with Shriek's limp body deposited at their feet. The noise of the shark people was steadily increasing, until Annabelle had to grit her teeth against the sound. It was painful—worse than feedback from her Les Paul—but it was also humiliating. She had the same feeling now as when she'd been on the receiving end of the chorusing boos her band had gotten the time they'd opened for Death Squad, whose neo-Nazi fans had eloquently expressed their impatience with the combination of music and theater that made up the Crackbelles' act.

Lookit the freaks.

When the sudden silence fell, it left a relief so profound that all Annabelle's limbs went weak. But she kept herself stiffly upright, for coming toward them through the parting crowd was an awesome figure that even the shark people seemed to hold with as much fear as they did respect.

He was a good foot taller than any of the other villagers, blue-skinned as well, but his entire body was covered with tiny white shells, which were attached by wires directly to his skin, like pierced earrings. His hair was long and braided with blue feathers. From a shell-festooned belt about his waist hung a small cluster of monkey skulls, and a flat fur pouch with a bluish tint to its pelage.

In one hand he carried a staff two feet taller than himself. From its head dangled more shells, these threaded on leather thongs, and the skeletal arms of what she assumed were monkeys, the bones wired loosely together so that the limbs swung back and forth with every movement of the staff.

He came to a stop directly in front of the captives and studied them with a considering gaze. His eyes were a cloudy white, like a blind man's, but it was obvious he could see.

"Hrak," he said suddenly, thumping his free hand against his chest.

The shells attached to his skin clattered at the impact. Annabelle winced at the pain it must have caused; but maybe these creatures didn't have nerves in their skin. When she thought about how she'd feel if her own flesh was like that, it seemed likely.

A chorus of subdued *chica-chics* arose from the crowd. The one who appeared to be the leader gazed at them expectantly, as though waiting for a response.

Great, Annabelle thought. What the hell's "hrak" supposed to mean? His name? His title? The kind of being his is? Hello? Howyadoin'?

Impatient with the silence of his captives, the leader poked Annabelle with a stiff finger.

"Folly!" he cried.

Jesus, Annabelle thought with sudden insight. He's trying to say Folliot. Clive's brother must have passed through here, and this geek thinks anybody with skin this white's a "folly." Now, the thing to figure out was, had Neville left these guys in a good mood, or had he been shitting on them like he did in almost every other place they'd tracked him to? Only one way to find out.

Annabelle took a steady breath. "Folly," she said, thumping her chest in a manner similar to the leader's.

He glared at her from his milky eyes. There was no question about his displeasure.

Way to go, Annabelle thought. Annie B. blows it again.

Without warning, the leader batted her across the head with his free fist. Arms bound behind her back so that she couldn't maintain her balance. Annabelle hit the ground, head ringing from the blow, shoulder bruised front the impact with the dirt. The leader spat down at her.

"Folly, folly!" he cried.

The surrounding crowd took up the cry, mixed with the rattling *chica-chics*. The leader thrust a hand toward a distant hut and then eager hands were hauling Annabelle to her feet, propelling her and her two standing companions toward it. Others dragged Shriek along, hauling her by one leg and a couple of her arms. Inside the hut, they were pushed to the ground. The door swung closed on leather hinges, and grinning shark faces pressed against it to look at the captives.

They hissed and spat, uvulas rattling.

Chica-chica-chica.

As Annabelle rose blearily into a sitting position, her vision swimming, a gob hit her on the cheek, the saliva leaving a slight burning sensation on her skin. She rubbed her cheek against her knee, then back-pedaled to the farthest corner of the hut, away from the crowd of creatures at the door.

"Why were you so *estúpido?*" Tomàs demanded.

Annabelle turned to look at him. "Blow it out your face," she told him. "I didn't see you coming up with anything better."

Tomàs's lips pulled into a snarl, but he made no reply, only turned his head away. Annabelle tested her bonds. The braided grass rope still held tight. She tried to ignore the crowd of leering faces at the door, and eventually they lost interest and drew away. It was then that the captives could see the stakes being raised in the square in the middle of the village, the wood being piled around their bases.

Four stakes. Four captives. No need to guess what they had to look forward to in the very near future.

"Aw, shit," Annabelle said. "What're we gonna do now?"

"Wait," Sidi told her.

"For what? The cavalry? I hate to break this to you, Sidi, but they're not going to show."

Sidi merely nodded to where Shriek lay, still unconscious. "If she were dead, they would not have thrown her in here with us. So we wait for the effect of the dart to wear off. She is not bound as we are."

Except, what if she didn't come round in time? Annabelle wanted to know, but she didn't speak her fear aloud. Instead, she leaned back against the wall of the hut and closed her eyes.

Annabelle tried not to think of the stakes, and the pyres being erected around them. From time to time she glanced at Shriek's limp body, but the spiderlike alien still showed no sign of life. Then she'd glance away again, catching Tomàs's gaze sliding from her own. Or meeting Sidi's, which was not quite resigned, but growing steadily less confident. Or seeing the stakes again, the blue-skinned shark people milling around them.

Those damned stakes.

She closed her eyes once more and thought of the last time she'd seen her daughter, out in front of her mother's place, where Amanda was staying with her Grannymums while the Crackbelles went on tour.

"Are you coming back, mommy?" Amanda had asked, her urchin face turned worriedly up to Annabelle's. "You won't forget me, will you?"

Amanda had a fear of being abandoned—because of all the band's touring. She thought one time that Annabelle just wouldn't come back. Like I'd ever dump her, Annabelle thought.

"No way, José," she'd told her daughter, mussing the short black curls. "I'll be back before you can say Jack Lippity Sprat."

Amanda's reply was to reach up for a tearful hug.

I'll be back, Annabelle thought, remembering. Right. She looked out at the stakes. I didn't mean to lie to you, sweetheart, but your mommy's never coming back.

"Life slips through our fingers," Annabelle's own mother had told her once. "Everyone says that—that time goes too quickly, that we never get to do everything we want to do in the time we have—but it's worse in our family, Annie. We never keep the things that are most precious to us—lovers, happiness. We never get to hold on to anything good for very long. Your grandmother used to say that there was a curse on the women of our line. 'Be happy with all your heart when you can be,' she told me, 'for it won't last. It never does. If you try to hold on, you'll only get hurt.'"

No kidding. Annabelle knew just what her mother had meant. Like saving up a lot of hard-earned cash for her first Les Paul, then getting mugged walking home with it from the store. Beautiful New York City. Like just having the Crackbelles finally start to get some decent gigs, and here she was, dusted off into Bizarro—Land of the Weird and Strange, where it looked like she was gonna end up as dinner for a bunch of monsters.

The Sharks That Walk Like Men. Now playing at a theater near you. Thrill to the chills. See the rock star and her friends become shark stew.

Aw, Jesus.

All she could see were Amanda's teary eyes. That sweet face turned up to hers.

You won't forget me, will you?

Never, sweetheart.

Are you coming back, mommy?

Tears were starting to leak from her eyes. She could feel Tomàs's disdainful gaze on her, Sidi's sympathetic one. Neither of them knew. They thought she was crying for herself, because she was scared, but it wasn't that. Not just that. It was the thought of leaving that big hole in her daughter's life. It was thinking of the poor kid growing up with first her old man, and then her old lady, dumping her.

I'm like the spell the fairies use, she thought, when they give humans gold in Fairyland and it turns out to be just dead leaves and crap when they get back to their own world. Everything I touch turns to shit.

Are you coming back, mommy?

She looked at the stakes, the wood piled up around their bases. Just waiting for her and her friends. They were probably due on that center stage at nightfall—at least, that's the way it usually worked in all the frigging movies.

You won't forget me, will you?

She looked at Shriek, still unconscious. Tomàs and Sidi watching her. The braided grass ropes around all their wrists, too tough to break. Maybe we could chew through them? Right. But then her gaze dropped down to the arms of her jacket, which was still tied around her waist.

Wake up, Annie B., she told herself.

"Sidi?"

"Yes?"

"Come help me get my jacket off, would you?"

Though he looked puzzled, the Indian slid himself over to where she was sitting and complied. When she had the jacket in her hands, she played around with it until she had a grip on one of the zippers. She held it firmly between her fingers.

"Get your hands around back here," she told him.

Sidi's eyes lit up as he understood. The metal zipper didn't have much bite, but it was going to be enough to saw through the grass ropes. It bloody well had to be.

It was tough going. The jacket kept slipping in her grip, and it was hard to work on something without being able to see what she was doing, but after a good fifteen minutes of sawing, the grass became weak enough for Sidi to break the remaining strands.

"All *right*," Annabelle said as he started to work on her own bonds.

The Indian was stronger, and he had her free in half the time, moving on to free Tomàs while she rubbed her chafed wrists and considered their next move. Shriek still wasn't moving. Should they try to make a break for it now—out the back of the hut, which faced the river, hauling Shriek as they went—or wait until the shark people came to get them, and try to take them down? There really wasn't any decision to make.

She moved to the back of the hut and explored the reed covering of the wooden frame. It'd be a piece of cake to get through that. When she looked back at the others, she saw that Tomàs was free now, as well. Sidi returned to her side, handing her back the jacket, which she retied around her waist.

"Good thinking."

"Yeah, well, I got lucky. But we're not outta here yet."

"We're going out the back?"

Annabelle nodded. "Only choice we've got, I figure. We'll hit the river and make a swim for it—it'll be easier pulling Shriek through the water than trying to haul her through the jungle. Can you swim?"

Sidi bobbed his head, white teeth flashing.

"How about you, Tomàs? A fine sailor like you—can you swim?"

Considering his aversion to bathing, it was just as likely that he couldn't.

"*Sim.*"

"Great." Annabelle glanced out the door, but no one seemed to be paying undue attention to them. "Let's get going, then. Sidi, you break down the wall—and quietly, please—while Tomàs gives me a hand with Shriek."

Tomàs shook his head. "Leave her."

"No way, pal."

"She is a monster."

"She's a friend. Now, either you give me a hand with her, or we'll knock you silly and leave you behind to be fish food—got it?"

"It is a waste of time," Tomàs argued. He gave Shriek's body a nudge with his toe that got no response. "She is already dead."

Sidi had broken a peephole through the reeds in the back of the hut. "All clear," he called softly over his shoulder.

"We've got a problem with the weasel here," Annabelle told him. "He won't help me with Shriek."

Sidi frowned and left the wall, brown fingers of either hand clenched into fists.

Tomàs quickly raised his hands protectively in front of him. "*Ja nao,*" he said. "I was only joking. I'm happy to help. *Verdade.*"

Annabelle gave him a hard stare. Yeah. Sure you are. Until someone offers you a better deal. But she motioned Sidi to return to the wall. While he continued to widen the small hole he'd made, she and Tomàs dragged Shriek's heavy body toward the back of the hut. When the hole was big enough, Sidi cautiously stuck his head outside.

"Still clear," he said.

He stepped through the opening, then helped the other two manhandle Shriek's body through. In moments they were all outside. The river bank was no more than fifteen feet directly behind the hut, hidden from the village's central square by a number of other huts.

Thank you, God, Annabelle said in silent prayer, eschewing her devout atheism. But then she heard the rattlesnake *chica-chic* of one of the shark people's uvulas. She turned, looking up from her half-crouch, to find a blue-skinned creature looming up directly behind her, obviously having just come around the hut to stumble upon them.

Shit, Annabelle thought. Everything I touch . . .

Chapter 11

Unarmed, and with nowhere to run, Clive's party awaited the approach of the herdsmen in their hovercraft—Clive, Smythe, and Finnbogg bunched together in a group, the cyborg standing off to one side on his own. Their helplessness chafed at them all, but considering their situation, the only reasonable course of action left open to them was to wait to see how events would unfold. For men who preferred to control their own destinies, it was not an easy course of action. But then, since entering the Dungeon, nothing had been simple or easy.

The hovercraft made next to no sound as they darted toward the party. Their riders gave the Englishmen the uneasy sense that they were defying the laws of science—a feeling that Finnbogg shared. The cyborg appeared unaffected by their fears.

Happily content to take advantage of another "observational opportunity," Clive thought with some bitterness, with no consideration of the possible danger it presented to them. The cyborg's next comments served only to confirm Clive's feelings.

"Fascinating," Guafe remarked, almost to himself. "The craft appear to be a form of scooter, utilizing an air cushion to keep them aloft, but still capable of great speed. I wonder what their method of propulsion would be."

The machines settled slowly to the ground in a half-circle facing the party, the low hum of their engines dying as their silver-suited riders switched off the ignitions and stepped down from the machines. Settled upon the ground, the flyers no longer appeared quite so marvelous. They were merely machines now—gleaming steel, and far beyond the technological capabilities of Clive's own England—but still machines.

It seemed, he realized at the present turn of his thoughts, that their continued tenure in this odd land was leaving him somewhat inured to its wonders.

He studied the approaching riders. At least they were humanoid—very much like Europeans, really—though it was hard to make much of their features behind the goggles and helmets they wore. The shimmery material of their suits clung to their bodies like a second skin, acquiring particularly intriguing shapes on the two women in the group.

One of the women was obviously the leader.

She took a few steps ahead of the others and removed her helmet and goggles. Her hair was blonde, and cropped to within a half-inch of her skull. Her eyes were the green-blue of the sky, her features not quite classically beautiful—due as much to her lack of hair to frame them, Clive thought, as to their actual proportions—but handsome all the same. Clipped to her belt was a holster that obviously held a firearm, though of what sort neither Clive nor Smythe could even make a guess.

A casual glance at the others of her party revealed that they all bore similar weapons. The woman regarded them each for a moment, then returned her attention to Clive. A friendly smile touched her lips.

"You will be Major Clive Folliot?" she asked.

Clive blinked with surprise. "How do you know my name?"

She gave a casual shrug of her shoulders, which gave her breasts an enticing bounce. Clive forced his gaze to remain on her face.

"We have been keeping a watch out for your party," she said. "You have been expected. We thought to find you sooner, but when we spied the porten herd, we delayed long enough to bring one down." She nodded over her shoulder. "Others of my company are butchering it as we speak. There is enough sustenance there to feed the city for a month. A worthy delay, don't you think?"

Confusion still reigned in Clive's mind, but he managed to school his features to give none of it away. "Certainly," he said. "But tell me, how did you know we were here?"

"Your brother, the priest, asked us to look for you—Father Neville."

The priest? Clive thought. Was Neville coming down in the world? The last they'd heard of his religious inclinations, he'd called himself a bishop.

"I see," he said. "And where is Father Neville? Can you take us to him?"

"Of course. That is the reason we have been looking for you."

"Who are you?"

The woman smiled again. "So many questions. Father Neville told us you would be full of them. I am Keoti Vichlo, First Scout of the Dramaran Dynasty."

"Dramaran—that is the ruined city a few days' journey to the east?"

Keoti frowned slightly. "Ruined, yes—but not for long. Now that your brother has raised us from the Long Sleep, we have begun to restore it to its former glory. Still, you must not worry that all is hardship in Dramaran at the moment. We have pleasant lodgings that are still intact, under the city."

"Long Sleep?" Clive couldn't help but ask, for all that he didn't wish the newcomers to realize just how ignorant of advanced technologies and this world his party was.

But Guafe understood immediately. "That would be a form of suspended animation, I presume," he said. "Can I assume that there was some form of malfunction with your equipment, effectively trapping you in that state until the fortunate arrival of . . . ah . . . Father Neville?"

Clive and Smythe shot the cyborg a curious look. Neither had ever heard Guafe hesitate in speech before and it jolted them. Keoti gave the cyborg a considering look as well. She seemed about to speak, but Clive was quicker.

"How do you come to speak English so well?" he asked.

"Father Neville taught us," she replied with a shrug. "We fed his language into our computers through a bio-feed link and received the data in a similar fashion. Is this not the way with your own people?"

Clive had only the vaguest notion as to what she was referring to, but he nodded. "Of course," he said.

Keoti turned her attention back to Chang Guafe. "What a superior piece of workmanship," she said. "Your humanotron appears so lifelike. One would almost believe that it was truly alive, rather than a construct."

"I am a self-aware cyborg," Guafe told her coldly. "Not a construct."

"Pardon me," she said. "I meant no offense."

"None taken," the cyborg replied, though it was obvious to all that exactly the opposite was the case.

Don't start now, Clive thought. The Dramaranians appeared to be quite friendly, and he preferred to leave things that way—not insult or anger them, as Guafe was apt to do if he began to argue.

"Yes, well," Clive said briskly. "It will be wonderful to see my good brother again. Let me introduce you to the rest of my companions. Chang Guafe you have just met. This gentleman on my right is my good companion Quartermaster Sergeant Horace Smythe."

"Yes," Keoti said. "Father Neville has spoken of you, Horace Smythe. You have some gift with . . . theatrics, I believe."

"I'm not sure what you mean, madam," Smythe said.

She smiled. "A talent that allows you to appear to be something other than you are."

"And this is our Friend Finnbogg," Clive said.

Keoti gave the dwarf a polite smile, but introduced none of her own companions. "We can take one passenger per flyer," she said. "If you are willing, we can begin the return flight to Dramaran as soon as I give my second-in-command—" she glanced back to where the greater number of Dramaranians were still at work on the porten's carcass "—his orders."

Clive glanced at Smythe and knew by the expression on his former batman's features that the same worries were troubling him. This Keoti woman was extremely friendly and forthcoming, but with Neville involved—and who knew what mischief he was up to—they might well be walking into yet another trap. Still, what choice did they have? When Smythe gave a brief shrug, Clive turned back to the woman.

"We'd be delighted to partake of your hospitality," he said.

Keoti smiled. "Will you ride with me?"

"I think we'd prefer to walk," Clive said. "At least as far as that . . . porten carcass your company is butchering. We'll join you there."

"As you wish."

She gave Clive a warm smile. Replacing her helmet and goggles, she returned to her flyer. Within moments the hovercraft were airborne once more, and speeding back to rejoin their companions.

"Well," Clive said, once they were gone. "They seem pleasant enough."

Smythe nodded. "Too pleasant, I'm thinking, sah. I don't like this—not with Sir Neville's hand in it, stirring the pot."

"At least they have some technology worth studying," Guafe offered, "even if their observational powers are somewhat limited."

They began to walk toward the dead behemoth, where the Dramaranians continued their harvesting work, busily surrounding the slain monster like a flock of flies.

"Did you know of any of this?" Clive asked Finnbogg. "Of this Long Sleep, or this second city, buried under the ruins of the first?"

"Not a whisper," the dwarf replied.

"What's Sir Neville up to?" Smythe wondered aloud. "'Father Neville,' indeed. The man's about as holy as a fat, pursy gunner, living high on the hog of his spoils."

"At least he's waiting for us," Clive said.

Smythe nodded. "As he's waited for us before. The thought doesn't give me much comfort, sah. I'd sooner just give him a few stout blows in the head than take the chance of falling victim to another of his jigamarees."

"I doubt our present hosts would allow that," Guafe said.

The carcass was looming closer—truly, if not a mountain, then a large hill of flesh, rising up from the flat surface of the veldt. The Dramaranians were cutting the huge slabs of meat from the monster's haunches with some form of saw that appeared to be composed of a tightly focused band of light.

"Lasers," Guafe said.

None of his companions bothered to ask him to explain. It was all simply too far out of their depth.

"Well, I, for one, will be very interested in hearing what Neville has to say for himself," Clive said. There was a hard look in his eyes as he spoke. "He has a great deal of explaining to do."

Smythe nodded. "Very interested," he agreed. "Just don't blink in his presence, or we might find ourselves whisked away to Lord knows where."

Keoti walked out to join them as they finally approached. They had to crane their necks to look at the top part of the porten's carcass.

"I am finished here," she said. "If you are ready to go now . . . ?"

She led the way back to her hovercraft without waiting for Clive's reply.

"Careful now," Smythe whispered quickly to Clive as another of the Dramaranians motioned to him.

"And you," Clive replied.

Finnbogg, however, wouldn't go with the Dramaranian who would be ferrying him to the ruined city.

"Finnboggi weren't meant to go floating in the air," he said. "It's not right."

"We won't be going very high," the Dramaranian coaxed him. "No more than a few feet above the ground."

"A few feet more than Finnbogg wants to be," the dwarf said. He stamped a foot against the ground. "Here's where Finnbogg is meant to be. With dirt in toes. Not playing bird."

Clive quickly interceded before Finnbogg shifted into one of his more belligerent moods. He put an arm around the dwarf's shoulder.

"It will be fine," he said. "We're all riding with them, Finn."

"It's not right," the dwarf repeated, though not so forcefully this time.

"Think of it as an adventure," Smythe said to him. "What a tale you'll have to tell—skimming for leagues over the veldt to a ruined city that's being rebuilt by its inhabitants." He rubbed the palms of his hands together. "Doesn't just the thought of it make you itch to get there the sooner?"

"We don't want to leave you behind," Clive added.

"Hrumph," Finnbogg said.

But though he walked stiffly, and frowned with every step, he let himself be led to the flyer. He mounted it gingerly, as though the machine would bite. Once he was seated, the others went to the flyers they would be riding.

It felt decidedly awkward, Clive thought as he sat behind Keoti, the machine straddled between his legs. It was like mounting a legless horse—and with nothing to hold on to, to keep from falling off. Keoti showed him where to put his feet—they went on small pegs, set into the side of the machine, that lifted his knees level with his buttocks—then placed his hands around her waist.

"Hold on," she said.

The material of her bodysuit had a metallic texture, but it was so supple that Clive could feel the bottom of her rib cage and the soft flesh of her waist, as though there was nothing between his hands and her skin. She looked over her shoulder at him, head like a bug with its helmet and goggles, but her lips were a woman's, and they smiled cheerfully at him.

The machine's engine set up a vibration against Clive's legs when it was turned on, then suddenly they were up in the air, hovering some three feet above the ground. He felt giddy at the sudden movement and clutched Keoti very tightly. Realizing what he was doing, he eased his grip. He looked around to see how his companions were doing. Finnbogg's face was blanched. Smythe's and Guafe's features were impassive.

Then the flyers shot off, and they were skimming across the veldt. They circled once around the brontosaur carcass, where the remainder of the Dramaranians continued their butchering work. The workers lifted bloody hands in greeting, and then the open plains were in front of Clive's party, and they settled down for the long trip to the ruined city, where Neville was waiting for them.

Chapter 12

Time took on a slow-motion quality for Annabelle. She and the shark man stared at each other as though they had just spotted each other's face in a crowd and were trying to place the half-familiar features. Annabelle knew she should be doing something—striking out at him, taking him down—but her limbs felt weighed down, heavy and dull.

She saw the shark man's mouth open wider. The first *chica-chic* of his approach had been a sound of surprise. Now he was going to call out a warning to the other villagers. She didn't feel she could do anything to stop him, but started to rise all the same, lead-heavy arms reaching toward him.

Then, one of Shriek's hair thorns sprouted suddenly from his throat. His eyes widened and his stillborn cry became a death gurgle. He toppled toward her.

Annabelle continued to reach for him, bracing herself to catch his weight as it fell. Before he landed, Sidi was there at her side, helping her. Together they lowered the dead shark man to the ground. Annabelle turned slowly to see Shriek half sitting up, her weight supported on three of her arms, the fourth just lowering from its upflung position. There was a dullness in most of her eyes, but one was already clear, the others clearing.

Whatever chemical she'd infused that particular spike with, it had done the job efficiently, and fast—very fast.

Is it dead? Shriek asked. Her voice echoed weakly in Annabelle's mind.

Annabelle nodded. "Thanks."

Shriek merely spat in the direction of the shark man's corpse. Sidi touched Annabelle's shoulder.

"We can't delay," he said.

Annabelle glanced down at the corpse, then gave a quick nod of agreement. While Sidi and Tomàs went on ahead to the river, she got her shoulder under one of Shriek's left arms and helped the alien to her feet. Together they hurried to join the others.

Just beyond the shielding wall of huts, they could hear the sound of the villagers—snatches of conversation in a language none of them could understand, the occasional, high-pitched bark of possum dogs, the nervegrating sound of their uvulas, the hollowed ends rattling, the shaking sound magnified by their mouth cavities.

Chica-chica-chica. . . .

Without bothering to strip off his clothes, Sidi lowered himself into the water. Annabelle and Shriek quickly followed suit, leaving Tomàs hesitating on the river bank.

"Come *on,*" Annabelle whispered sharply.

Plainly unhappy, the Portuguese slipped into the water with them. Sidi took the lead, walking them out at a right angle away from the village until the water was level with his neck. Then he kicked his feet free of the river bottom and began to swim, careful not to break the water with a splash that would alert their captors.

Annabelle and Shriek moved through the water closer to the river bank, as Shriek couldn't swim. Instead, with Annabelle there to help support her weight in the water, she half walked, half kicked herself along, using the river bottom as a springboard. Tomàs took up the rear.

Soon the village was out of view, and then even its sounds faded. The bugs were worse than ever this close to the river, and time and again they had to dunk their heads to get rid of the clouds of mosquitoes that were settling on their faces and neck, even in their hair.

"The sooner we get to that gate and outta this jungle," Annabelle muttered, "the happier I'm gonna be. I don't care where it takes us."

"At least we're free of our captors," Sidi remarked.

But he spoke too soon. Even with the distance that they'd put between them and the village, the sudden cries of outraged anger carried dearly toward them.

"Shit."

Sidi glanced at Annabelle and nodded. "We'd best get out of the river," he said. "Considering what they are, I don't doubt that they'll be able to track us through the water—just like the sharks of our own world."

"You're kidding. I thought water was supposed to throw off your scent."

Sidi nodded, then lifted his arm to show the tiny cuts and bruises there, like those they all had. "But a shark can track blood for miles."

They made their way to the shore, clambering up among the thick vines and vegetation. Low-hanging boughs hid them from view, but their trail led directly to where they stood.

Look, Shriek said.

She pointed with one arm to where the first of the shark people had come into view. He swam with an undulating motion of his body, arms kept close to his side, dorsal fin breaking the water, head bobbing up and down with the movement. In moments there were three more, close behind, then another pair.

Shriek plucked a hair spike from her thigh and, holding back a bough to give herself room, threw it at the foremost of their pursuers with a sharp snapping movement of her arm. The spike struck true. The creature began to thrash in the water, limbs convulsing, blood coughing up from his lungs. The others immediately attacked him, tearing at his thrashing limbs with their powerful jaws.

Annabelle turned away, a sick taste coming up her throat.

Shriek flung a second spike, and then the creatures were tearing at that victim as well, fighting among themselves in a feeding frenzy.

That should keep them, Shriek said.

"More will be coming by land," Sidi warned.

Nodding in dull agreement, Annabelle let the Indian lead them deeper into the jungle, away from the river. Some twenty paces in, they stumbled over the game trail, which appeared to have entered the village and then continued on to meet them here. With its more solid footing, and its overhang relatively clear compared to the surrounding forest, they set off at a mile-eating gait, trying to put as much distance between themselves and their pursuit as they could.

They paced themselves, trotting for a quarter of a mile, then walking, then trotting again. The distance fell away behind them, but they were all worn out now. Annabelle knew that they wouldn't be able to maintain this pace very much longer. She clutched the stitch in her side, waiting for her second wind to cut in. All she wanted to do was throw herself down and collapse where she lay. The heat and humidity made her mind dull and sapped the strength from her limbs.

Ahead of her she could see Tomàs lagging. Shriek, still recovering from the effects of the shark people's treated dart, had little of her usual resilience left either. Only Sidi seemed able to keep up the pace forever, if need be, but he held himself back, matching his speed to that of his slower companions.

There was no sign or sound of pursuit yet—neither on the trail behind them, nor in the occasional glimpses of the river they caught where the jungle's dense growth cleared for a moment. But they'd be coming. None of them doubted the tenacity of the shark people. They just had that look about them, Annabelle thought. They weren't the kind to give up.

Yeah, well, neither are we.

But a half-hour later her legs simply gave out from under her, and she went toppling to the ground, only just saving herself from a bad fall by grabbing onto a low-hanging vine. She lost her grip on it almost immediately, but it had been enough to break her fall. When she hit the ground, she didn't hit hard.

She tried to get up, but her calves and thighs were locked with cramps. When the others turned back to help her, she tried to wave them on.

"Go on," she said. "Get outta here."

Sidi shook his head. While Tomàs and Shriek literally collapsed where they stood, he knelt by her and began to massage her legs with his quick, long fingers, kneading the muscles through her leather jeans until they began to unlock. Her eyes teared with pain, but she didn't complain. The relief was profound as Sidi worked out the cramps, even though the muscles continued to throb.

"Anybody ever tell you that you're a godsend?" Annabelle asked him.

Sidi grinned. *"Keh.* Not recently."

Annabelle smiled back at him, but her moment of good humor was short-lived. "I don't know if I can go on right away," she said. "I'm mean, I've always been in pretty good shape—you go on a tour that's lasting a few months, and you'd *better* be in shape—but the old bod's been taking too much abuse lately."

"We'll rest here for a little while—a half-hour."

"Those shark guys . . ."

"I observed them carefully when they caught us," Sidi replied. "Though they have a very liquid style of movement, they don't appear to have a great deal of speed on land. I think we're well ahead of them, for the moment."

"What about on the river?"

The Indian shrugged. "We'll face that when the time comes. Shriek's stopped them for a while, I think. Rest now, Annabelle, while I see to the others."

"I'm too wound up to rest," Annabelle told him, but she dozed off before Sidi had taken the two steps to where Shriek was lying.

By nightfall they'd put at least six more miles behind them. Exhausted, they sprawled around a small campfire set well east of the game trail—on the side opposite from the river. Twice they had thought they'd heard the grating *chica-chic* rattle of the shark people on the trail behind them. Both times they hid alongside the path, clutching the spears that Sidi had cut for each of them; both times they were false alarms. The second time they found the source of the sound—a small, scorpionlike creature about eleven inches long, with a rattlesnake rattle on the end of its tail in place of a stinger.

For supper they had baked fish that Sidi had speared in the river after he'd set up camp for the others. Now he was hardening the points of their spears in the fire. When he finished the last one, he covered the fire with dirt and they sat in the darkness.

Annabelle had gotten her second wind. Supper had helped, and she felt stronger now, but guilty that so much of the day's decisions and work had fallen on Sidi's slender shoulders. She was determined to pull her own weight the next day—*if* she could find the energy to get up in the morning, that is.

Tomàs sat by himself, away from the rest of them, muttering to himself in Portuguese for a time, then lapsing into a sullen silence. Shriek was grooming herself, carefully working at her hair spikes. The faint rustling of the spikes was the only unnatural sound to be heard against the noise of the jungle until Sidi came to sit beside Annabelle.

His footsteps were muffled, but sounded very loud to her, all wired up as she was, listening to the sounds of night, waiting for the jungle noises to cease at the *chica-chic* of the shark people. She shifted a little to give him room to lean against the tree trunk she'd claimed for a backrest. Their shoulders touched companionably.

"Tomorrow," Sidi asked, "we go on to Quan?"

"Christ, I don't know anymore. I'm tempted to backtrack and try to catch up with Clive and the rest of them."

"The veldt is wide, Annabelle—we could easily miss them."

"Yeah. And spend the rest of our lives wandering around out there. What do you think we should do, Sidi?"

"Go on."

"I suppose." She sighed. "Do you think they're still following us— the shark people?"

"I think so, yes,"

"We need some defense against their blowguns. I mean, these spears of yours are good and all that, but we gotta get in close to use them. By the time we do, they could've taken us all down."

She wondered about the spear lying there on the ground beside her. Could she stick it into somebody—even one of the shark people? She supposed she could, if she had to, but she wasn't really sure. She just wasn't really cut out for this kind of thing.

"I could make us shields," Sidi said. "If we had the skins, the wood for the framework, the time."

"Time. Yeah. Maybe heading for Quan's a big mistake, Sidi. What if the people there are no better than what we've got tracking us down right now? And didn't Finn say something about there being ghosts or something there? Maybe we're just walking into more trouble."

"Unfortunately, from our experiences in this Dungeon so far, that seems quite likely."

"I wonder how Clive's doing."

"Surviving, I hope. But the veldt will have its own dangers, Annabelle."

"I suppose. Okay. We go on to Quan. How far do you think it still is?"

"Three and a half, four days."

"I don't know if I can take another minute of this frigging jungle. I feel like one huge mosquito bite."

"You attract them to you by the tension you project—your irritation with them. Ignore them, and you will find they trouble you less."

"Easy for you to say—they're not bothering you."

"Because I—"

Annabelle laughed. "I know. Because you ignore them—like you do the heat. It's a cute trick, Sidi. Wish it could work for me, you know?"

"It works, Annabelle," he insisted. "Just try it."

"You can't teach an old dog new tricks," she said. "They say that where you come from?"

"No. We say, 'The cautious seldom err.' It's not really the same thing."

"Same things are boring," she told him. "They gotta be different if they're gonna spark."

She turned toward him and could just make out the shadow shape of his head next to hers. His closeness gave her a warm feeling, made her forget the bugs and the heat.

"I like you, Sidi," she said softly. "I like you a lot."

She started to lift a hand to his cheek, but then the sounds of the jungle night went still all around them. Annabelle and Sidi moved apart, reaching for their spears. Tomàs sat up suddenly, his own weapon clutched in sweaty palms. Shriek froze, then swiftly plucked hair thorns—one to hold in each of her four hands.

Chica-chica-chica-chica . . .

The sound seemed to come from all around them. The night was filled with it. Annabelle felt her chest go all tight, then realized she'd been holding her breath. She let it out slowly, tried to regulate her breathing to a slow rhythm, but all her lungs wanted to do was hyperventilate.

They rose to their feet, each of the four facing a different section of the jungle.

Chica-chica-chica . . .

"Been nice knowing you, kids," Annabelle said softly.

Her skin crawled with tension. Any moment she expected to feel one of the shark people's darts hitting her. She kept changing the way she held the spear, trying to find a comfortable way to hold it, settling for a Little John/Robin Hood kind of grip, where she could use the thing like a staff.

Silence fell suddenly.

"What the—" Annabelle began, but then she realized that there'd been another sound behind that of their pursuers' shaking uvulas.

A drumming. It seemed to come from the trees above them—a booming, hollow sound from all sides.

Now what? she wondered.

A shape moved in the corner of her vision. She turned toward it, sighting on the shadowy, streamlined head that was there above the shadow of a dorsal fin. She lifted up her spear, ready to strike, when something dropped out of the trees above her, landing directly on her attacker.

Chapter 13

Except for the wind in his face and the faint vibration of the machine between his legs, Clive could feel no sense of motion, of traveling— at least, not of a manner with which he was familiar. There wasn't the sway of a ship's deck underfoot, the jolting of a carriage seat, the rhythm of a horse's gait. Instead, he was carried along, like a leaf on the wind, or like a kite, floating just above ground that sped by so quickly it was a blur.

The entire concept was decidedly disconcerting, but while he grew used to it in time, he wasn't sure he would ever like it. In that sense he sided more with Finnbogg than with Smythe and Guafe, both of whom appeared to be enjoying the ride—the one immensely, as one does a pleasurable new experience, the other as a convenient method of locomotion, far superior to that of placing one foot before the other. For Clive, it remained too unnatural.

They darted across the veldt, following the track of the brontosaur herd until the trail of flattened grass that marked their route turned to the south, back toward the mountains. The flyers continued straight, rising above the height of the tall, mauve-yellow vegetation that was here unmarred by the behemoths' passage. The grasses whipped against each other as the flyers rushed by above them.

Their party was made up of five of the small hovercraft—one each to bear the members of Clive's company, and a fifth that scouted ahead, keeping in touch with the other flyers through something Keoti called radio contact. Clive assumed it was a variation of a telegraph system, and was startled to learn that actual words could be transmitted in this manner.

When they made camp that evening, the ground seemed to sway under Clive's feet for the first ten minutes or so, but he soon recovered his land legs. From compartments under the seats of the flyers, the Dramaranians brought out tents that appeared almost to set themselves up. Provisions followed, and small portable stoves to cook them with that had no source of heat Clive could perceive. The term *microwave* meant nothing to him.

"Explain to me," the cyborg Guafe asked of their hosts, after they had all eaten, "these flyers of yours. Why do you not use larger craft? Surely your technology is such that you could manufacture larger and quicker airships—ones that ride higher in the atmosphere?"

Keoti's lieutenant, Abro L'Hami, replied. He was a tall, black-haired man with a day's growth of beard and startling dark eyes. Like the other Dramaranians, he had become much friendlier to Clive's party as the day progressed.

"Most of what you see above," Abro said, "is not true sky. While there are patches that rise straight up to the upper levels of the world, most of what is above is actually a thin layer of some sticky substance that we have yet to identify. We have managed to force ships into that layer, but inevitably their engines become gummed up with the substance, causing the ships to crash."

Guafe looked up at the night skies, dotted with unfamiliar constellations. The sliver of a moon was rising in the east.

"Curious," he said.

"But what about the stars?" Smythe asked. "The sun we've seen each day, and the moon just rising now?"

Abro shrugged. "If we knew everything about the Dungeon, we would rule it. But we don't."

Keoti nodded. "Mostly, we believe that there are some things men were never meant to know. Travelers between the levels, such as yourself, are not merely rare—we find it difficult to understand why anyone would assume such a dangerous undertaking."

"We want to go home," Clive said. "It's that simple. We're not here by our own will, and we wish to return to our own world."

The Dramaranians regarded him curiously.

"This is a good world," Keoti said finally, "so long as one avoids the jungle."

Clive and Smythe exchanged worried glances.

"The jungle?" Clive asked, fear rising inside him. "Why would that be?"

"The jungle holds many strange and primitive tribes—they grow stranger the deeper one fares. They make constant war with each other, and against any strangers who trespass on their lands. Why do you look so worried?"

"We have . . . companions who entered the jungle."

Keoti gave him a sympathetic look. "They will not survive, Major Folliot."

"Please, call me Clive," he said absently. His worry for Annabelle and the others was intensifying. "With these flying ships of yours—could you take us into the jungle to rescue them?"

"Impossible. We do not go into the jungle . . . Clive. To do so is certain death. We leave the tribes alone, as they do us. We have no need to enter their jungle. We have our veldt and our own forests beyond Dramaran. We have the porten for meat—Walking Mountains of protein. All else we need, we raise for ourselves.

"It is not a bad life, Clive, and because of your relationship with our savior, you will be well treated there."

"Just how did Sir Neville become your savior?" Smythe asked.

"I told you earlier about our Long Sleep," Keoti replied. "Our seasons are long here, summer and winter each lasting for many—" she paused, as though searching for a word "—of what Father Neville calls centuries. When the portens migrate and the ice comes, we retire to our Long Sleep. It's a form of mechanically induced hibernation. Last spring, the mechanism that rouses us failed, and we slept on through the spring and well into summer.

"It was Father Neville who woke us once more."

"How long ago was that?" Clive asked.

It seemed odd to him that Neville could have accomplished so much in such a short time on this level. To begin with, how had he reached Dramaran so quickly?

"Almost five years ago now," Abro said.

"As you reckon time," Keoti added.

The shock of that statement struck Clive and the others of his party profoundly.

"Five years?" Clive asked slowly.

The Dramaranian lieutenant nodded.

That was impossible, Clive thought. Unless there had been some flux in time that had sent Neville here years before his own party had arrived, even though they had left the previous level within moments of each other. Was such a thing possible? In the Dungeon, who could tell?

"You've been looking for us all that time?" Smythe asked.

Keoti shook her head. "Oh, no. It's only been a few weeks now since Father Neville told us you would be coming."

Later, when Smythe and Clive lay in the tent they were sharing, they spoke of that.

"There's another possibility, sah," Smythe said after both had run out of speculations and they had lain in silence for a time. His voice floated toward Clive from the darkness, a disembodied sound. "It might not be Neville waiting for us in Dramaran. It wouldn't be the first time he's played that trick on us."

"But the Dramaranians know me—and you. It has to be my brother. How could a stranger be expecting us?"

Neither man had an answer. Eventually, they let silence fall between them again. Smythe's breathing grew more regular and he fell asleep, but Clive lay awake for a long time, staring up at the darkened roof of the tent.

He was thinking of Annabelle now, wishing he'd been more forceful in convincing her to stay with him.

She had been a small, nagging worry in his thoughts, ever since the two parties had gone their own ways, but while he'd worried, he'd held firm the knowledge that she was a resourceful woman, with—barring the Portuguese—trustworthy companions. He'd been able to hold out hope for their survival. But now, with the finality of Keoti's tone as she spoke of the certain fate of any who dared the jungle ringing in his mind, hope had fled.

The hard truth lay like a rock in his stomach. He would never see Annabelle or any of her companions again. It was a bitter realization, made worse by the sense of guilt he felt for letting them go off on their own. As leader, it had been his responsibility to keep the company together, yet he had failed to do so, sealing their fate.

I should have tried harder, he thought unhappily.

But now it was too late.

Not one of Clive's party—not even Chang Guafe—was prepared for the sheer immensity of the ruined city of Dramaran when they

reached it late in the following afternoon. They flew over acre upon
acre of abandoned buildings, pillars that lay fallen across roadways,
collapsed walls that had scattered their enormous stone blocks willy-
nilly wherever they might land, floors that had fallen through to
shadowed basements. Here and there tall towers still remained, but
most of the city had the look of a child's toy village, flattened by a
large boot.

They saw no people until they reached the center of the city, where
the work of reconstruction was being undertaken. Hundreds of
Dramaranians bustled like ants about the building they were repairing.
Strange mechanical devices were being used to lift the stone blocks
and set them into place. Clive could have watched the curious work
for hours, but then their flight took them to a docking area near a huge,
upright thrust of rock, where the flyers landed, one after the other.

The party was conveyed inside what appeared to be a cave that was
brightly lit by bulbous globes hanging from its ceiling. Keoti ushered
them into a small room that could barely hold the nine of them. When
the doors hissed shut and the room began to move downward, Clive
knew a sudden moment of panic. The swiftness of their descent left
him with the feeling of leaving his stomach in his throat. Beside him,
Finnbogg made a low moaning sound.

Clive learned later that that had been his first introduction to an
elevator, a conveyance that moved one from floor to floor in a building
without the necessity for stairs. It was only the beginning of the
mechanical marvels to be discovered in this wondrous city.

The elevator let them out at a junction of large hallways, many
levels below where they had left the flyers, Abro told them. Three
corridors led away from where they stood, with the elevator situated
at the joining of the "T" where they met. The walls were smooth here,
and the lighting came from the ceiling itself, rather than globes.

"Where can we find Father Neville?" Clive asked finally.

"He will see you tomorrow," Keoti replied. "First, I will show you to
your rooms, where you may bathe and eat. If you'll follow me?"

They left the remainder of the Dramaranians there and followed
Keoti down a bewildering series of corridors. Finally, she stopped at a
door, which hissed open when she laid her palm against a metal plate
set in the wall beside the frame.

"This will be your room," she told Guafe. "If you are unfamiliar with the workings of any of the devices, you have only to speak into this grille and someone will come to help you."

One by one she showed Finnbogg and Smythe to their rooms. Smythe hesitated at the door of his.

"Well, then, sah," Smythe said. "I will see you later."

As the door hissed shut behind him, Keoti led Clive on to his room. When they reached it, she came in with him. Clive stared in open-eyed wonder. The furnishings were spare, but luxurious. A large comfortable bed. Over-stuffed chairs. A false mantel with a mechanism under it that gave the impression that there was a fire burning there.

Much of what he saw now, he had no vocabulary for. He learned later that the realistic, full-color pictures hanging from the wall—with brushstrokes so tiny he could not spy them and too sharp and colorful to be daguerreotypes—were actually photographs. That the curious, windowlike affair in the corner was a video screen. That the feather-soft carpeting underfoot was not wool, but some synthetic material.

He turned at the sound of a zipper, to see Keoti stripping off her silver bodysuit. She wore nothing underneath it.

"Shall we bathe?" she asked with a smile.

"I . . . that is . . ."

Her matter-of-fact boldness left Clive speechless for a few moments. Keoti stepped out of the suit and tossed it onto a chair. Turning from him, she went into another small room that proved to be a washroom. Clive watched the movement of her buttocks as she walked, lifting his gaze when she turned her head slightly toward him.

"Are you coming?" she asked over her shoulder.

When he nodded, she disappeared from view. Clive hastily removed his own clothing. By the time he joined her, she was standing in a small stall, water showering over her from a faucet overhead. She drew him inside with her and handed him a bar of soap. It made her skin wonderfully slippery to the touch.

After a long, messy shower, which left as much water on the floor as had been on them, Keoti shaved his beard and trimmed the wild tangle of his hair. Clive felt like a new man—clean-shaven and civilized—as they retired to the bed. Keoti pressed him down upon the mattress and straddled him.

"You certainly are a hospitable people," he said, looking up at her.

She lowered her face to give him a long kiss. He closed his arms around her, drawing her close.

"Remarkably so," he added.

"Stop talking," she told him, then indicated other ways in which he could be occupied.

Chapter 14

As Annabelle's attacker went down, something small whistled quickly by her ear. *Poisoned dart*, she thought. She ducked instinctively, though the dart had already passed her, so close she'd almost been able to feel it go by. Shaking her head, she moved closer, spear still raised.

She wanted to help, but all she could see of the two struggling figures was a confusing mix of shadows. She was just as likely to strike her benefactor as the shark man who'd been attacking her. Then someone caught her about the knees and brought her down. She fought the grip until she heard Sidi's voice.

"Stay down! Let them fight it out, Annabelle—they seem to know who's who better than we could."

She relaxed in his grip. When he loosed his hand and crawled back toward the tree they'd been leaning against earlier, she followed him, keeping her head low. Sidi was right. The best they could do right now was just stay out of the way.

Shriek was already there, hunched in a half-crouch, trying to pierce the confusion with her multifaceted eyes, but doing no better than Annabelle had, even with six extra eyes.

All around them, figures struggled. They heard the familiar, guttural voices of the shark people, raised in cries of both pain and anger. Mixed with them was the sound of drums and different voices that sounded human and almost decipherable. Shapes continued to drop from the trees. Then, suddenly, the surviving shark people broke away.

Annabelle and Sidi joined Shriek, who had already risen to her feet. As torches flared, they spied Tomàs curled up into a ball near another tree, hands wrapped over his head.

"It's over now, hero," Annabelle called to him.

God, what a weasel.

She turned away as their benefactors approached. Above them, drums continued to sound, but their rhythm was different now—no longer menacing, but joyous. The torches lit up their campsite, scaring away the shadows. And the newcomers . . .

How come I'm not surprised? she thought.

They were ape-men—a whole troop of them. More humanoid in shape than the gorillas and other great apes of her own world, but definitely simian, all the same. As though their evolution from monkeys had taken them along a different route, or wasn't quite fully advanced yet.

Their brows were high, lower parts of their faces protruding slightly in a chimplike fashion. The eyes were set close together over a broad nose. Their bodies were covered with fur, but they wore various pieces of clothing. All had loincloths, arm bracelets, and neck torcs. Some had sashes worn over their shoulders; others, scarves around their necks. Some wore strips of cloth about their brows, or tied on their upper arms or thighs. Earrings glistened in their large earlobes, some having a series that ran up the edge of their ears, as Annabelle's own did.

Some carried what looked like a kind of throwing stick—foot-long, with a knob at either end. All had knives at their belts or in their hands.

The foremost one stopped a few feet away from them and said something. Again, it sounded almost familiar, but Annabelle had to shake her head to indicate she didn't understand.

"We fren'," the ape-man said then. He gave them a wide, toothy grin. "En-mee of—" he said something she didn't quite catch, that sounded like *chasuck* "—fren' we." "You speak English?"

The Dungeon threw more curves at her than she was ready to catch. With everything that had already happened to them—ape-men who spoke a kind of bastard English?

He bobbed his head. "En'lish—talk good, yuh?"

"Very good."

"Yoo cum we, yuh?"

Annabelle glanced at her companions. Tomàs was shaking his head no, but the other two indicated their agreement.

"We'll come with you," she said. "Thank you for your help. What . . . ah . . . should we call you?"

"Huh?"

"Name you?"

The ape-man grinned hugely. "Me Chobba. Big cheef. Kill chasuck—yuh?"

Annabelle pointed at the dead shark man that had almost gotten her. "That chasuck?"

The ape-man nodded and spat on the corpse. Kneeling beside it, he drew a knife from his belt and began to saw off the dorsal fin. Many of the other ape-men were already carrying similar trophies. She thought of the leader of the shark people with his staff, and what hung from his belt.

"Those skulls we saw back at the shark people's village," she said to Sidi.

He nodded. "Were the shrunken skulls of these ape people, Annabelle."

When Chobba had the fin cut free, he offered it to Annabelle. She shook her head quickly, but made sure she kept smiling at him as she did so. Annie B.'s rules of etiquette for meeting ape-men in strange jungles number one: Until you figured out the customs, it never hurt to just keep grinning like a loon.

"No thank you, Chobba. You keep it."

He nodded. Puncturing it with the tip of his knife, he tied it to his belt with a thong, then replaced the blade in its sheath.

"Cum," he said. "We go."

He leapt into the lowest branches of the tree directly above him. All around the clearing, the rest of the troop that was on the ground swung into the trees, joining those who were waiting for them above, drums quiet now, slung onto their backs.

"Chobba!" Annabelle cried.

He looked down at her, face wrinkled with a puzzled expression that was almost comical in its broadness.

"You no cum?"

Annabelle opened her hands before her in a helpless gesture. "Not good tree cheef like you," she said.

The look that came into his face then was one that Annabelle had seen before: it was the way a healthy person looked at a cripple. Chobba dropped back down to the ground and approached her slowly. She kept herself still as he reached out and squeezed her upper arm. He shook his head slowly, brows lifting in a question.

"Sick?" he asked.

She shook her head. "Just not good in tree."

"Chobba walk you," he said.

He turned and called up to his companions. A few torchbearers and one drummer dropped down to the ground. The remainder of the troop swung off into the night, their torches bobbing in among the trees, winking like fireflies as they disappeared behind branches, then reappeared again.

"We go now," Chobba told her. "Walk on legs, yuh?"

Annabelle smiled. "Yes," she said. "We'll walk on legs. You don't know a guy named Tarzan, do you?"

"He is rogha—like me?"

"No. He's a man in a story—like me. But big and strong, and he can swing through the trees like you."

Chobba looked around. "He cum soon?"

Annabelle laughed and shook her head. "It's just us, Chobba."

He scratched at his temple, then shrugged. Leading them back to the game trail, he set off at a pace they could all keep. As they followed him, Annabelle walked at Shriek's side.

Walking on legs, Shriek said with a grin. *What does the Chobba being think of all of mine?*

Annabelle laughed. "What a place. More fun than a barrel of . . ."

"A barrel of what, Annabelle?" Sidi wanted to know when she just let her voice trail off.

Annabelle looked at Chobba's broad back in front of her. Another rogha walked right behind her, abreast of Sidi. Others ranged farther behind, one tapping a soft rhythm from his drum. Annie B.'s rule of etiquette number two: don't make fun of anyone who's just saved your ass.

"Never you mind," she told him.

Naturally, the rogha village was up in the trees—high up in the trees.

They reached it just as dawn was breaking, the salmon-colored sun waking sharp shadows in the blue-green and burgundy vegetation. Annabelle craned her neck and peered up among the gaps in the leaves to the boughs some sixty feet above to make out the reed huts on platforms. There were already cooking fires, sending their morning smoke into the sky.

"Home now," Chobba said.

Annabelle looked away from the village, lowering her gaze to his features.

"It's very private," she said.

He blinked, not understanding.

"Safe," she tried.

"Many safe," he assured her.

"And high."

Chobba squeezed her upper arms again. "Carry yoo, yuh?"

Annabelle swallowed thickly. "Ah . . . sure. Why not?"

"What's the matter, Annabelle?" Sidi asked.

"Well, you know. Heights scare the shit out of me."

She remembered the descent from the plateau where they'd first arrived on this level. It had been a little easier to ignore the crawling fear, because the rocks were solid, the grade not too steep, and there were people there to grab onto if she got to feeling too weird. This was going up, and staying there, their destination a bunch of swaying platforms near the top of some of the biggest trees she'd ever seen.

Sidi gave her a worried look. "Maybe we should make our own camp here below."

"Right. Where the shark men can come crawling all over us—or Christ knows what else."

"But if you can't go up . . ."

Annabelle drew a steadying breath. "Oh, I can go up," she said. "I just don't know how bad I'm gonna freak once I get there, that's all."

"No happy?" Chobba asked.

"I'm delirious with joy," she replied.

Again, that uncomprehending blink.

"Many happy."

Chobba grinned. "Cum," he said.

He motioned for her to wrap her arms around his neck. Annabelle took a couple more slow breaths, trying to still the sudden, rapid tattoo of her heartbeat. Chobba bent his knees, lowering himself to make it easier for her. She got her arms around his neck, surprised at the clean smell of his fur—it had none of the reek of a zoo monkey house—and the softness of its texture. He indicated that she should wrap her legs around his middle.

She tried not to let her fear force her to hold him so tightly that she'd choke him. He straightened for a moment, bouncing lightly on his heels to adjust himself to her weight, then leapt for the lowest branch. Annabelle left her heart behind her on the ground.

The ascent up through the jungle boughs was just a dizzying blur. She closed her eyes after the first couple of stomach-lurching springs, and kept them tightly shut until they had stopped moving and Chobba was trying to pry her fingers loose. She let her muscles go slack and stumbled. Another of the rogha caught her before she could fall, but not before she had a heart-spinning view of the drop to the jungle floor below.

A low moan escaped her, and she moved away from the edge of the platform, her grip now desperately tight on the arm of the second rogha. The ape-man grinned reassuringly at her. Gently disengaging her fingers, he steered her to the side of a hut and lowered her down so that she was sitting with her back to the reed wall, the edge of the platform a good ten feet from her.

Another rogha appeared at the edge then, a scowling Tomàs clinging to his back. As soon as they reached the platform, Tomàs stepped free and nonchalantly swaggered back toward the edge, where he peered down. Years of scrambling through ship's rigging had long ago rid him of any acrophobia he might have had.

Sidi was next, his brown face creased with worry when he looked in Annabelle's direction.

"Annabelle," he began as he hurried over to her.

She tried to copy Tomàs's cool and give Sidi a little careless wave of her hand, but all she could feel was the sway of the platform under her. Her chest was so tight she could hardly breathe.

"I . . . I'll be okay. No problem." She gave him what she hoped was a bright smile, but knew it had come out as a grimace. "Where's Shriek?"

"On her way."

"Right."

Of course. Being more spider than human, the arachnid would have no trouble coming up on her own.

Annabelle worked at calming herself. Breathe in, hold it there for a few counts, breathe out. She tried looking around at what she could see of the village from her perch, legs drawn in close to her chest, arms locked around her knees.

The huts were similar to those of the shark people—even to the possum dogs hanging from branches and poles by the doors. But there was nothing of the sense of menace that had been in that other village. Here, the people regarded them with friendly curiosity—furry women and little children, older men and women, their body fur grizzling and gray. She realized then that Chobba was missing.

Just as Shriek pulled herself up over the lip of the edge, Chobba reappeared at Annabelle's side. He was carrying a pouch from which he drew a small thick leaf, which he offered to her.

"Stop scare," he said, pushing the leaf into her hands when she didn't take it right way. "Yoo feel hokay. No more scare, yuh?"

Annabelle took the leaf dubiously. Oh, yeah? And just what the hell was it, anyway? If it was going to make her feel "hokay," it was probably some kind of drug—and sick though she was, she wasn't into getting freaked out on the local version of who-knew-what.

"I . . . I don't think so," she said. "Don't want too much happy."

How did she tell him that she wasn't into dope?

"Not happy," Chobba told her. His face wrinkled comically as he tried to find the right words. "Fetta cheef—she find. Stop scare is all."

The tree swayed, making her stomach lurch.

What the hell, she thought.

She lifted the leaf and put it in her mouth. It was pulpy, juice squeezing out as soon as she bit down on it. The taste was sweet and tart, all at the same time, and went down her throat with a numbing sensation. After a moment, she took the second leaf Chobba offered her.

"Glad now?" he asked.

It's a little early, don't you think? Annabelle thought, but then she realized that she did feel better already. Not high—not like taking some hallucinogenic, as she'd feared—but calm. Muscles unknotting, chest loosening, the panic fading. The leaves didn't give her any kind of a buzz at all. They just relaxed her.

"What do you call this stuff?" she asked.

"Byrr." Chobba said. "Yoo like?"

"It's all right," she said.

She was about to add to that, when a commotion at the far end of the platform caught her attention. She was surprised to see a white man pushing his way through the crowd of rogha. He was slender and wiry, at least in his late fifties, early sixties. A snow white mane of hair and full beard gave him the look of a small, skinny Santa Claus, but he wasn't wearing red.

He stopped short when he reached Annabelle and her company, looking from one to the other.

"My God," he said finally. "Do any of you speak English?"

Chapter 15

When Clive woke the next morning, he was alone in the bed. All that remained of Keoti's presence was the indentation left by her head on her pillow.

Looking around the room for her, he found Smythe instead, sitting at the table by the video screen, sipping tea from a white porcelain mug. He, too, was cleanshaven again, except for his bushy mustache; his hair was neatly trimmed. The remains of breakfast sat on a tray before him. At the setting across from him was another tray, covered with a metal hood.

Clive thought about the night before and guilt arose inside him. How could he have forgotten Annabella so easily? And for what? A tumble in the hay with some woman—all right, a damnably attractive woman—that he'd only just met. It was true that Annabella was out there—in the world beyond the Dungeon—and he was here, with little hope of seeing her again, but still. . . .

As he thought of Annabella, an odd sensation came over him. He seemed to remember a night with her. . . . They were in her rooms, then went out to a party with George du Maurier—a party thrown in honor of a promotion he'd received, and for his and Annabella's engagement.

Just a dream, of course.

But it had gone on. He seemed to remember walking by himself, later that same night, through the slums of London, and being confronted by Annabella again—only this time, she was in the guise of a prostitute. . . .

Impossible. It had to have been a dream.

But it seemed terribly real. And, hard on the heels of those recollections, other dreamlike memories fluttered. An odd conversation . . . overheard in the dark. . . . But, as soon as he tried to concentrate upon it, it was gone.

He sighed and sat up in the bed. Smythe looked up as he stirred and gave him a grin.

"Busy night, then, gov'nor?" he asked.

With an effort, Clive put away the strange feelings.

"It's too early for me to face your cockney imitation," he told him.

Smythe gave a quick tug at his forelock. "Sorry, gov'nor. Just trying to get along."

Clive couldn't help but laugh at Smythe's mock self-effacement.

"Incorrigible," he said. "That's the only term that properly describes you, Horace."

"Right you are, gov'nor. Shall I be throwing myself in the Thames for troubling your morning? Just say the word."

"No doubt picking my pocket as you fling yourself from the bridge?"

"Jerusalem! The thought never crossed me mind, gov'nor. How to regain your trust?"

"You could pour me some of that tea you're keeping to yourself."

Swinging his legs to the floor, Clive tugged on his trousers, surprised to find them clean.

"Washed, pressed, and mended while we slept," Smythe said, plucking at his own shirt. "Can't fault our hosts for their hospitality."

Clive joined his companion at the table. Lifting the hood from his tray, he found a breakfast of eggs, fried strips of what must have been porten meat, biscuits, and fresh fruit staring up at him. Smythe handed him a mug of tea.

"It's like the finest hotel back home," he said.

Clive nodded. He took a sip of the tea and was again surprised. It had the aromatic flavor of an Indian brew.

"Did Keoti show you how to work this?" Smythe asked, pointing at the video screen.

"No. We were . . . otherwise occupied. She did describe it to me as some form of window. . . ." He shrugged, the terminology she'd used to describe its functions escaping him at the moment.

"It's a marvelous machine. It can bring words up onto its screen—as a book—but it also has illustrations. Not static ones, but moving pictures that have somehow been recorded and stored inside it—somewhat in the way that our friend Guafe has described the workings of his memory, I assume."

"And what of our companions?" Clive asked. He set aside the tea and started at his breakfast. The porten meat had a delicate texture, for all the creature's immense bulk. It was tender, without a touch of gaminess about it, having a domesticated flavor, rather than that of a wild beast. "Have you spoken to them yet today?"

Smythe nodded. "Guafe's gone on a tour with a pair of the Dramaranians. I believe they're as interested in observing him as he is their machines. As for Finn—he won't leave his room."

Clive's eyebrows lifted. "Why not?"

"He now believes this level to be the realm of the Dungeon's dead. The Dramaranians are spirits of the dead, he told me—judges measuring our worth. He's waiting for them to take him away for judgment."

"Didn't he say something about a white stone that held dead spirits?"

Smythe nodded. "But that's in Quan—or so he said earlier."

Silence fell between them as they thought of the other half of their company, lost now in the jungles. Loyal Sidi. The arachnid, Shriek. And Annabelle.

Clive set aside his fork, appetite fled. He didn't care much what happened to the Portuguese, but the others . . . especially his descendant. . . .

"We made a bad mistake letting them go off on their own," he said.

"It wasn't our choice to make, sah. They are all thinking, rational adults with minds of their own."

"I was responsible—"

"For yourself, sah. You are only responsible for yourself."

"But Annabelle. She's. . . ."

"A capable young lady to do you proud. I'm not so ready to write any of them off as our hosts are. We've come through some other bad times in this place and survived. I'm not prepared to give up on them until I see the bodies."

An image flashed into Clive's head, of Annabelle torn apart by wild beasts. Or lying hurt somewhere in that jungle, her companions slain, danger closing in.

Smythe reached across the table and touched Clive's hand. "Don't think about them," he said softly.

"How can I help *but* think of them?"

Smythe sighed. "Here," he said, turning to the video screen. "Watch how this works."

He manipulated the controls as one of the Dramaranians had shown him and the screen suddenly flooded with images in full color. The picture on the screen gave them the impression of looking out a moving window, the view slowly panning across a windswept, frozen plain. Then, disconcertingly, as the view continued to shift, it proved to be one of the borderland between jungle and veldt, where they'd left their companions, though obviously at some other time from when they had seen it, for the veldt was a frozen waste, while the jungle retained all its tropical glory.

There was no sound, but only because Smythe had left it turned down.

"This machine brings to life the past," he said. "Anything that's been recorded upon it can be called up on that screen, at any time."

The two men watched as the camera continued to pan across the scene—jungle and ice fields, side by side.

"That doesn't seem possible," Clive said. "The vegetation should be dead—withered by that cold."

"This is the Dungeon," Smythe reminded him. "Anything seems possible here."

"Within reason," a new voice said.

So entranced were they with what was on the screen that neither man had heard the door hiss open behind them. They turned now to find Keoti standing there. Today her bodysuit was a bewildering pattern of blacks and reds, a swirling design that caught the eye and led it this way and that, but never let the full pattern emerge. Her weapon was no longer in its holster, clipped to her belt.

"But this," Clive said. "It defies the laws of nature."

Keoti smiled. "What you see was recorded by a remote scouting unit that was sent out while we were in our Long Sleep. Apparently an invisible barrier—made of a material that we have yet to identify—comes between the jungle and the plains at that time so that the two environments do not affect each other. Curious, isn't it?"

Both men nodded.

"Have you come to bring us to my brother?" Clive asked.

Keoti shook her head. "He wishes to see you this afternoon. I merely came by to see how you were doing, and to ask if you would like to see more of Dramaran."

"I don't think so," Clive replied.

He looked from her to the screen, but neither was enough to take his mind from the fate of Annabelle and the others of her party. A tour of the city would merely aggravate his sense of loss, for he'd always be thinking, If only Annabelle were here, to share this with me.

Damn him for not keeping their group together. He should have stood firm when the suggestion first arose, but somehow, it was all discussed and done before he'd really had a chance to think through all of its ramifications.

"I don't feel in a very . . . companionable mood," he added. "I'd just make for poor company. But you go ahead, Horace."

Keoti gave him a considering look. "You are worrying about your friends," she said with quick insight. "The ones who entered the jungle."

"I can't forget them."

"And so you shouldn't. But brooding does no one any good." Her brow wrinkled for a moment, then she smiled. "Come with me anyway, Clive. I know something that will help you deal with what's troubling you."

"I'm not sure. . . ."

"Humor me."

Clive sat for a long moment, then finally nodded and started to rise. As he pushed his chair back from the table, he suddenly realized that all he was wearing was his trousers. A blush crept up the back of his neck—foolish, for she'd seen him in far more revealing circumstances—but he felt awkward all the same. Crossing the room to the bed, he gathered up the bundle of his clothes and fled for the washroom.

"Just let me get dressed," he called over his shoulder.

Behind him, Keoti and Smythe shared a smile.

"Will you look at this, sah," Smythe said. "A bloody gymnasium. Who'd of thought it?"

Keoti led them to a locker room, where she took two sets of matched fencing gear from a locker—foils, gloves, masks, and metallic plastrons.

When she presented one set to Clive, he laid everything down on a bench except for the foil. He tested its spring and balance, enjoying the feel of the handle in his hand. The tip of the blade was capped with a button.

"Do you fence?" he asked her.

Keoti shook her head. "I have a friend who will be meeting us—ah, there you are, Naree."

The man who entered the locker room was lean as a whip, with expressive, mobile features. His black hair was long and tied back in a ponytail, and there was a scar under his left eye. He smiled as Keoti introduced them, giving Smythe a quick glance, then focusing all of his attention on Clive.

"Finally, some new blood," he said as he took the other set of fencing gear from Keoti.

His full name, they learned, was Naree Terin, and he was a biological research scientist.

"The pleasure is all mine," Clive replied.

Keoti and Smythe took seats on one side of the gym as the two men donned their gear. Each went through a series of warming-up exercises. When they were ready to fence, Naree attached body wires to the rear of each of their metallic plastrons. The wires were fed out of reels that sat at either end of the fencing area.

"It's for scoring," Naree explained at Clive's puzzled look.

He touched the tip of his foil against Clive's chest and a small bell rang on the electronic scoring apparatus that was on a table near where Keoti and Smythe were sitting. Keoti rose and cleared the counter back to zero once more. When she sat down, the two men began to fence.

"This was kindly thought of you," Smythe remarked to her.

She smiled. "I know what it is like to have tension build up in you—the mind knots as much as the muscles."

"And what do you do to relax?"

"Are you familiar with gymnastics?"

Smythe nodded. "They can be very demanding."

"They have to be—or what would be the challenge?"

"Of course."

Smythe looked back to where Clive and Naree were fencing. The whip-quick clang of the foils rang in the large room, the two figures weaving a pattern as intricate as a set dance with their feet, back and forth along the marked-out fencing area. Neither man had scored yet.

"Naree is very good," he said.

"As is Clive. To be honest, I hadn't thought he would do so well. Naree is the best in Dramaran."

"But to him it's a sport, am I correct?"

"Yes."

Smythe smiled. "For Clive, it has been a matter of life and death—his skill being all that kept him alive." Keoti regarded the fencers in a new light.

"I see," she said softly.

There was just time for Clive to have a shower after his workout, before Keoti collected them for the meeting with Neville. Clive was in much better spirits, muscles tender and sore in spots, but the pain honestly earned. He had won the match, seven to zero, leaving Naree puzzled, and not a little in awe.

"Now they judge us," Finnbogg said mournfully as he joined them in the corridor outside his room.

"We're just going to meet Sir—Father Neville," Smythe reassured him. "There'll be no judgments, Finn."

Perhaps, perhaps not, Clive thought. There was still the puzzle as to how his brother had arrived here five years before them when they had entered the gateway literally within minutes of each other. And considering the traps Neville had left in their way before—if, in fact, he *had* been responsible for them—Clive meant to be prepared for anything.

"Clive will see, Clive will see," Finnbogg muttered as they went down the hall to where Guafe was waiting for them. "All dead now—blue limbo was boundary between being alive and dying. And now they judge us."

"Nonsense," Guafe told the dwarf when they reached him. "They have made some remarkable technological advances, but they are hardly deities."

"Been having a good time, then?" Smythe asked.

The cyborg caught the thinly veiled hostility of Smythe's tone. "It's been a pleasure dealing with other than primitive minds," he replied.

"I think we're ready to meet my brother," Clive said before they went any further.

They rode the elevator once more, all the way up to the floor just below the ground level of the city. Though he was prepared for the sensation of the small room's movement this time, Clive was still uncomfortable in the elevator. He doubted that he would ever be comfortable with some of the Dramaranian mechanisms, but he schooled his features to remain impassive.

When they disembarked from the elevator, Smythe touched his arm, holding him back so that they took up the rear of the group.

"We'd best be ready for anything," he whispered.

Clive nodded. "I am."

Keoti had opened a door in the corridor ahead of them, and they hurried to catch up as she ushered them in. Clive's heartbeat sped up as he went through the door.

Now, Neville, he thought. Now, we'll find out the meaning behind all these games of yours.

But the man behind the desk was a stranger.

Not again, was all Clive could think as he stared at him.

He was a rotund man with cheery features, pate shaved like a friar's, blue eyes bright and curious as he looked up to meet his guests. He wore a Dramaranian bodysuit that was stretched too tight across his stomach, giving him a somewhat comical air.

A pleasant-enough looking fellow, but he wasn't Sir Neville Folliot, no matter how much one might attempt to stretch the imagination. If anything, he reminded Clive of that damnable Philo B. Goode. There was enough familial resemblance to make him at least Goode's brother.

Clive and Smythe exchanged worried glances.

Even though Clive had been expecting this—or something like it— from the moment that he had learned that his brother was in Dramaran, the fact that he'd been duped again still hit him with a hard jolt. He stood with his back straight and met the stranger's gaze— an increasingly puzzled frown. He could feel Smythe's tension, Keoti's confusion.

"You are not my brother," Clive said.

"Indeed, I am not," the stranger said. "But I *am* Father Neville Folliot. And who are you, sir?"

Chapter 16

His name was Luke Drew.

"Call me Lukey," he told Annabelle as he sat down on the platform near where she was sitting, his blue eyes glinting merrily in the torchlight.

The rogha treated him with a friendly familiarity, making room for him in the circle of furry bodies that were sitting cross-legged or slouched around Annabelle's party. The old man presented an incongruous picture among all those brown apes, his bony limbs protruding from the cloak of animal pelts he was wearing.

Tarzan in his fifties, Annabelle thought with a smile. This was probably what he'd really look like—forget all the muscles.

"Hell," the old man went on, "call me anythin' you like so long's you know some words that ain't monkey talk. Now, don't get me wrong. These monkeys are all Lukey's pals, you bet. But a soul gets tired a' listenin' to all their jabberin', you be here as long as me. I bin tryin' to teach some of 'em English, but I ain't had much luck. You get a good of boy like Chobba here, an' he's for learning, but most a' them can't be bothered to take the time, so mostly I'm jabberin' away in their lingo."

"Are you a native?" Annabelle asked.

"Hell, no. I'm a Newfie, born an' bred. Lived an' woulda died in Freshwater, Bell Island—little place smack dab in the middle a' Conception Bay—'cept a blue bogey light snatched me right out of my ol' boat one night an' dumped me here. I never seen anythin' so spooky before—though I bin seein' things since that'd make your toes curl."

"How long have you been here?"

"Don't rightly know. I used ta keep track, but I kind a' lost interest. Let's see. It was just after the big war when that blue light gobbled me up. . . ."

"Which war?"

Lukey blinked. "The big W.W. Two, girl. Is there any other?"

" 'Fraid so," Annabelle said.

"Don't tell me about 'em—I don't want to know. Just tell me, the ol' Rock—Newfoundland—she's still in one piece?"

"So far as I know."

"Well, that's somethin'. What year was it when you got snatched?"

"Nineteen hundred ninety-nine."

For a long moment, Lukey didn't say anything. Then, he slowly shook his head.

"I can't a' bin here that long. I figured maybe twenty years. . . ."

"We've all come from different times," Annabelle told him. "Sidi here's from the nineteenth century. Tomàs goes all the way back to the fifteenth. And Shriek. . . ."

Lukey looked at the alien. "She ain't even from our world—not 'less things a' changed a helluva lot more'n I'd want ta think was possible."

"How did you come to live with the rogha?" Annabelle asked.

"Damn lucky—that's all. Just like you, girl."

"My name's Annabelle."

"Hokay—Anniebelle it is. Anyways, that blue light gobbled me up an' spat me out a ways from here. You bin in the upper levels a' this place?"

Annabelle nodded.

"Took me a half-year ta get this far, an' I guess I'd just be shark food if the monkeys hadn't been out raidin' the chasuck an' brought me back with 'em. Same deal as happened ta you. You folks were just plain lucky Chobba an' his boys was out huntin' some fins tonight."

"What does that mean—chasuck?"

Lukey grinned. "Well, pardon my French, but I guess the closest I can come in plain English is 'shit for brains.' That's what the monkeys figure the chasuck to be. They bin fightin' each other for years—least, they do 'round here. You get deeper inta rogha country, an' you could go your whole life without seein' one a' them land sharks. 'Course, you go too far, an' then you run into the gree."

He paused expectantly.

"And what are the gree?" Annabelle asked, taking her cue.

"Thought you'd never ask. The rogha call 'em 'dick-faces,' if you'll pardon—"

"Your French. Sure."

Lukey wagged a finger at her. "Let a man tell his story in his own way, Anniebelle. Anyways, they call 'em that 'cause they look like birds—you know, all full a' black feathers an' with big yellow beaks in the middle of their fares."

"Can they fly?"

"Nah. Well, not really. Though they can glide somethin' fierce. See, they got hands, sort a', but they're at the ends of these long black wings. They're a mean bunch—almost as bad as the chasuck—though they don't go in much for live meat. Feed on carrion, that kind a' thing."

"I don't believe this place," Annabelle said.

"You're tellin' me. Gets so you'd welcome anybody that was human."

"So, why do you stay?"

"Where'm I goin' ta go?"

"You could come with us," Annabelle said. "We're going to the gateway in Quan."

"Quan? Not an' keep your skin in one piece, you ain't. You got somethin' against livin'?"

"What's wrong with Quan?"

"Haunts. That's the only thing you'll find in there. Nobody goes there. Damn things'll strip the flesh from your bones like you was dipped in acid. Like those pie-ee-raner fish they got in Africa. Eat you up like there ain't no tomorra."

He made snapping motions with both hands, bringing them up close to Annabelle's face. She backed quickly away, and was suddenly aware again of the height of the platform as it swayed underneath her. Her face went pale, the forgotten fears rising up in a spinning whirl. Chobba plucked the pouch of byrr leaves from her frozen fingers and pressed one leaf between her lips.

She was too scared to even chew, but just the mixture of her saliva with the pulpy flesh of the leaf that slid down her throat was enough to unlock her jaws after a few moments. Relief came quickly again—no high, just a calmness that brought her heartbeat back down to normal and loosened the sudden tightness in her chest.

Just don't think about what's underneath you, she told herself. But then, she *was* thinking about it. She chewed another leaf.

"I used to chew a lot a' that," Lukey said, "when I first got here. But you get used ta the sway an' the height. In a couple a' months, you won't even notice it anymore."

"We don't plan to be here for longer than it takes to get ready to go on to Quan," Annabelle told him.

"Much bad place, Quan," Chobba said.

Annabelle glanced at him. She'd been wondering how much he and the other rogha had been following of their conversation, and decided now that Chobba, at least, understood English better than he spoke it.

"We gotta go," she said.

"Speak for yourself," Tomàs said.

She turned to look at him. "I've told you before, no one's making you tag along, pal."

"I am part of the company," the Portuguese said. "I should have a say in what we do, and I say is *estúpido* to go on."

"Blow it out your face," Annabelle told him, and looked back at Chobba. "We don't belong here," she said. "At this point, the gateway in Quan is our only hope of getting back home."

Chobba stroked his furry forearm and muttered something in his native tongue.

"What'd he say?" Annabelle asked Lukey.

The old man smiled as he translated. "'Brains must grow in hair because you don't have much of either.'"

"Do you see?" Tomàs said.

"Only that you're looking for a fat lip," Annabelle told him. "Won't you help us, Chobba?"

"Sleep yoo," he replied. "Dark bye-bye, we talk."

"Okay. That's fair enough."

Chobba nodded, grinning again. "Hokay," he said.

His good humor was so infectious that Annabelle couldn't help but smile back at him. He handed her his pouch of byrr leaves and indicated she should keep it. As the troop of rogha began to break up, he showed Annabelle's party to the hut they'd be sleeping in. Happily, it was on the same platform that they were already on.

Thank God they didn't have to do any more climbing, Annabelle thought. She'd been eyeing the other platforms, and had not been too thrilled to see that the only connections between them were swaying rope bridges—which appeared to be mostly for the very old or the very young—or the *boughs* of the trees, which the majority of rogha used.

She just couldn't have done it.

Later, in their hut, she sat up with Shriek. Holding hands, they could speak mind to mind and not disturb the others as they talked over what they'd learned from Lukey and Chobba. Tomàs sat glowering in a corner, muttering about how spiders were only good for being stepped on, and that went double for women who thought wearing pants gave them a man's wisdom, until Annabelle gave him one of her hard stares and he fell quiet. But she could tell by the glower in his eyes that his monologue was still going on inside his head.

We were lucky, Shriek said finally. *The Chobba being and his people arrived at a most opportune time.*

Tell me about it, Annabelle replied.

But still . . . we cannot remain here.

Thinking about living up on these platforms made Annabelle's stomach go all queasy again. *We'll leave soon,* she said.

Shriek nodded. *Soon,* she agreed.

She touched Annabelle's cheek in a friendly gesture, then turned in on the mattress, stuffed with leaves, that the rogha had provided for each of them.

Annabelle pulled her own mattress in closer to where Sidi was already sleeping and gave him a chaste kiss good night—chaste only because Tomàs's gaze was fixed upon them.

No cheap thrills for you, you little weasel, she thought.

Sidi woke to catch both looks—hers and Tomàs's. "You make a good boss, Annabelle," he said quietly before he rolled over once more.

Annabelle sat up, staring at Tomàs, until he finally lay down—face pointed at the wall, away from hers—Chen tried to get some sleep herself.

Gotta do something about Tomàs, she thought as she was drifting off. He was only going to get worse.

Annabelle spent an uneasy few hours, her sleep disturbed by a series of dreams in which she kept falling from a great height. Sometimes she was trying to get from one platform to another, and the rope or branch she was holding on to simply broke. Other times, she tripped on the platform and just tumbled off. Once it was Tomàs pushing her.

Each time she woke, she was sweaty and wide-eyed, the start of a scream just building up in her throat. She'd lie there, trying not to feel the sway of the platform under her. If she didn't move, she told herself—if she just lay where she was—nothing could happen to her. She couldn't just fall off.

But then the platform would shift slightly underneath her again and she'd sit up, arms wrapped around her chest, shivering. She fumbled for the pouch of byrr leaves that Chobba had left with her, then remembered she'd left it where they'd been sitting on the platform outside.

She stared at the rectangle of lighter darkness that the door made in one wall. Nope, she thought. There was no way she could face going out there to get the pouch.

Oh, Annie B. You gotta do it.

Outside, a wind moved in the trees. This high up, it wasn't impeded by the thick tangle of underbrush that was on the jungle floor. The platform moved with it, yawing only slightly, but it might as well have just tipped her right over the side, for the way her stomach felt.

Sidi stirred on his mattress beside her, turning in her direction.

"Annabelle?" he asked.

She hated to admit it—somehow it was worse that she had to admit her weakness to him because she wanted him to think of her as a strong person—but it was all she could do to keep her breathing relatively normal. She kept wanting to hyperventilate—to just run out there and throw herself over the edge of the platform and get it all over with.

Sidi realized her problem immediately. He moved like a shadow across the room, out the door. Moments later he was back, the pouch in his hand. He placed a leaf between her lips, as Chobba had done earlier.

"Chew," her ordered her.

Again she had to wait for her saliva and the leaf juice to mingle and trickle down her throat before she could unclench her jaws enough to chew. But finally, she did. Sidi sat close, an arm around her shoulder, holding her while she chewed, then giving her another leaf when she was finished with the first.

"Take your time with it," he said.

She chewed more slowly. By now, the effect had kicked in. The tension washed out of her limbs, the tightness from her chest. She could breathe again. Her stomach stopped churning.

Calmer now, she shook her head when Sidi offered her a third leaf. Ducking under his arm, she rose to her feet. The slight sway of the platform didn't even faze her.

"Annabelle?" Sidi asked, the worry plain in his voice.

"I gotta sit outside," she said. "Thanks, Sidi. You're a bloody lifesaver."

It was cooler outside—still warm by any normal standards, but not so close as in the hut, and a hundred times better than it had been down on the forest floor. There were next to no mosquitoes, for one thing. And the humidity was at least bearable.

She sat down, back against the hut, and looked out at the jungle night spread around her. A moment later, Sidi joined her. She reached out and captured his hand.

"Not doing too good, am I?" she said.

She could feel him shrug. "No one is free of fear."

"Yeah, but it gets pretty bad when the only way you can handle it's with something like this." She shook the pouch of byrr leaves.

"We could ask the rogha to bring us down to the jungle floor," Sidi said. "It's not long until morning anyway."

Annabelle shook her head. "Nah. I'm just gonna sit out here and wait for it to get light. When I start to get weirded out again, I'll just chew another of these. You go on and get some sleep."

"I'd rather sit out here with you."

Annabelle turned to look at him. "You're something else, you know that?"

"Something good, I hope."

"Real good."

He put his arm around her shoulder and she snuggled in close. It felt good to be held.

It was kinda weird, she thought, remembering Sidi as he'd been when she'd first met him—a sixty-year-old man, who'd looked his years. Dark-skinned and lean, worn by time, yet tough as nails, as the old saying went. Now he looked about her age—still tough, but the dark skin was free of wrinkles, the webwork of laugh lines around his eyes all smoothed away.

She'd liked him before the change, and liked him better now. In a different way.

Don't go getting all involved now, Annie B., she told herself.

But it was hard not to. It was lonely in the Dungeon, cut off from everything she knew. When she thought of all the time she'd spent on her own in that prison a few levels back, before Sidi and the rest showed up. . . . She didn't want to feel that cut off from people she could relate to. Not ever again.

So Sidi was an old man in a young man's body. So what? We should all be so lucky.

She lifted her head, bringing her face close to his.

"Remember just before the chasuck attacked us earlier?" She asked.

"I remember."

"Now, exactly where were we?" she murmured.

She brought a hand up behind his head and pulled him toward her until their lips met. Sidi pulled back, gently disengaging her hand.

"What's the problem?" Annabelle asked.

"This isn't right," he replied.

"Says who?"

"I'm old enough to be your grandfather."

"You'd never know from looking at you."

Sidi shook his head. "That still doesn't make it right."

"It doesn't matter to me."

"But it matters to me," he said. "Please understand, Annabelle. It's not just the age difference, but that we come from such vastly different worlds, as well. Here and now, it might not seem of much importance, but in the long run, it would set us against one another, and I would not wish to lose such a good friend."

Annabelle wanted to rail at him, but she knew he was right. It wasn't just age or race. It was everything that they were. A rock 'n' roller, and an Indian who was more a Zen sensei than a Hindu. Friends could bridge the differences that would have to arise as time went by. But lovers?

She leaned against his shoulder again. "Okay, Sidi," she said. "But friends can comfort each other, can't they?"

He gave her shoulder a squeeze.

Chapter 17

For Clive, it was as though he was in the middle of a bad dream—a nightmare in which everything familiar had been given a twist to set it slightly askew. Here was a man who claimed to be Neville Folliot, who was expecting his brother Clive—yet he was not Clive's twin. He was a complete stranger.

Given the man's poise and assurance, one could almost believe that he spoke the truth, and that all of their own memories were a lie.

Clive glanced at Smythe, but his former batman's face remained impassive, his stance that of a man prepared to defend himself at the drop of a glove. Keoti had taken a few steps away from them, and was now watching the party warily. The distrust with which she now regarded him pained Clive.

"Doomed," Finnbogg muttered mournfully.

So it seems, Clive thought. We are in desperate straits, perhaps, but not for the reason you think, Finn.

Their best course of action was to beat a hasty retreat, but that was, no doubt, already impossible. They were underground, at the mercy of the Dramaranians and their technological wonders. Even if they should manage to escape to the ground level, the Dramaranians undoubtedly had mechanical bloodhounds with which they could track them down.

As though reading Clive's mind, the man behind the desk smiled. Though he made no motion that Clive could see, some signal must have been given, for there was a stirring in the doorway behind them through which they had entered. When Clive turned to look, he saw a number of the silversuited Dramaranians blocking their escape. Each of them held one of those curiously shaped pistols in their hands. He remembered the blades of light with which the Dramaranians had been carving up the carcass of the brontosaur. It seemed likely that these weapons would be equally marvelous and strange. And deadly.

"What manner of game are you playing?" he asked the man behind the desk.

"Game?" The man's amusement faded from his features. "We play no game. We haven't sought guesting under false pretenses, claiming to be who we are not. 'Fess up, now. Who are you, and what do you want from me?"

"My name is Clive Folliot. I am a major of Her Majesty Queen Victoria's Fifth Imperial Horse Guards. I am searching for my brother, Major Neville Folliot of the Royal Somerset Grenadier Guards, who is currently on an extended leave of absence for the purpose of exploring East Africa. Upon his disappearance, I applied for and received detached service for the purpose of seeking him out."

The man at the desk leaned back in his chair. "Very pretty. You have all the facts correct—learned by rote, I imagine—but it will do you no good, sir, for you remain a stranger to me while my brother, for all our differences, is decidedly not."

"This man is not your brother?" Guafe asked.

"He most certainly is not."

"I had no idea," the cyborg said. "I took him at his word that he was who he said he was—there was no way I could look into the facts, and I had no reason to disbelieve him before, but I now disown all association with him."

"Well played," the man behind the desk said, "and it certainly sheds light upon the purity of your dedication and loyalty to your companions, but you are a touch too late, don't you think? It's very easy to step forth now and disclaim any guilt that might be associated with the others of your party."

"I had no way of knowing the truth until this very moment."

"Yes, well. That is a shame, isn't it? But we can't simply set you free now, can we? Seeing as how you arrived here with them, being a potential enemy and all?"

"I tell you I had no knowledge of this man's true motives."

The man behind the desk raised his eyebrows. "And I suppose we'll just have to take your word for that?"

"I do not lie," Guafe said stiffly.

"Ah. Well, that is welcome news, isn't it? Quickly, my friends, allow the cyborg his freedom. Open the doors to all our secrets to him, for he is an honorable being—or, at least, the part of him which is not a machine—and he means us no ill."

Not one of the Dramaranians stirred. Guafe's cybernetic eyes flashed red, but he kept his own counsel now in the face of their captor's sarcasm.

Clive wasn't particularly surprised, or even hurt, by Guafe's attempt to dissociate himself from the rest of the party. What hurt more was the recrimination that lay plain in Keoti's eyes. But, who was she to believe? he asked himself reasonably. A stranger she had known for a day or so—intimately, yes, but a stranger all the same—or a man who was the savior of her people and had lived among them for the past five years?

There was no question. But he wished there was some way that she could learn the truth, could know that he hadn't come all this way on false pretenses, his life a lie.

She would not meet his gaze anymore, so he returned his attention to the man behind the desk.

"What do you mean to do with us?" he asked.

"That is the question, isn't it? What would you do in my circumstance?"

Clive shrugged, pretending a nonchalance he didn't feel. "It would depend upon how I would expect my lies to best serve me—if I were a man such as you, which I am not."

The man behind the desk smiled. "Ah. So you mean to continue to press your claim—that you are the true Folliot, and I the pretender?"

"I know who I am," Clive replied.

"Yes, of course you do. The trouble is, we do not."

"That is not my concern. You can believe me or not, but who I am will not change."

"Oh, yes. You assume Clive Folliot to be an honorable man, so you mean to play your role to the end, not giving an inch. What will you do next? Challenge me to a duel to settle our differences—the winner being he with the greater skill?"

Clive could not hide the momentary hope that leapt inside him. With sword in hand, just the two of them, he and this fat man with the look of a friar about him, how could he not prevail?

The man behind the desk laughed. "Poppycock! I saw the videotape of your workout with Naree this afternoon. You're very skilled, but it means nothing. Might does not make right. Truth does."

"You're frightened," Clive said. "The real Neville Folliot—my brother—never refused a challenge in his life."

"Then this 'brother' of your imagination is a fool, something Neville Folliot—myself, sir—most assuredly is not."

Clive nodded. Fine. If this was how the game was to be played, then he would play along.

"You've had your fun with us," he tried, "now, why don't you let us go peacefully on our way? We've certainly no reason to remain here to cause you any further trouble—not with our quest still unresolved."

"I can't very well have you wandering about the Dungeon besmirching my good name, now, can I?"

"What do you *want* from us?"

"Your true identities—the real reason you've come to this place."

Clive realized that there was nothing more he could say. He could argue forever, but it would do absolutely no good.

He glanced at the others in the room. Guafe still glared at the man behind the desk, the metal dome of his head gleaming under the lights, one mechanical hand twitching at his side. Finnbogg stood with his head bowed, awaiting his judgment at the hands of what he thought were the spirits of the dead. Keoti, standing stiffly beside the desk, now wore a stranger's mask on her features. Clive remembered the softness of her lips, but there was no memory of them in the thin, hard line they now formed. Behind him, he could feel the weight of the guards' gazes, prepared for any untoward move.

Smythe stirred beside him. "And what then?" he asked the man behind the desk.

"What do you mean?"

"We give you what you want to know—then, what happens to us?"

"I might simply set you free."

Clive frowned at his companion, but Smythe turned his head slightly away from the desk so that neither the man behind it nor Keoti could see him give Clive a wink.

"Well, then, gov'nor," he said. "I suppose we'd better come clean. Now, Finn and our mechanical friend here are just what they say they are—or, at least they are so far as we know, for we only met 'em on route, as it were. 'Course, Guafe's got a mind as busy as a hurry-whore—it never stops whirling—so who knows who he really is, or what he's thinking, if you follow me?"

"Yes, yes. I'm not so concerned with them, except insofar as their plans coincide with yours."

"Well, I'm getting to that now, gov'nor. I'm not a man of many morns. I speak to the point and do what needs doing straightaway—no sense in making folks wait, that's what I always say. I remember a time in Newgate, when I was sitting in for a pint with a couple of the lads, and Casey, he turns to me and he says to me, like, 'Jim, when you take on a job, you do it quick, and you do it right, or you don't do it at all.' A right good bit of advice, that. Well, I look him straight back in the eye—don't I just?—and I says back to—"

The man rapped the desk top with his fist. "Will you please get on with it."

"Easy now, gov'nor. Don't be such a surly boots. A proper tale takes time to set up, as I'm sure you know. You don't go rushing blindly in, or the tale will just lie there looking like a dying duck in a thunderstorm—all pitiful and forlornlike."

Smythe shot the man behind the desk a quick grin, then plunged on before he could be interrupted again. "So what I'm saying is, though I know who I am, and I know the Cap'n here, the long and short of it is, I don't know these other two lads at all—except for what they've told me, and as Guafe himself's already mentioned to yourself, gov'nor, it could all be a pack of lies."

"Just tell me who you are."

"Well, gov'nor, I'm getting to that, aren't I now?"

"Your names."

Smythe straightened up. "Well, I'm Jim Scarpery—and that's the truth—and this here's the cap'n of the best band that ever plagued England's roads—Jack Roper. We're highwaymen, gov'nor, and proud of it."

"Highwaymen," the man behind the desk said. His tone was dry, and he eyed the pair of them with an expression that Clive couldn't decipher.

Madness, Clive thought. Horace had taken complete leave of his senses. Too many years of dissembling and mimicry had finally made him lose touch with reality.

But then he realized just what it was that Smythe was up to, and he was hard put to hide a grin. Lord help them all, it *was* madness. But the Dungeon was a Bedlam house, where perhaps only the play-acting of madness could see one through.

"The Devil's own, and a pair of the best, gov'nor," Smythe said with a nod. "'Least, we were till that damned blue light snatched us away

and brought us here. We ran into your brother in a prison on one of
the upper levels and got the whole tale of his search and all from him.
Then, when we escaped—leaving him and his sergeant behind, didn't
we just?—we thought we'd take their names and continue their quest.
The cap'n here always fancied being a major."

The man behind the desk pursed his lips. Elbows on the desk top,
he cradled his chin on his hands.

"Why" he asked.

"Well, you know why, gov'nor. Old Clive told us that you knew the
tricks of getting in and out of this place. We want to go back home,
the cap'n and me—take us a load of booty and stand with both feet
firm on England's green shores. There's not much for a good
Englishman in this place, be they a highwayman or a peer of the
realm—am I right?"

"He's telling more lies," Keoti broke in. "They demanded to see you.
Why would they take such a chance, knowing you'd see through them
as soon as they were brought before you?"

Smythe never gave anyone else a chance to reply. "Well, we had
to, didn't we?" he said. "We had to play the game out. In for a
penny, in for it all. There was a chance we could win you over—"
he gave the man behind the desk a quick, ingratiating smile "—or
maybe catch you unawares and then lean on you a bit till you
delivered us up a secret or two.

"We're not greedy, gov'nor—I'll tell you that straightaway. We
didn't want much. Right now, we'll settle for our lives. We never
meant any real harm."

Smythe bowed his head then and looked at the floor, wringing his
hands.

"You can't be taking him seriously," Keoti said. "The man obviously
wouldn't know the truth if he tripped over it."

The man behind the desk shook his head. "I believe him."

"Thank you, gov'nor," Smythe told him. "Now, we'd be eternally
grateful if you'd just let us go on our way, and we'd never be troubling
you anymore, would we, Jack?"

"Take them away," the man behind the desk said, waving them off.

The guards marched them out of the office and down the corridor,
Keoti and the man behind the desk following them at a slower pace.
Clive leaned closer to Smythe.

"Well played," he whispered, "but do you think he truly believed you?"

Smythe shrugged. "I just gave him what he wanted, sah. Think about it—our man there is the pretender. Do you think he wants the Dramaranians to know that? All he wants from us is proof that he is who he says he is—or, conversely, that we're not who we said we were."

"And now what?"

"Now we look to escape before we lose our heads, for you can count on this: he won't keep us around."

"Cap'n Jack," Clive muttered. "Jim Scarpery. Highwaymen."

"He wanted a tale, and any tale would do," Smythe said, "so I gave him the first that came to mind. I always had a hankering to be considered a bold highwayman."

Clive thought of the hate for him that was now in Keoti's eyes. "I'd rather you had put your quick thinking to considering a way that they might have believed us."

"'Father Neville' would never have allowed it," Smythe said.

"I know," Clive conceded. "Now, if we can just make an opportunity to escape this mess, rather than getting ourselves in even deeper. . . ."

But that moment never arrived. They were marched through a number of corridors, taken down many levels in an elevator, then marched down more corridors, until the way was blocked by an enormous metal door. The guards kept them all bunched together until Keoti and the man who called himself Father Neville joined them.

"I'm not an unfair man," the pretender said. "There's a way to the sixth level through the caverns that you will find behind this door."

Hope rose in Clive. Horace had been correct. The man *had* just wanted a tale, any tale, and now he was going to let them go.

"I might add, however," the pretender went on, "that there are . . . *things* in there that enjoy the taste of human flesh." He nodded to the guards. "I wish you luck."

Like hell you do, Clive thought. He looked at Keoti, but saw from her expression that so far as she was concerned, he no longer existed.

"You'll pay for this," Clive told "Father Neville" as the guards opened the door just wide enough to push their small company through.

The pretender came to stand beside the door. "I doubt that," he said.

It was dark in the cavern—dark, cold, and damp. Clive was the last to be hauled to the door and then pushed inside. Just as the door was closing, "Father Neville" leaned close to the crack.

"Your brother sends his regards," he said in a voice pitched just low enough to carry to Clive's ears, but no farther.

Clive lunged for him, but the fat man danced nimbly back, and the great metal door closed with a clang that echoed on and on through the dark cavern in which they were imprisoned.

Chapter 18

Head pillowed against Sidi's shoulder, Annabelle managed to get in a couple of hours of dreamless sleep before she was awakened by a whooping gang of young rogha who were playing a mad game of tag in the trees around the platform she and Sidi were sitting on. As she watched their acrobatics, her stomach began a series of flips. She quickly reached for the byrr pouch. Taking out a leaf, she began to chew.

By the time her unreasonable fears had retreated enough to be bearable, Chobba arrived. He swung down from a branch, neatly balancing a tray laden with what looked like little breakfast cakes, fruit, fired-clay mugs, and a steaming pot of tea. The mugs didn't rattle against each other, and not a drop of the tea was spilled.

"Show-off," she told him as he settled on his haunches in front of them.

The big rogha grinned. "Sleep hokay?" he asked.

"I think I'd like to get back on the ground now, if I could," she said.

She winced as the shrieking troop of children suddenly swooped by again. They didn't so much seem to swing between branches as tumble. Chobba, obviously thinking they were bothering her with their nose, stood up and began to shout at them, until she tugged on his furry arm.

"No, no," she said. "It's not them—it's just the height. It makes me . . . sick."

"Yoo chew byrr?"

"Yeah, but I still want down."

"Yoo eat first. Loo-kee cum. Fetta cheef cum. We all talk. Then yoo go. Hokay?"

"Fetta chief?" Annabelle asked. She remembered him using the term last night, but she'd been too out of it to ask him what it meant.

"She make fetta," Chobba explained. "Plenty smart."

"I think he means a rootman," Sidi said. "Someone who makes fetishes and speaks with the spirits."

131

"Like a shaman," Annabelle said.

Sidi shrugged, but Chobba was nodding in response to what the Indian had said.

"Named Reena," he said. "Fetta cheef. Talk with dead rogha—read sign in root and leaf. Cum plenty soon."

Drawn by the sound of their conversation, Shriek and Tomàs emerged from the hut. At the sight of the four-armed alien, the younger rogha came bouncing through the tree boughs to peer more closely, scrambling away when she turned toward them, then creeping forward again once she looked away. Shriek laughed at their antics, the high chittering sound cutting across the young roghas' shrieks.

"Eat—drink!" Chobba said. He sat on his haunches again and pushed the tray forward, smacking his lips. "Plenty good, yuh?"

Lukey joined them while they were eating, his arrival sparking what appeared to be a good-natured series of teasing remarks that flew between the younger rogha and himself. The children hung from their perches with one hand, or one leg, waving their free limbs as they chattered.

"What does that mean, *bishii?*" Annabelle asked. It was the term that the younger rogha used to refer to the old man.

Lukey smiled. "Well, they say it means 'hairless ape', but Chobba here told me after I was here a while that it really means 'old fart.'"

"Bishii, bishii!" the children chorused.

Lukey stood up and shook his fists at them with mock severity as he tried to shoo them away, but he need not have bothered. The young rogha were already falling silent. In moments they had all fled quickly away.

Turning, Annabelle saw that it was the arrival of the fetish chief that had sent them scurrying. Taking off right now, she thought, looking at the strange rogha, might not be such a bad idea.

Reena had no legs, but it didn't stop her progress through the trees. She landed on the platform and propelled herself toward them on her powerful arms. She wore a short skirt of leather, which just covered her leg stumps, and a vest of woven grass, under which her furry breasts bounced. The vest was decorated with beadwork, feathers, and hundreds of tiny bird bones that rattled when she moved. Hanging from her neck was a large, beaded leather pouch. Dozens of bracelets jangled on her arms. Her fur smelled strongly of incense.

Her face was hidden behind a shockingly ugly mask. The mask itself was wooden—a grotesque exaggeration of a rogha's features—with copper, cowrie shells, and beads covering everything but its crown, which was a square of plain, dark, blue-green cloth. A thick fringe of antelope hair bearded the bottom of the mask, and rising like an elephant's trunk behind the plain crown was a beaded headpiece tufted with raffia.

She stopped in front of Annabelle and her party, the dark eyes in the eyeholes glittering as she studied the four of them.

"What does the mask signify?" Annabelle asked Lukey.

"A spirit of the darkworld that watches you through my eyes," the fetish chief replied. Her voice had a hollow sound, coming out from behind the mast as it did.

"You speak English?" Annabelle asked.

Stupid question, she thought as soon as she'd asked it, but Reena shook her head.

"She doesn't speak your language," that same hollow voice said. "But I do."

"Ah. . . ."

Annabelle glanced at Sidi, but he shook his head, understanding as little as she did of what was going on. Neither Lukey nor Chobba would meet her gaze.

"Who . . . ah . . . are you, then?" she asked the voice behind the mask.

"A spirit of the darkworld."

Right. Seance time in the jungle. Just what they needed.

"Can you be a little more specific?" Annabelle tried.

"The darkworld lies all about you—invisible, yet always present. We watch you, through the eyes of our mouthpieces."

"Like a ghost?"

"We are not dead, but yes, like a ghost."

"What's your name?"

"We don't have names."

"Then, how do you tell each other apart?" Annabelle asked.

"We know who we are—that is sufficient, don't you think?"

"I suppose. . . ."

"You wish to go to Quan," the voice continued, issuing hollowly from behind the mask, "to enter the gateway that lies there, which you believe will take you back to your own worlds. But I tell you now,

Annabelly—" it said her first and surname as though it were all one word "—that if you go on from here, you will never see your child Amanda again."

"How can you know all that stuff?" Annabelle demanded.

"From the darkworld, we can see you as you truly are—your complete history as a whole, rather than just the outer face you present to the immediate world around you."

This was really weird, Annabelle thought. She'd never been one to go in for mumbo-jumbo stuff. Everything had a reasonable explanation. You might not have the right data to work it out at any given time, but you could count on it all making logical sense somewhere along the line. But this . . . this was just spooky.

"So, you're reading my mind?"

"I am reading your essence."

"Wonderful. And after having a good long poke around in there, the best you can come up with is to tell me that Quan's dangerous? I hate to break this to you, pal, but that's not exactly a hot news flash."

"I understand your desire to return to your home-world, but you must accept the impossibility of that. The deeper you go through the Dungeon's levels, the more danger you are placing yourself in, and the less chance you have of surviving. Quan is extremely dangerous, but it is nothing compared to what lies in the gateway and beyond it."

"Okay," Annabelle said. "But, why don't you humor me? Tell me what's waiting for us."

"In Quan, certain death at the hands of an illusion. In the gateway, certain death caused by your greatest fear made real. In the next level, certain death brought on by madness."

"Wait a sec," Annabelle said. "You keep saying 'certain death.' How can I find certain death in the gateway when I've already died in Quan?"

There was a long pause, then finally, the hollow voice admitted, "Should you go on, it is possible, though extremely unlikely, for you to survive one, or another, but not all of the dooms that lie in your way."

"But we could go on and have a chance?"

"The possibility is so slight that it is not worth considering."

"Still, you wouldn't try to stop us—I mean, physically?"

"Each individual is free to make his or her own choices in this world. That can never be taken away."

"Okay, so you won't stop us. Can you help us some more? Give us some more info? I mean, come on. What's it gonna hurt you?"

There was no reply.

"Spirit?" Annabelle asked.

Still silence.

Annabelle reached forward and touched Reena on the shoulder. The fetish chief started, then spoke to her in the language of the rogha. The voice, while it had a hollowness to its tone, was nothing like the one with which she'd been speaking moments before.

"What's she saying now?" Annabelle asked.

"'What do you wish of me?'" Lukey translated.

"We were talking . . ." Annabelle began. Her voice trailed off as Lukey shook his head.

"Nope. You were talkin' to the darkworld spirit that gives Reena her powers—not to Reena herself. I've seen it before. Bin through the same thing myself when I first got here."

"What the hell's going on?" Annabelle demanded.

Sidi touched her arm. "I have heard of this before—among the rootmen of the Africans. The spirits fill the rootman's body like water filling a vessel. When the spirit departs, the rootman remembers nothing."

"But that's not real," Annabelle protested. "Spirits . . . ghosts. It's just not real."

"There are too many mysteries in the world," Sidi said, "for me to be able to decide which of them are illusions and which are real. In this Dungeon we have already seen what we thought to be impossible become real. When the bizarre is commonplace, who can honestly say what is or is not possible?"

Annabelle nodded. "Okay. You got me on that one. But I'm still going on."

"I would not think to argue with you, otherwise," Sidi said.

Annabelle turned to Chobba. "And I'd like to get down to the ground now, if I could."

"Sorry yoo go," Chobba said. "Chobba take yoo down. Chobba and yoo walk on legs to Quan, yuh? Hokay?"

"Wish I could think of a way ta get you ta stay," Lukey said, "but damned if I can think o' one—not when you got your mind set on goin'."

Annabelle started to rise, but the fetish chief suddenly thrust out a strong hand and gripped Annabelle's arm. She spoke quickly in rogha, masked face close, dark eyes glittering in their slits, inches from Annabelle's own.

"What's she saying?"

Lukey translated. "That even though you ain't got nothin' ta ask her, she's goin' ta tell you somethin' all the same. She sees in your white face a . . ." The old man paused, looking for a word. "Not a destiny. More like a mess a' hard times comin', an' if you want ta make out okay, you got ta be willin' to depend on other people's strength, 'stead a' just tryin' ta pull the weight on your own. An' don't go lookin' too hard for what you think you want, 'cause you just might get it."

Tomàs, who had remained silent through all the various exchanges, spoke up now. "So, will you listen to me now? I say we go back to find others, *sim?* They are not so *estúpido* as you."

"Go back," Annabelle said. "Right. You ready to take on the chasucks, pal?"

"We will go carefully."

Annabelle shook her head. *"You* go, and anybody else who wants to go with you. Me, I'm going on. I'm getting outta this place, and the only way I see to pull that off is to keep on going."

Shriek moved to Annabelle's side, her multifaceted gaze fixed unpleasantly on the Portuguese. *And she will not go alone,* the arachnid said.

Annabelle smiled, and turned back to look at the fetish chief.

"Thank you," she said. "You and your spirits." She waited for Lukey to translate. "Though we must go on, I will remember your advice."

Reena nodded. She spoke softly.

"'You are a strong woman with much pride,'" Lukey translated, "'an' that, too, will be a great help.' An' then she gave you her blessin'."

The fetish chief walked away on her hands, then swung into the nearest branch and was gone.

"That's really something," Annabelle said. "The way she moves."

"Reena plenty strong," Chobba said, flexing his arm muscles. "Plenty smart. Big cheef. Like Chobba, yuh?"

Annabelle grinned. "You got it," she said. "Can we get down to the ground now? It's either that, or I'll be falling off in another minute."

With what passed for a smile on her alien features, Shriek swung over the side of the platform and started down. By the time Annabelle and the others of her party reached the ground, Shriek was there waiting for them. Chobba and a number of his warriors were planning to guide them to Quan. Surprisingly, Lukey joined the group as well.

"Well, I'm not sayin' I'm goin' all the way," he said, "but I wouldn't mind catchin' just a peek a' the place, an'—oh, hell, you never know. I might just find I'm ready to do some travelin' my own self. Bin livin' like a monkey for an awful lot a' years. Maybe it's time I learned ta live like a man again."

"We're happy to have you," Annabelle said.

"Oh, yes," Tomàs said. "*Muito feliz*. Very happy."

Annabelle turned to the Portuguese, then frowned when she saw the guileless look on his face. The little bugger acted like he'd had a change of heart and meant it. Well, who knows? she thought. Nobody says he's gotta stay a sullen little weasel.

"Walk on legs now, yuh?" Chobba said when they were all gathered on the game trail.

They each had a new pack to carry, filled with provisions and water sacks. Annabelle's also had the pouch of byrr leaves, which Chobba had insisted she keep.

"You guys know any walking songs?" she asked.

When Chobba shook his head, she taught him and his warriors the chorus for "Da Doo Ron Ron." Making up words to fit their present situation, with the rogha answering her back with a lusty if slightly off-key chorus, Annabelle walked beside Chobba and Sidi as they set off for Quan. Even with the warnings of danger that lay ahead, she still felt better than she had in a long time.

It's the ground under your feet, Annie B., she told herself. Don't go getting too cocky now.

Maybe, maybe not. All she knew was that it was good to be moving under her own steam, their party strengthened, and no pack of land sharks on their ass.

Things could be better, she thought. But then again, they could be a helluva lot worse.

Chapter 19

They were trapped in utter darkness. Clive ran his hands along the metal door that had sealed them in, but could find no handle or bolt on this side to let them back out again.

"Damn the man!" he cried, and hammered a fist against the door.

A dull, hollow boom rang through the darkness.

"Need light," Finnbogg said.

"I've got the spark for a torch," Smythe said, taking flint and steel from the pocket of his jacket. "Let's see if we can find something to burn."

"What did he mean by *things?*" Clive said.

Smythe's shrug was lost in the blackness. "In this place, it could be anything," he said. "Wouldn't surprise me to trip over a band of kobolds."

"Can't find even a scrap of wood," Finnbogg said.

His voice came from farther out in the darkness, where he was carefully feeling his way about, looking for fuel to burn.

"Don't wander too far," Smythe warned him. "I caught a glimpse of the size of this place just before they shut us in, and it's big enough to get easily lost in."

"Perhaps I can help," Guafe said.

Clive and Smythe turned in the direction of the cyborg's metallic voice.

"God save us," Smythe muttered.

He'd forgotten one of the uses of having a cyborg as part of their company. Guafe's eyes began to glow red, then redder, casting a dim light wherever he turned his gaze.

"Nice of you to help," Clive said dryly, "all things considered."

But he was happy for the light, no matter how dim it was.

"We are in this together," Guafe replied.

"Funny how you forgot that a few minutes ago, when we were talking to the fat pretender."

"He was most . . . convincing."

"Do tell," Smythe said. "Pity for you that you weren't. You might have been spared our company."

"What we think of each other has no relevance to our situation," the cyborg said. "I merely wish to observe as much of this curious world as I may before I make my escape. This particular place holds little of interest."

Clive nodded to himself. He tended to forget that while the cyborg looked human enough, the workings of his mind would no doubt always remain unfathomable. In some ways, the cyborg was less human than either Finnbogg or Shriek, he reminded himself. It would serve them all well if he didn't forget that.

"Here, what's this?" Smythe said.

Guafe turned his gaze in the Englishman's direction, illuminating a heap of what appeared to be discarded mining gear. Smythe picked a lantern out of the debris. Checking inside, he found the stub of a candle. More searching found a number of other lanterns—most broken, but all with bits of candle in them that could be salvaged.

"The equipment seems rather primitive," Guafe said.

Considering the technological marvels of their captors, Clive had to agree.

"Perhaps that's why it's here," he said. "It's of no more use to them."

"Perhaps," the cyborg said.

Or perhaps, Clive added to himself, the *things* that the pretender had spoken of had made the Dramaranians abandon this mine a very long time ago. Though he wasn't given to either claustrophobia or a fear of the dark, he found himself keeping one ear constantly alert for any sound that they didn't make themselves. Whatever the Dramaranians kept down here to prey on their captives had to be extremely unpleasant if the best description of them was *things*.

"Look," Finnbogg exclaimed, holding up a box of unused candles.

"Good work, Finn," Smythe said.

With bits of shaved wood and some straw padding from the seat of an old mine cart, he now had enough of a fire going to light the first candle stub. Setting it back into place inside the lantern, he held the lantern up so that they could get a better look at their surroundings, but while it illuminated their immediate area, its light was simply not strong enough to penetrate the cavern's deeper shadows.

"There are rails here," Guafe said.

He was pointing to where narrow rails, set on wooden ties, led off into the cavern, disappearing into the darkness some ten feet from where they stood.

"We can follow them," he added.

Clive nodded, but first, he held up the lantern that he'd lit for himself, turning its light to the door. The face of the massive door was utterly blank, one solid sheet of metal fit so snugly into the stone walls of the cavern that it would be a very long job to try to attempt to chip their way out, even with the use of the tools that lay in the heap of discarded gear. And there was another good reason for not attempting such an escape, he realized. The sound of their work would surely draw the Dramaranians back to investigate. They might be able to overcome a small party, but then they would have the entire complex of the underground city to transverse.

No. They had to go on.

"Does Neville's journal say anything of this place?" Smythe asked.

Clive shook his head. "It was not mentioned in the last message." There was no point in looking for that entry again. He had almost become used to the way in which entries appeared and disappeared unexpectedly, impossibly, in the slim journal. Somehow Neville—or the Ren or the Chaffri, the rulers of the Dungeon—had found a way to write in the book while it rested in Clive's possession. Perhaps something had been added. He patted his jacket pocket and frowned. "Damn. I left it in my room. The Dramaranians have it now."

Smythe shrugged. "It caused us as much trouble as it helped us."

Thinking of Annabelle and the rest of her party, lost—more likely dead—in the jungles, Clive could only agree. If they had kept together. . . .

"We should follow the rails," Guafe said. "They must lead somewhere."

"They'll only take us to wherever they were mining," Smythe said.

"Not necessarily. In the Dungeon—"

"Any-bloody-thing's possible," Smythe finished. "Right. But these rails. . . ."

"Do you have a better idea?" the cyborg asked.

"This place our tomb," Finnbogg said suddenly. "Judgment of dead was that we be entombed alive, or eaten by creatures that live down here."

"Those were living, breathing men and women that put us in here," Clive said. "They were no more spirits of the dead than we are."

But again he tried to pierce the deeper darkness beyond the glow of their lanterns, an uncomfortable sensation of being spied upon crawling up his spine. *Things*, the pretender had said. Damn him. What manner of *things*?

"We have no water, no provisions," Smythe said, "and these candles won't last forever."

The stub he'd first lit was already guttering in its lantern. He lit a fresh one, then paused.

"Look at this," he said.

The candle's flame was being drawn away from the door where they were standing, deeper into the cavern, in the same direction that the rails led.

"An air draft," Guafe said. "Created by an opening to the outside farther in. So the rails do lead somewhere other than merely the last shaft in which they were working."

Smythe nodded. "Well, that's settled, at least. We follow the rails."

They salvaged what they could from the discarded mining gear. Candles filled their pockets. Finnbogg, Clive, and Smythe each carried a lantern. The dwarf took a small sledgehammer for a weapon, the others pry-bars. Smythe added a discarded tin container to his gear, tying it to his belt with a length of twine that he'd also discovered. He meant to use it to hold water, if they came across any. Over his shoulder, tied at each end with more of the twine, he carried a strip of sturdy canvas that he'd found bunched up in a corner.

"I'd feel better with a rope," he said.

"I'd feel better to simply be quit of this place," Clive said.

"There's that."

They set off then, following the two metal rails, their boots sending up hollow echoes as they tramped along the wooden ties.

With no way to measure time, it was difficult to tell how long they followed the rails across that immense cavern, but eventually, they came to its farther side. As the dark bulk of the walls rose before them, disappearing into a darkness that their lights could not penetrate, they saw that the rails entered a large cleft in the wall. Stepping through, they now found the rails leading them through a series of smaller galleries that began to slope gently downward.

Here, dripstone covered the rails in places, spindly stalagmites rising from the ties, forcing them to make detours from the actual path the rails took. Some of the galleries were small enough that their light reached to the walls on either side and the ceilings above, hung heavily with stalactites.

In one gallery they came upon the first branching of the rails. They went along the ones that led to the right, but these followed a sudden dip, leading the party into a gallery where the walls and floor were heavily covered with knobby calcite growths. Here the stalactites had grown all the way to the floor, forming a bewildering series of columns. The cave coral on the floor made the footing very unsteady.

In places the rails vanished under the dripstone growths, so thick had they become. The party retraced their path back to where the track had initially split, taking the left turn this time. Here, the downward incline continued at a gentler slope, though the farther they went, the damper the air grew about them.

They stopped twice to rest, once simply on the rails, the second time following the sound of water to the far side of a larger gallery where they found a pool of water, fed by an overhead drip. They drank there and rested again. Smythe filled his tin container before they pressed on.

Clive's sense of the party being under observation by hidden viewers neither increased nor decreased, but the farther they went, coming upon no sign of any living creature, the more ill at ease he felt. The darkness beyond their lantern lights, the soft echoing shuffle of their footsteps rebounding hollowly from the walls, all added to his discomfort, making him brood.

He worried about Annabelle and her party, his guilt at letting them go off on their own made worse by what Keoti had told him of the jungles and Annabelle's chance of surviving their dangers. Time and again he berated himself for not being firmer with her and keeping the two parties as one.

The fact that they had had to leave Dramaran in disgrace irked him as well, and not just because of how poorly Keoti had been made to see him. It was more the thought of that fat pretender sitting safely amid all those technological wonders, wearing Neville's name like a badge of honor, his lies being accepted as truth, while the truth was made a mockery. . . .

It made Clive grit his teeth. He wished that there had been an opportunity for him to cross swords with the pretender to his brother's name. He would have enjoyed seeing that smirking smile wiped from the man's fat-jowled features.

But thinking of the pretender brought thoughts of his twin to mind, as well. Ever since he and Horace had entered this damned Dungeon, Neville had been playing them for a pair of fools. Everything that happened to them seemed to be a part of some elaborate game, only no one had been kind enough to allow Clive and his party in on its rules. Finding that journal, mysterious voices, all that had happened to them following the advice that Neville had written in it. . . .

Perhaps Horace was right—they were better off without the damned thing. For if it was to have been of any use, why couldn't it have been more clearly written? Instead of riddles and vagaries, a few hard facts would have been far more than useful. Such as what this cavern entailed for them. Where would it take them? And what inhabited it?

It was Finnbogg who stumbled upon the bones.

The dwarf was walking on one side of the rails when he gave a cry and would have fallen, his lantern smashing on the rocks, if Guafe hadn't caught his arm and helped him to regain his balance. As it was, the lantern swung wildly, making the shadows dance like dervishes, and then they all saw what the dwarf had stumbled upon.

All along the left side of the rails in this newest gallery, bones lay scattered from the track to the far wall. Skulls and rib cages, the bones of arms and legs. Others that were not readily recognizable—perhaps not even human. And there were some—clearly the skeletons of humanlike creatures, with hands like men, or legs and torsos, only their sizes were wrong. Most of these were too small even to have been children's. One, if it had been a part of a humanoid, then it had belonged to a giant at least eleven feet tall.

"It's some kind of graveyard," Smythe said.

"More a feeding ground, I would say," Guafe remarked.

Finnbogg shuddered, and Clive could feel a shiver travel up his own spine. As Smythe moved closer, holding his lantern high to cast more light, Clive followed suit, though he couldn't shake that sense of being spied upon by hidden watchers. It was stronger now than it had ever been since they'd entered the cavern. A crawling sensation that traveled up his spine and settled at the nape of his neck, knotting his muscles.

For a long time the party regarded the bone Field, none of them speaking, each keeping his own counsel. Then, just as Guafe turned to him to make a remark, Clive held up a hand.

"Hist!" he said softly. "What was that?"

"I heard nothing," the cyborg began, but then his gaze traveled past Clive, his eyes widening.

Turning himself, Clive saw that dozens of pairs of small, slitted eyes watched them from the farther side of the gallery, retinas reflecting back at the party like a fox's or cat's would in the light of their lanterns.

Smythe pulled his pry-bar from where it had been thrust in his belt. "Now we'll see what manner of creatures haunts this place," he said.

"Wait a moment," Clive said. He held out a hand to stop Smythe's advance. "Let's see if we can pass them by."

Smythe hesitated, then nodded. Slowly, the party backed toward the narrow entryway that led into the next gallery, feeling their way with their feet as they went, unwilling to lift their gazes from those that were watching them from the darkness. Just as they reached the entrance, a blood-curdling shriek, like that torn from the throat of a man being disemboweled, shattered the darkness.

"Well, that's cut it," Smythe said.

As one, the members of the party lifted their weapons and prepared to meet the creatures' attack.

Chapter 20

With the presence of the rogha, Annabelle felt as though their journey had turned into an outing. It was hard not to have fun with the good-natured ape-men around. They laughed and joked among themselves, making Lukey translate what they thought were the particularly good lines. They loved to sing, especially to the rhythm of R&B, so the songs that Annabelle taught them were all old Motown numbers and Fifties rock music with lots of doo-wops, she-bops, and the like.

Their own music was harder for her to follow. It involved a lot of sharp clicks that were made in the back of the throat, and sounds that were like short coughs, mixed in with a rhythmical chanting. But she loved listening to it and trying to follow its odd tempos.

By the end of the first day, she found it easy to tell the various rogha apart. Chobba had never been a problem—he hulked over the others, and there was no mistaking his toothy grin. Through variation in fur coloring at first, and then the facial features, as she grew used to them, she soon learned to keep all the rest of them straight as well.

Ghes was smaller than the rest, with a large nose and a henna tint to his fur. He was quiet-spoken and the best singer. Ninga had black and silver streaks in his head fur, and large eyes set wide apart. A practical joker, he loved to have a good trick played on him as much as playing the trick on someone else. Tarit and Nog were the hardest to tell apart, because they were identical twins, but Tarit wore a brightly colored scarf along with his neck torc, and Nog had a shrill laugh that couldn't be mistaken for anyone else's.

The only female among the rogha accompanying them was Yssi, with her light, tan-colored fur and soft, dark-brown eyes. Next to Chobba, she was the strongest of their little troop, and like Ghes, she was quiet-spoken, but she had a dry wit, so that when she did make a comment, all the rogha invariably broke up. She also wasn't averse to a little common tomfoolery, either.

She was the one who, when they camped that first night, tried to get Annabelle and her party to eat from a bowl of wriggling white worms and slugs that she'd collected on the journey, insisting that they were a delicacy that shouldn't be missed, and yes, they were supposed to be eaten while still alive. That was, in fact, half the charm of them.

Annabelle was disgusted, but since she prided herself on her willingness to try any native food, no matter where she traveled, she almost swallowed one of the squirming creatures. All that stopped her were the stifled giggles of the other rogha, who eventually let her in on the joke.

Ninga took to calling her Ilkgar after that, which Lukey translated for her as "eater of worms."

"Cute," she told both Ninga and Yssi. "Just remember, kids: I don't get mad, I just get even."

The rogha hooted with appreciative laughter when Lukey translated what she'd said.

The real dinner that night was a kind of jambalaya of vegetables, with the meat of a wading bird that Shriek had brought down just before they camped. The camp itself was well off the game trail, in a clearing on the veldt side of the path. The strip of jungle on this side of the river was so wide now that they no longer caught brief glimpses of the plains through the trees, as they had on their first day after leaving Clive's party. The undergrowth was thick off the game trail, while the trail itself was heavily overhung with drooping boughs and vines.

The one thing Annabelle missed about the rogha village was the wind that moved through the treetops. Here, the air was still and humid again, the heat draining. Mosquitoes were a problem until Ghes pointed out the black mud that formed at the roots of a reedlike flowering plant growing in thick stands along the river bank. A thick white juice secreted from the roots of the plant made an excellent bug repellent when mixed with the mud. Although it did have a certain pungent odor that was almost, though not quite, unpleasant, it was better than constantly trying to fend off the bugs.

The silliest thing about it, Annabelle decided, was the way that it made them all look like a motley bunch of commandos in camouflage gear.

When they were finally ready to turn in that first night, the rogha and Lukey all swung into the trees, where they made nests for themselves, wedged in the crooks where branches thrust out from the main trunk. After the night she'd spent in the rogha village, nothing could convince Annabelle to follow suit. She, Sidi, and Shriek made their beds on the ground around the dying embers of their fire. Tomàs, however, climbed up into the lower branches of one of the trees and, after much twisting about and adjusting of his limbs, fell asleep as though he'd been born to life in the trees.

Wasn't much different from a ship's rigging, Annabelle thought.

It was during her watch that she heard the cough of a monkey-cat. It came from a good distance away in the jungle, but each subsequent time she heard it, it sounded closer. With her spear, she poked up into the boughs above her, where the nearest of the rogha was sleeping. Ghes stirred, then called down softly.

Though she was trying to pick up the language, Annabelle still had a long way to go with it. But while she didn't understand what Ghes had said, she did catch the rogha's questioning tone.

"Hear that?" she called back in very badly accented rogha. "Bad sound?"

The monkey-cat coughed again. This time it was no farther than a few trees away.

Ghes cocked his head. Hearing the monkey-cat, he made a low, warbling sound, like that of a night bird. Instantly, the other rogha were awake. They had a hurried conference, shadowy heads bent together, then swung off in various directions.

Annabelle blinked at their sudden disappearance. She clutched her spear, wondering if she should get the fire going again, when there came a sudden chorus of shrieks from the forest all around them, followed by an abrupt silence.

Sidi and Shriek leapt to their feet, brandishing their own weapons. In their tree perches, Lukey and Tomàs stirred. Then, before Annabelle could explain, a long, wailing cry broke the jungle night, followed by another silence.

"Annabelle?" Sidi asked. "What's happened? Where are the rogha?"

"There was one of those monkey-cats coming near the camp," Annabelle started to explain, but then the rogha were back.

They swung down from the trees, hooting with pleasure. Chobba was holding the slain monkey-cat by its tail.

"Lookit that!" Lukey cried. He started down from his perch. "Those damn things'd tear your heart out as soon as look at you. They like to sneak up on the baby rogha an' carry 'em away."

Annabelle slowly lowered her spear. "It's like killing a cousin," she said.

"It's killin' a varmint, that's all," Lukey said. "They're tough little buggers—mean as sin. Guess this one wasn't expectin' us to be ready for him."

Chobba was thumping his chest. "Big cheef, yuh!" he cried.

The rogha pounded each other's shoulders, all of them grinning. As Yssi and Nog started to skin the animal, Annabelle looked away. She couldn't shake the feeling that the monkey-cat, like the rogha and the flying monkeys, were all related in a way. To her, what they'd done was the same as if she'd killed a chimp. Up close, the monkey-cat didn't appear much bigger than that.

"Different customs," Sidi said from beside her.

Annabelle nodded. "Yeah. I know. It's just, when you think of the rogha or Shriek, or even Finnbogg, you get confused as to what's an animal and what's . . . a person."

Even though they'd just eaten, the rogha built up the fire once more. When the monkey-cat was skinned and gutted, its paws and head kept aside so that the teeth and claws could be collected later, the rogha thrust a spit through the animal's torso and set to roasting it over the fire.

"Eat heart—be strong," Chobba told her. "Stronger, yuh?"

"I guess," Annabelle said, regretting that she'd ever wakened anybody in the first place. Maybe she could just have shooed it away.

"Hell," Lukey said, forcing open the monkey-cat's jaws. "Will you lookit the teeth on this bugger." He showed them to Annabelle. "It could rip your arm off without even blinkin', an' that's God's own truth."

If the journey had seemed like an outing before, now it had gained a completely festive—if somewhat macabre, by Annabelle's reckoning—air. The rogha laughed and told jokes, and later, they feasted on the roasted cat. When Chobba offered a piece of the cooked heart to her, Annabelle shook her head, but she did try some of the meat. It was gamy, with a coarse texture, but surprisingly good. She found she couldn't eat very much, and what she had eaten left her feeling a little queasy.

It was a long time before the camp settled down again, with only a few hours left until daybreak. The rogha told tales, which Lukey translated, and the songs went on until near dawn. They all slept late that morning, not getting back to the game trail until well after noon.

* * *

The following days fell into a pattern of marching by day and camping by night that was broken only a few times. Once, when they were washing up at the river bank on the third morning out from the village, the rogha withdrew back into the jungle, quickly pulling Annabelle and her companions into the undergrowth with them. When Annabelle questioned them, Ninga pointed at the sky above the river. Peering through the bushes, Annabelle could just make out a small black dot floating there, its wings still, riding the air currents like a falcon.

"Gree," Ninga explained.

"They spot us," Lukey added, "an' there'll be hell ta pay."

"I thought you said they were scavengers," Annabelle said.

"Well, they are. Thing is, they don't mind killin' somethin' an' waitin' for it ta rot properly, an' they plain hate anybody wanderin' through their territory."

"This is their territory?"

"Close enough so's it don't matter."

Another time they came across the recent scent trail of a monkey-cat, and the rogha argued about whether or not they should track the animal down. Their disagreement grew so profound that Annabelle was sure that they were going to come to blows, but as suddenly as it had started, it was over, and the rogha were laughing again as they continued on their journey.

As they came closer to Quan, the rogha grew increasingly wary. Twice they had the party circumvent elaborate traps laid on the game trail. One was a pit with sharpened stakes at the bottom, covered with leaves and made to look like a part of the trail. The other was a series of nets, ready to fall on the unwary traveler when set off by a trip string. The second time they came upon a pit, it held the impaled body of one of the tapirlike creatures. The rogha descended into the pit and stole the body, and that night they had another feast.

"Who is setting these traps?" Sidi asked Lukey that night.

"Quanians, I guess. Me, I've never bin this far from the village. Just heard about what it's like, that's all."

Chobba, overhearing them, nodded solemnly. "Bad place, yuh?" he said. "Plenty trouble."

It was when they were within a day's march of the village that Annabelle spied a piece of torn cloth caught in a branch alongside the trail. It looked to be fine linen—a piece of a sleeve, torn from a shirt, with part of a frayed cuff still attached.

"I thought you said the Quanians were ghosts," she said. "But this didn't belong to any ghost, and ghosts didn't set those traps back there, either."

Lukey took the piece of cloth from her. "Guess this belonged to that other feller," he said.

"What other feller? You never said anything about somebody else coming this way."

"Didn't really think to tell you about it," Lukey replied. "It was a while ago—a couple a' weeks, maybe less? Feller came through an' we tried to stop him, but he wouldn't take no. Said he had to get to Quan, an' wasn't nothin' goin' to stop him from gettin' there."

"What was his name?" Annabelle asked.

She had a sneaking suspicion as to who it had been, even though the time frame was wrong. But then again, who knew how time worked in this place? When you considered the spread of centuries from which people were plucked, it made sense that time worked differently here as well.

"His name was Folly," Lukey said. "Neville Folly."

Annabelle remembered the chasuck, with their cries of "folly, folly." She should have remembered to ask about Clive's brother when she'd first arrived at the rogha village.

"Do you mean Folliot?" she asked.

Lukey nodded. "That's the name, all right. You know that feller?"

"We've been chasing him forever, it seems."

"Well, you can stop lookin' for him now," Lukey said. "Ain't no way he'd've survived in Quan. No way anybody can."

"Yet, you're coming with us."

"Well, now, I'm goin' to have me a look-see; that's all I'll swear to right now."

Annabelle exchanged glances with others of her party, and saw the same knowledge reflected in their eyes that she knew was in her own. Clive's party was completely off track.

"What did this feller do, anyway?" Lukey asked.

"He's supposed to know how to get out of this place," Annabelle replied, "so you can bet that if anyone gets through Quan and its ghosts, it'll be him."

"He knows for sure?"

"To the best of our knowledge," Sidi said, "he's been all the way through and back once already."

"An' now he's goin' back through a second time? Feller needs his head examined, I'm thinkin'."

"And we'll be happy to do it for him," Annabelle said.

She wondered if she'd ever see Clive and Finnbogg and the rest of them again. She'd half expected their trails to cross once more, but now she knew that the other party was so far off base that they might as well be on another planet. She even missed Finnbogg, for all that it was his fault that she was still stuck in this place.

"Bad place now," Chobba called back from where he walked ahead.

"Quan?" Annabelle asked.

The rogha shook his head. "Big trap. Go by tree now, yuh?"

Annabelle pushed ahead to where Chobba had stopped and looked ahead. She couldn't see anything on the trail at all.

"What is it?" she asked, carefully poking her foot forward in the dirt.

"No!" Chobba cried.

But he was too late. The touch of Annabelle's foot had tripped the trap. A cord whipped out of the ground, snagging her foot. Before anyone could grab her, she was jerked off her feet and pulled high into the air. The abruptness of the trap as it whipped her into the air just about dislocated her hip joint.

"Get me down!" she cried.

But then, from somewhere high above them in the trees, a bell sounded to let whoever had set the trap know that it had been sprung.

Swinging upside down, with the world swirling and spinning below her, Annabelle's fear of heights filled her with a panicking rush that left her absolutely numb.

Chapter 21

As the creatures charged them, Clive and his party had time to set their lanterns down and bring out their makeshift weapons, but that was all. Finnbogg raised his sledgehammer, the others their pry-bars, and then the swarm was upon them.

The light of the lanterns cast an uneven glow on the creatures as they came at the party in a skittering wave. They were barely three feet tall, spindly limbed, and with no color to them at all, except for the red flash of their eyes. Corpse-pale flesh covered torsos and limbs. Their hair hung in greasy, pale strands, tangled and knotted like snakes. The faces were flat, features more vestigial than pronounced: flat noses, lipless slits for mouths, eyes set against the slope of their brows.

They were unclad and weaponless, though they made up for the latter with rows of sharp teeth and knife-sharp claws on fingers and toes. After that first bloodcurdling scream, their advance was a silent rush. The only sound they made was the soft padding of their feet on the cavern floor, the click of claws against stone.

Clive braced himself for their attack, then swung his pry-bar as the nearest creature leapt at him. His weapon caught it across the side of its head, splitting the skull with an unpleasant, wet cracking sound. The creature dropped, but there was no opportunity for Clive to regard his handiwork, for a pair of the creatures immediately took the place of the one he'd just slain.

In moments, all four of them were fighting for their lives against the swarming horde.

Because of their position in the entryway to the next gallery, the creatures could only attack them from the front and sides, so the party ranged itself, with Finnbogg and Smythe on either flank, Clive and Guafe in the center. They presented a solid face to their enemy, weapons rising and falling as they met the wave of horrid creatures. It took no time at all before each member of the party bore numerous claw cuts on their arms, while the sleeves of their jackets and shirts were torn into shredded strips that flapped when they swung their weapons.

It was steady, unpleasant work. The creatures died quickly—there was soon a mound of bodies underfoot—but their numbers were such that for long, wearying minutes, Clive and his party had no moment to even catch their breath, they were kept so busy. Then, finally, as some twenty or so of the small bodies lay strewn about them, the remaining attackers withdrew. Their wounded attempted to retreat as well, but Guafe immediately stepped forward and killed them as they tried to crawl away.

The creatures were vocal now. They hissed and spat at the party as they gathered themselves for another charge, jabbering to each other in high-pitched voices that grated on the ear. One or another would charge forward, almost within range of the party's weapons, then dart back as quickly.

"This isn't a battle," Clive said. "It's simple butchery."

"Better them than us," Smythe said.

Clive nodded. "But it's distasteful all the same."

He wiped his palms on his trousers. The blood of the creatures had sprayed all over the party, and they had the look of messy butchers about them.

"At least now we know what the pretender was speaking of," Clive added.

"They'll have to do a better job than this to stop us," Smythe said. "They have the numbers, but even with the numbers, they don't have the strength to stop us."

True, Clive thought, but the creatures could wear them out.

At the other end of the line they made, Finnbogg brandished his bloodied sledgehammer at the creatures.

"Come *on*!" he shouted at them. "Spineless worms!"

Clive toed one of the nearby corpses with his boot, starting when the creature stirred and made a feeble grab for his foot. Smythe brought down his pry-bar, splitting the creature's skull. Clive started to nod his thanks, but the horde chose that moment to renew their frantic attack.

They swarmed forward in a living wave of pale flesh, hissing and jabbering, claws flashing, jaws snapping. Clive killed two, three, then one slipped through and fastened its jaws on his shoulder. Mostly it got just a mouthful of jacket, but the teeth nipped into Clive's flesh, and the force of the creature's lunge, and its impact on his shoulder, was enough to turn Clive around.

He tore the creature off and heaved it to the ground. The thing scrambled toward his legs. As he brought up his pry-bar to kill it, he lost his footing on the blood-slick stones, and his feet went out from under him. He managed to bring down his weapon with enough force to stun the creature, but as soon as he fell, there were suddenly two more of them leaping for him, claws ripping at his chest, catching in the fabric of his jacket, jaws snapping inches from his face.

He kept them from his throat by holding the pry-bar in a two-handed grip and pushing it up against their torsos. Spittle sprayed his face as the creatures fought to get at him, but then Guafe was there. Two quick blows killed them. The cyborg took a stance that covered Clive long enough for him to regain his feet.

He glanced in Finnbogg's direction and saw the dwarf go down under four or five of the creatures. He started forward to help, but Finnbogg shrugged them off, his sledgehammer rising, killing a pair for each blow. The fifth he kicked in its stomach, then brought his weapon down on the top of its skull. Brain matter and blood sprayed from the force of the blow.

Clive turned to renew his own attack against the creatures then, fighting beside the dwarf now, as Guafe had taken his own position beside Smythe. His arms were wearying under the work, but still the creatures kept coming, snarling and spitting, dying quickly enough, but for each that fell, there was another there immediately to take its place.

The air reeked of blood. Sweat dripped from Clive's brow, stinging his eyes. He found it more and more difficult to swing the pry-bar. Once a comfortable weight, it grew more leaden with each passing moment. Glancing at Smythe, Clive saw that he, too, was wearying. His blows had less force to them, and his responses to each attack were slowing.

But Finnbogg maintained his strength, weapon rising and falling in an untiring rhythm, while Guafe was a killing machine. The heap of corpses rose waist-high around the party, and still the creatures came. They scrambled over the wall of their dead comrades, launching themselves over the top with a ferocity that Clive had never encountered before. On and on they came, until he was sure he could lift his arms no more.

And then, suddenly, they withdrew a second time, this time vanishing into the shadows beyond the light of the party's lanterns.

"Quickly, now," Smythe said wearily. "Through to the next cave."

Guafe kept watch while the others stumbled through. There was still no sign of renewed activity in the darkness where their foes had fled.

"There!" Smythe called.

He pointed to a heap of rubble. Setting down his pry-bar and lantern, he went over and began to manhandle a rock toward the entryway through which they'd just come. Clive immediately came to help him roll the huge stone across the cavern floor.

Once they saw what he was about, Finnbogg and Guafe quickly lent their strength to the task. Taking turns watching for the creatures, they built up a wall of stone to block the narrow entryway. In the end it was only Guafe who had the strength to lift the stones up to close the final few feet of the gap. The others brought the rocks over. When the entryway was finally sealed, the party collapsed where they stood.

"God," Clive said, "I've never seen such creatures."

Smythe nodded. "If the attack had lasted much longer, they would have had us."

"Perhaps," Guafe said.

Clive felt a momentary irritation at the cyborg's calm control. Although he looked as bloody and disheveled as the rest of them, he wasn't even breathing hard. He stood, gazing off to where the rails led on across this new gallery, the battle apparently already forgotten.

But then Clive remembered who it was that had saved his life not twenty minutes ago, whose strength—along with Finn's—had been the telling point of their surviving the battle.

"Thank you," he told the cyborg.

Guafe merely shrugged. "I wish to be quit of these caverns and see what the next level holds," he said. "And I would rather travel in your company."

Why? Clive wanted to ask, but he realized that this wasn't the time to get into an argument with Guafe. Though he held no great affection for the cyborg, he was pragmatic enough to know that they would more than likely need Guafe's strength again before they were free of this place.

"Hear water dripping," Finnbogg said.

In a weary group, the party made their way across the gallery to the pool that was the source of the sound. The roof of the cavern over the pool rose in a high, dark shaft, and it was from it that the water was dripping.

They drank deeply, then stripped and cleaned the gore from their bodies and clothes. Smythe was the first to be done. Shivering in his wet clothes, he used his pry-bar to work free a couple of the wooden ties on which the rails lay. With the sledgehammer and bar, he broke one up enough to get kindling, with which he started a fire. Slowly, he fed wood to it. By the time the rest were finished cleaning themselves, he had a good blaze burning, around which they all gathered.

"We should have brought in a few of the dead creatures to roast," Guafe remarked.

Clive blanched. "We couldn't eat them—they were almost human."

The cyborg shrugged. "We have to eat."

"I think I'd prefer simply to tighten my belt for now," Smythe said.

"Suit yourselves," Guafe said. "But if we run into more of the creatures, I, at least, plan to see how they taste."

They rested by the fire long after their clothes were dry. Tearing the shredded strips from their sleeves, they bandaged the cuts on their forearms. Clive's shoulder was beginning to stiffen up where the creature had bitten him, and both Smythe and Finnbogg had wounds on their legs that were sore, but not deep.

Their greatest worry, Clive thought, was the danger of infection, but there was little they could do about it, except what they already had done—clean the wounds and bandage them.

When the fire died down, they returned to the rails and went on.

Time passed, but they had no way of telling day from night, or how long they had been traveling. They rested when they were weary, walked on when they had rested. Twice, they came upon pools in which fat, white, eyeless fish swam. The creatures were easy to catch, but they had little taste and, though they were nourishing, all were aware of a constant sense of gnawing hunger that could not be appeased. Their wounds continued to itch, but seemed to be healing. Their supply of candles was dwindling—so much, and with no end to their journey in sight, that they were using only one lantern.

They kept a firm lookout for more of the murderous creatures who had attacked them, but they suffered no further attacks after that first one. Either the cleft they had blocked had been enough to stop them, or the creatures simply didn't fare this deeply into the cavern. None of the party really wanted to dwell on why that might be, but it was something that couldn't easily be put aside. Was there something still worse waiting for them?

The rails continued on. Sometimes the track split, leading them into more than one blind alley, but mostly it took them deeper and deeper underground.

"What can we look to find on the next level?" Smythe asked Finnbogg at one point.

"A big city," the dwarf replied.

"Another ruin?"

"No. Many people there, just like us—" Which could mean just about any sort of being, Clive thought. "—ruled by the Lords of Thunder."

"And who are they?" Guafe asked.

The dwarf shrugged. "Finnbogg doesn't know."

"And what is their level of technology?"

"Finnbogg doesn't *know*."

Smythe gave Clive a quick glance. "Best leave off, sah."

Clive nodded. There was no sense in getting Finnbogg into one of his states.

"I remember hearing of these Lords of Thunder," Guafe said slowly. "From a being I traveled with on one of the upper levels. They are elected to their position, but the elections are held every seven days, so the actual lords change from week to week. Then again, the same being told me at another time that the city holds a lottery every seven days, and that the winners—or maybe I should say losers—are fed to the Lords of Thunder."

"Wonderful," Clive said.

"Sounds as though your source was about as reliable as ours can be," Smythe said.

"It's not Finnbogg's fault Finnbogg doesn't know everything," the dwarf said.

"This is true," Guafe said. "With so many levels, and everything in such a confusion, a human would find it impossible to keep it all straight."

Finnbogg still looked glum—almost on the verge of tears.

"There, there, Finn," Smythe said soothingly. "We know you're doing your best."

That was the day—as they referred to their waking periods—that the rails simply stopped.

They gave out on the far side of another enormous cavern, at a cleft that dropped at a steep angle into yet another gallery. Standing at the opening of the new gallery, they discovered that this one was blocked with a wall. The light from their lantern was strong enough to show them that the wall was twelve to fifteen feet high. Beyond its height, the gallery's roof was lost in the darkness. On the left side of the cleft was a corridor that took an immediate sharp turn some ten feet down its length.

Having come this far, there was no turning back. They set off down the corridor, taking its turn, to find themselves presented with a choice of three corridors.

"Now what?" Smythe muttered.

But Clive had a sinking feeling that was soon proved all too prophetic. "It's a maze," he said.

Smythe held the lantern into each opening. From its light they could all see that each corridor opened on to others.

"Bloody hell," he said.

"There is usually some logical method of making one's way through such a thing," Guafe said.

"In this Dungeon?" Smythe asked.

The cyborg nodded. "There is that."

"Which way to go?" Finnbogg asked.

"We'll be in here forever," Smythe said.

But Clive wasn't listening to any of them. Instead, he was remembering a Midsummer's Eve when he was ten years old, and the maze that he and his brother had walked through that day. Neville, as always in such situations, had had absolutely no trouble working his way to the end, but Clive had been trapped in there for hours, eventually driven to tears of frustration by his failure to win free.

Until the voice had spoken to him.

That mysterious voice.

You may face the moon, or you can have it at your left shoulder, it had said.

Following the voice's advice, he had made his way safely through.

But something nagged at Clive as he remembered.

That voice. . . .

In a hazy fashion, he could recall another instance when it had spoken to him, in another garden. Or at least he could recall the fact that it had—not the details. Tied up that recollection was a mixture of other dreamlike memories . . . of Annabella, of London, and of pain.

He rubbed at his upper left arm.

He'd been swallowed by darkness, and there had been voices bidding him to forget. . . .

He shook his head. Now wasn't the time for reverie. All it was giving him was a headache. Instead, he put his mind to the task at hand.

You may face the moon, or you can have it at your left shoulder. . . .

Clive took the lantern from Smythe's hand and lifted it above his shoulder. High above, somewhere on the roof of the cavern, he saw a glint of reflected light. It wasn't a moon, but. . . .

That voice had helped him more than once. But, he wondered, that first time . . . could that early hedge maze have been merely a preparation for the Dungeon? How could that be possible?

He was loath to put their fates on such a flimsy hope, but when he looked at his companions, and saw that none of them had anything better to offer, he squared his shoulders. Following that old advice was as likely a solution as their other options would be, which amounted to either guesswork or blind luck. So, what did they have to lose?

Realizing that it was up to him, as leader of the party, to take command of the situation—even if the source of information on which he made his decision was somewhat suspect—he faced the "moon" and started off down the left-hand corridor.

"This way," he said.

Chapter 22

Annabelle swung back and forth on the rope, like a weight at the end of a pendulum. She kept her eyes shut. Her face was bleached with fear. After her first startled cry, she kept quiet, trying to hold in the contents of her stomach as the rope spun her in a dizzying arc, back and forth across the trail.

The alarm bell in the trees above had stopped tolling, but its echo continued on in their minds. The Quanians, or whoever it was who had set the trap, would not be long in getting here—not with an alarm system rigged up.

The rogha came scrambling up through the branches of the trees around Annabelle. Yssi climbed to where the rope holding her was tied to the tree, and swung it until Tarit and Chobba could catch Annabelle. They quickly cut her free. Chobba put her on his back.

"Hold hard, yuh?" he told her.

Annabelle put her arms around his neck, but she didn't think she had the strength to hold on, until the first time Chobba launched himself through the air from one branch to another. Heart in her throat, Annabelle gripped his neck so tightly she had to be choking him, but Chobba didn't even seem to notice.

Warning cries came from the rest of the party still on the ground. Chobba swung onto a perch in the crook of two branches. Through her unreasoning panic, Annabelle managed to crack open her eyes and look over Chobba's shoulder, to see what the cries were about.

A small, round, metal ball the size of a softball hovered in the air near the sprung trap. There were various small, tubelike protrusions sticking out from its surface, none of them longer than an inch. A faint whine came from the ball as it slowly spun around.

It was taking stock, Annabelle realized. A new fear cut through the haze of her panic.

"That's a mobile scouting unit," she told Chobba. "It'll have visual and audio input—probably heat sensors, as well. We've gotta get out of here. Pronto."

Chobba turned to her, his face inches from her own, the confusion in his features plain.

He didn't understand a word of what I said, Annabelle realized.

"Plenty bad," she said. "Go quick. Hide."

He nodded, but the scouting unit chose that moment to make the very real danger it presented to them apparent in a less nebulous fashion. A thin red beam issued from one of its tubelike projections. It moved in the direction where Nog was perched.

"Oh, Jesus," Annabelle cried. "It's armed!"

The laser burned through leaves and branches as it sought its target. Nog leapt away, but the scouting unit immediately tracked his sudden motion. The laser sliced a swath through the vegetation in the rogha's direction, cutting across his torso in midleap. Nog screamed, then plummeted to the ground, bouncing off branches on the way down. He was dead long before he reached the jungle floor.

The remaining rogha howled their rage. As they began to move in toward the scouting unit, Annabelle tugged on Chobba's fur.

"No!" she told him. "It will kill you all. We have to go deeper into the jungle, where the branches grow too thick for it to follow. Maybe some of the bigger animals'll screw up its heat sensors. Chobba, please."

The rogha hesitated. He started to shout out an order to the others, but when he saw Tarit launch himself at his twin's killer, Chobba leapt forward as well. All Annabelle could do was cling to his back.

The scouting unit swiveled in a quick circle, momentarily distracted by the presence of so many different targets. Shriek chose that moment to throw one of her well-aimed hair spikes at the ball-like machine.

The spike bounced harmlessly off, but it brought the party on the ground to the machine's attention. It dropped from the sky, laser burning up the floor of the game trail in a straight line that led directly for Shriek.

Sidi stepped in and threw his spear. It was a clean miss as the scouting unit spun on its axis and darted to one side to avoid the weapon, laser cutting the spear in two. Shriek threw more spikes, then plunged into the nearest undergrowth as the unit turned back to her. It dropped at a sharp angle, laser searing the brush as it looked for her. Then, suddenly, Tomàs was there.

The unit turned, sensing his presence, but the little Portuguese was too fast for it. He swung his spear like a bat. The weapon hit the unit with a sharp crack that sent it spinning out of control. It hit a tree, then dropped to the ground, laser spraying a random pattern all around it. Before it could correct itself, Tarit dropped to the game trail beside it.

The scouting unit tried to turn in the dirt to train its laser on the rogha, but Tarit simply smashed the machine with his club. He pounded it into the dirt, arm rising and falling. He wept as he continued to club the unit, crying Nog's name. The unit had split open under his blows, flashing with sparks and smoking.

Chobba dropped to the game trail and set Annabelle on the ground. She staggered, her right leg giving out from under her. Tomàs stepped quickly forward and put his shoulder under her arm.

Jesus, she remembered thinking through her pain. First he saves our asses, and now he's helping me. What's the matter with the guy?

The other rogha descended from the trees and joined Chobba and Tarit in beating what was left of the machine. They kept it up for long moments, then finally stepped away from the small ruin of wiring, circuitry, and metal. Tears streaked their facial fur. Tarit disappeared into the forest to return with Nog's body. He laid it gently on the ground.

Giving Tomàs her thanks, Annabelle hobbled forward under her own steam. "God, I'm so sorry," she said. "I never thought anybody'd get hurt. . . ."

"Nog die like cheef," Chobba said.

The other rogha all cried Nog's name again.

"We go now," Chobba told her.

Tarit clasped his twin's corpse under one arm and swung back into the trees, followed by Chobba and the other rogha. In moments they were gone.

Annabelle turned slowly to look at her companions. Lukey, who was still with them, sat down on the side of the trail and put his back up against a tree.

"What's happening now?" she asked him.

"He was a real good monkey-man," Lukey said. "Hell, I really liked him."

"Lukey, where have they gone?"

"To bury him, rogha-fashion. They'll stick him up in a treetop—the highest they can climb—an' leave him there so's his soul can rise up into the sky real easy."

"What was this thing?" Sidi asked, toeing the remains of the machine.

Annabelle glanced at him. "A kind of scouting device. A mobile unit—remote-controlled. It'd have a kind of an eye in it, so whoever sent it's gonna know we're here. We've got to get moving. When will the rogha be back, Lukey?"

The old man shrugged. "A day or two, I guess. They've got ta talk through his life up there where they leave him, so that the ancestors know who he is an' can see he's the kind a' guy that they should take up there inta the sky with 'em. Takes time."

"You say whoever sent this thing knows we are here?" Sidi asked.

Annabelle nodded.

"Then, we must go. Can you travel?"

Annabelle rubbed her leg. It ached something fierce. Her ankle, where the rope had encircled her leg, was rubbed raw. She tested her weight on it. That first moment on the ground, when it had buckled under her, had been due more to surprise at the pain than because the leg wouldn't hold her weight.

"I can manage," she said. "But what about the rogha? We can't just take off on them, after all they've done for us. And poor Nog. . . ."

"If we stay here," Sidi said, "won't the Quanians just send more of these things?"

"I guess. . . ."

We should go on, Shriek said. *Immediately.*

"Yeah," Annabelle said. "Are you coming with us, Lukey?"

"Don't have a whole lot a' choice, seems."

"We should travel quickly, *sim?*" Tomàs said. "By river, perhaps?"

Annabelle and Sidi exchanged puzzled looks. Neither of them could figure Tomàs's sudden shift in mood, from surly to friendly.

"Are you feeling okay?" Annabelle asked him.

"I feel fine," Tomàs said. "Why do you ask?"

"You're just not acting like yourself."

"I have been thinking. You—Sidi and Shriek—we are all in this place together—*comaradas, sim?* So we must be good *amigos* and help each other."

Annabelle found that she distrusted this new face of Tomàs's more than the old, but she didn't let any of that show. She simply nodded.

"Well, thanks for the vote of confidence," she said.

"Vote—*sim,*" the Portuguese said, obviously remembering Annabelle calling a vote back on the cliffs, to separate the two parties. It was clearly a new concept to him. "I vote we go by the river. This path is *muito perigoso.* Too dangerous."

It turned out that they were much closer to Quan than they had supposed. They waded through the water by the river bank, and after only an hour or so, they came upon a sudden drop in the land. They left the river where it turned into rapids, and made their way to a vantage point where they could look down on the clearing that lay ahead of them.

Quan.

It was a collection of mud and wattle huts, except for a white stone building at the far side of the village. Aerials and a satellite dish protruded from its roof. To one side of the building was the ghost stone of which Finnbogg had told them. It was a tall white column of rock, sticking out of the ground much like a Celtic standing stone. Figures moved about the village. They flickered strangely, winking in and out of view as the party watched.

"I can't figure this place at all," Annabelle said. "I mean, they've got the tech for a satellite dish and that mobile scouting unit, yet back on the trail they're screwing around with primitive traps and—Look at this village—mud and straw huts. What gives?"

Her companions weren't nearly so blasé.

"There really are ghosts," Sidi said.

Surprised, Annabelle looked at him. "Those aren't ghosts. They're just 3-D holograms—sort of like moving pictures, except they've got depth, as well. But whoever's running this show's working with faulty equipment, 'cause those things shouldn't be flickering like that."

"They aren't ghosts?" Sidi asked.

Well, why am I surprised? Annabelle thought. Sure, Sidi was smart and capable, but he did come from the nineteenth century— nineteenth century India, to boot. How the hell was he supposed to know about these kinds of things?

"They're projections," she explained. "Paintings that move, made by a machine—that's all. They can't hurt us."

"But something can," Lukey said. "Someone wants to hurt anyone who comes near a' this place."

"I suppose," Annabelle said. "But I've got a gut feeling that everything's just running on a program that someone set up. If there's anybody left, it's just a skeleton crew to run the place, and they're not doing such a good job."

"Tell that to Nog," Lukey said.

Annabelle's face clouded. "Yeah," she said softly. "There's that. So we gotta go careful. I wonder where the gateway is."

She returned her attention to the village. The ground sloped steeply from their vantage point in a rough rock face that ran from the jungle where they were hidden, down to the cleared fields around the village. The river was on the left. On the right and behind the village, the jungle marched on again.

Although they were high up, her acrophobia wasn't bothering her here. It only hit her bad when she was in an exposed position—like a tall bridge, or up in a tree. Here, with lots of good, solid earth around her, all she felt was a vague sense of wanting to lean out far— really far.

She pulled herself back and looked at her companions. "So, what do we do, kids? Check it out, or go back the way we came?"

Shriek pointed forward. *That is where our road lies, Being Annabelle. Not behind us.*

"One vote to go on," Annabelle said. "What about the rest of you?"

Tomàs and Sidi both nodded their agreement. Lukey said nothing.

"I feel bad about just taking off on Chobba and the others without saying goodbye," Annabelle added. "They were good people."

Lukey sighed. "Hell, I'll say your goodbyes for you."

"You're not coming?"

He shook his head. "I'm too old ta start all over somewhere else," he said.

"We should make a plan," Tomàs said.

Annabelle nodded. "I'm not big on exploring this place, myself—who knows what kinda booby traps they've got rigged. I'm for finding the gateway and getting outta here."

It will either be in that building, Shriek said, *or below us, at the bottom of this cliff. I see no other choices.*

"'Cept that stone," Annabelle said.

They waited until dark, and then, after saying their farewells to Lukey, cautiously made their way down the rock decline. Although the angle was fairly steep, there were so many handholds that it was not much different from going down a ladder. Even Annabelle had no trouble with it. When they reached the bottom, they carefully checked it for a cave or opening, foot by foot, but came up blank.

"Looks like it's the building," Annabelle whispered.

Even though she knew the figures were holographs, the idea of walking among them didn't exactly appeal to her: But she didn't see any other options. They decided to circle around by the river and approach the building from the left, but as they passed the standing stone, its surface began to glow.

"What the hell . . . ?" Annabelle murmured.

In the middle of the stone's pale white glow, a dark opening was appearing. *The gateway,* Annabelle thought. It had to be. Cautiously, they approached it. Fingers tingling with nervous anticipation, Annabelle reached out toward the dark, door-shaped opening. There was a momentary buzz of a shock—no stronger than picking up static electricity from a carpet—and then her fingers entered the rock.

"This is it—" Annabelle began.

At that same moment, the alarms went off.

Bells rang. A piercing siren sounded. Floodlights awoke from the sides of the white building, turning the night into day all around them. Figures in metallic bodysuits issued in a stream from the building. They carried laser rifles. When they fired, the air around the party crackled.

"We've got no time to pussyfoot around," Annabelle cried. "Let's go!"

She stepped inside and found herself on a small platform, the others following on her heels. She'd been expecting it to be dark inside, but a dull, phosphorescent glow lit what appeared to be a vast cavern. The roof and sides stretched impossibly huge all around them—as did the drop below. There was only the small platform on which they were standing, and a narrow band of a path that led straight across the chasm. It was no more than a foot wide, dropping immediately on either side to unguessed depths.

Platform and path. There was no other place to go.

"I can't do it," Annabelle said.

She was already trembling violently.

"We have no choice," Sidi cried.

Behind them, the sirens and alarms were still sounding. They could hear the voices of the Quanians raised in angry shouts.

"I . . . I just can't. . . ." Annabelle mumbled.

Chapter 23

"We are simply going in circles," Guafe said after long hours in the maze.

"I don't think so," Smythe said. "I don't sense the walls of the cavern to be that close to us anymore. I believe we've come a good way through."

Guafe shook his head. "We—"

"It's just the winding of our route," Smythe broke in, "that's giving you that impression. Besides," he added, glancing at Clive, "the major knows what he's doing."

I wish, Clive thought. But he had to be doing something right. By either facing the "moon," or keeping it to his left shoulder whenever there was a choice to be made in their route, they'd fared steadily, if tiresomely, onward. There had been no blind alleys, except for the one time Guafe had argued that they should take a different turn from the one Clive had chosen for them, and they'd wound up in a dead end.

The cyborg had kept his own counsel after that—at least, until now.

"There seems to be a kind of a spiral effect," Clive said in answer to Guafe's comment, "but I think we've come a fair distance across— even with the twisting back and forth."

Finnbogg nodded. "Who knows how big this place is?"

But Guafe had lost his patience again. "You say we turn right here," he said, "but I believe the other side of the cavern lies straight ahead— down this central corridor."

"The last time we followed your lead," Smythe said, "we wasted a good half-hour backtracking our way out of that dead end."

"No maze can be as large as this one appears to be," the cyborg replied. "We are going in circles, and getting nowhere. I say we go straight now."

Finnbogg and Smythe both turned to Clive, who simply shrugged. They *had* been traveling through the maze for a very long time, and all he was using to lead them was old advice from a mysterious voice he'd heard in another maze when he was a child. While the voice's advice had been enough to free him from that hedge maze, and had helped him again since then, there really was no logical reason that it should be effective here as well. And while it was true that they hadn't run into any dead ends following his route, they didn't really seem to be getting anywhere, either.

"We might as well try it," he said.

Guafe nodded brusquely, pleased to be leading, and set off at a brisk walk down the corridor he'd chosen. It twisted and turned on them, but there were no branches running off, and they did seem to be generally heading in one direction. When they reached the first split, the party paused while Guafe studied each corridor.

At length he nodded. "Left, I say."

It was not what Clive would have chosen, but he said nothing.

Guafe gave them each a questioning look, then, satisfied that he was still in charge, led them on again. A half-dozen paces down the new corridor, it took a sharp right turn. As they entered it, one of the stone blocks shifted under their weight.

A loud grinding noise arose all around them, like sudden thunder.

"Move!" Smythe cried.

He gave Clive and Guafe a shove forward, then darted after them, Finnbogg hard on his heels. The stone that had been underfoot dropped away with a resounding, hollow crash, and one of the walls behind them groaned, then slid across the corridor, effectively blocking any retreat.

Stone dust filled the air, the motes dancing in the light of their lantern. They coughed and stared back through the dancing cloud at the new wall that filled the corridor behind them.

"Well, that's done it," Smythe said, turning to Guafe. "Well-led."

"Finnbogg want Clive-friend to lead," the dwarf said.

For once, the cyborg seemed completely taken aback. "I had no idea . . ." he began.

Though he agreed with the others, Clive saw no reason to take it out on Guafe at this point. The deed was done now, and there was nothing they could do about it.

"We've no choice now but to go on," he said.

Finnbogg turned to him. "Yes, but—"

"There's nothing we can do about that," Clive said, indicating the new wall blocking their retreat. "Lead on, Chang," he called ahead.

Guafe nodded and led the way once more, but the corridor soon ended against another blank wall.

"I fear my miscalculations have done far more harm than good," he said.

It was the closest Clive had ever heard him come to an apology.

"It wasn't your fault," he told the cyborg. "We're all going blindly in the dark here, and—"

"Hsst!" Smythe said suddenly.

They could all hear it—a whispering sound, like a great soft weight being pulled across the stone floor.

"Is it those creatures?" Clive asked softly, reaching for the pry-bar in his belt.

Smythe shook his head. "No. It doesn't sound quite right."

He took the lantern from Finnbogg, who had been holding it, and held it up at arm's length to investigate the walls above them. He moved the lantern slowly along until he saw what looked like a break in the stone, high up in one part of the wall. It was a place where the stones weren't set quite properly together, leaving an indentation between the blocks. "Could you lift me toward that?" he asked Guafe.

The cyborg nodded. "What do you mean to do?"

"Get us out of this trap you've put us in. If I can get up on top of the wall—" he tapped the sheet of canvas that he'd been carrying all this time in a rolled-up bundle "—I could lower this to the rest of you and pull you up."

"And we could follow the maze simply by walking on top of the walls," Clive finished. "That's a capital idea, Horace."

With Clive holding the lantern and Finnbogg bracing Guafe, Smythe stepped onto the cyborg's shoulders. Guafe straightened to his full height, but the mis-set blocks Smythe was aiming for were still out of reach. Guafe slipped his hands under Smythe's feet and then straight-armed him up.

"Got it," Smythe said as he scrabbled for a hold. "Just don't let go yet. Wait a bit. All right . . . now."

Guafe gave a final upward surge, and Smythe scrambled the rest of the way, scaling the wall like a monkey.

"What do you see?" Clive called up to him.

"Nothing. I need a lantern. Pass it up to me."

He dropped the twine with which he'd rolled up the canvas, then lowered the canvas down the side of the wall. It came to just above Guafe's head. Using the twine, they tied the lantern to the canvas, and Smythe hauled it up.

"Can you see anything now?" Clive called.

"My God," Smythe said.

"What is it, man?"

Smythe shook his head. "There's no time to talk. Quick. All of you, up here!"

He lowered the canvas, bracing it on top of the wall with his weight. Clive was next, pulling himself up with handfuls of canvas. Finnbogg was next. The material of their makeshift ladder made ominous tearing sounds under the dwarf's weight. Both Clive and Smythe braced the canvas at the top of the wall until Finnbogg was in reach of Clive's hand. As the dwarf scrambled up the last few feet and took Clive's place bracing the canvas, Clive picked up the lantern to see what had alarmed his fellow soldier.

"Come on now, Guafe," Smythe was saying.

The light of the lantern wasn't strong enough to travel far. It showed the tops of the walls, running in all directions like elevated paths, but the spaces on either side of them were lost in shadow, and the paths soon disappeared into darknesses beyond the reach of the lantern. He saw nothing alarming until he turned in the direction from which they'd come.

There, he saw a huge white shape that seemed to fill the corridor.

Clive took a few steps closer, holding the lantern high. When the massive head lifted from the corridor, he almost dropped the light.

Things, the man pretending to be his brother had said. He hadn't been referring to the feral pack of creatures that had attacked them days ago. No. It had been *this*.

It was monstrous—a cross between an enormous snake and a slug. The flesh was pale and slimy, but scaled as well. It was from the latter that the heavy whispering sound came, as they rustled against the stone. The head was a good yard across in width, stubby and square in shape. It had large, milky-colored eyes, with a pair of antennae above each—one large feeler, and one smaller one. The mouth, when it opened its huge jaws, showed three series of barracudalike teeth.

As Clive watched, it began to undulate up from the corridor, the enormous weight of its body rising to the top of the wall, then straddling it with a huge coil of its pale body. The head moved toward him, but the monster's bulk was too much for it to balance easily on the wall, which was only a foot and a half wide.

As it lost its balance, it coiled its body to fill the corridor. Using those coils as a lever, it flexed suddenly. The stones on either side of it groaned under the pressure.

Fascinated despite himself, Clive watched the creature relax its muscles, then flex them again. This time, the walls of the corridor on either side of it collapsed under the pressure.

The stone blocks that fell on it seemed to give the creature no discomfort whatsoever. It merely shrugged them off. More of the wall fell in, and the creature began to rise, using the rubble as a ramp to slide up.

As it approached him, Clive remained spellbound, staring. There was a terrible beauty in its ugliness, in its sheer physical power.

"Sah!"

He set down the lantern and then stepped over it, moving toward the creature. The sudden urge to feel that slick hide, the muscles running underneath it, was too strong to ignore.

"Sah! Have you taken leave of your senses?"

The large milky eyes were blind, he was sure, but they impressed him with their hypnotic spell all the same. He could hear Smythe calling him, but his companion's voice was strangely distant, as though he heard it from under water, or in a dream.

At this moment, it was the creature that took up all of his attention.

Demanded it.

Would not be denied.

He stepped closer still, almost within the reach of those immense jaws, then suddenly, Smythe had a grip on his shoulder and was pulling him back. Clive protested, until he began to lose his balance. Then he was forced to look away, and the creature's blind eyes no longer filled his sight. Suddenly, his will was his own again.

The monster lunged forward at being denied its prey, but Smythe had already pulled Clive out of its reach. The new wall on which the creature found itself buckled under its weight, and down it plunged once more. The walls shook at the impact this time; clouds of dust rose about them like a thick London fog.

"'Ware its gaze," Clive warned as he followed Smythe back to where the others waited. "The damn thing looks blind, but it hypnotized me all the same."

"Quick," Smythe merely said. "Take the lead, sah, and get us out of here."

Behind them, the monstrous snake was rising from the rubble once more—a huge, pale shape moving in the clouds of stone dust. Rocks ground under its weight, and the wall trembled as it once again attempted to get at them.

"Sah!" Smythe cried, as Clive continued to stand in place.

"Let me get my bearings," Clive told him.

He searched the vault of the dark cavern roof above them, looking for the reflective "moon" that had guided him earlier. When he finally had it, he set off at as brisk a walk as he dared along the narrow width of the wall's top.

They heard another rumbling crash behind them. Guafe, who was in the rear, turned. The red beams of his gaze pierced a new cloud of stone dust, to show that the monstrous snake had broken from the cul-de-sac and was now slithering along a corridor toward them.

"Let's get some walls between that monster and us," Clive said.

Ignoring his guide in the ceiling of the cavern for the moment, Clive led them off at a sharp angle. Due to the way the maze was laid out, they were soon able to put a number of walls between themselves and the creature. As they paused to catch their breath, they could hear the huge snake battering at one of those walls.

"It's fiendishly clever, really," Smythe said. "The design of this place, I mean. Obviously, we were meant to be kept trapped by that sliding wall until the creature arrived. Then, I don't doubt, it would trip some mechanism that would shift the wall back into place, allowing the creature access to where its prey was trapped."

"Only this time, its prey escaped," Guafe said.

Smythe nodded. "Exactly. And it's driven the bloody thing mad. Having its prey light out on it is something that's never happened to it before, I'll wager. Have you got your bearings again, sah?"

"I think so—yes."

With the "moon" at his left shoulder, Clive led them off. They kept up a brisk pace, for they could still hear the monster following them, battering down the walls as it made its own blundering route through the maze.

There'd be little left of the place when the monster was finished with it, Clive thought. Not that it was any of his concern. It was just that the next party faring through would have an even rougher time of it than they had.

"How are we doing?" he called back to Guafe, who was still in the rear.

"Well enough," the cyborg said. "We seem to be leaving it far behind."

"Behind?" Finnbogg asked. "Then what does Finnbogg hear over there?"

He pointed to his right.

"Echoes," Smythe began.

But Guafe was already shaking his head. With his sharper senses, he was already aware of what the others were not.

"No," he said. "It's another of the creatures. Heading our way." He pointed to their left and ahead now. "And there's a third, approaching us from that direction, as well."

"Wonderful," Clive said.

Chapter 24

Your greatest fear made real.

That's what the darkworld spirit had told her through the medium of the rogha fetish chief. How could it have *known*? Because here that fear was, in all its dark glory.

Annabelle swayed on the ledge. The chasm that dropped suddenly on both sides and in front worked on her acrophobia, calling her down into its black depths.

Come to me, it called. *Accept your destiny. Be one with me. There is nothing to fear.*

And she wanted to. She wanted to just let herself go and fall into the blackness.

Come to me. To a better place.

She needed a better place. Where she could be with her daughter and her friends, where all of this, the Dungeon, and its incomprehensible madness, was just a bad dream.

Come to me.

She wanted to. Desperately. But just as she couldn't back away, she couldn't move forward, either. She was paralyzed with fear.

Dimly, through the ghostly outline of the gateway, she could hear the shouts of the Quanians growing closer. Around her, the voices of her companions were nothing more than a babble of unintelligible sounds as they tried to get her to set foot on the narrow pathway that led across the chasm. But she couldn't do it. And there wasn't time to get out the byrr pouch.

No time to pull out a leaf.

No time to chew it.

No time.

Only the chasm, calling out to her as she swayed at its lip.

Come to me.

"Annabelle, *please*," Sidi said.

She tried to turn her head to tell him how she just couldn't, but she was unable to tear her gaze from the chasm. She could barely hear anything except its hypnotic voice, calling out to her.

Her throat was thick and blocked, swollen with fear. Her chest was a knot of tension, lungs desperate for air. Every muscle in her body locked tight.

"Annabelle," Sidi said. "Just take my hand."

I can't move, she wanted to tell him, but she barely formed the words in her mind. Voicing them was impossible.

Get outta here . . . Sidi . . . all of you. . . . Leave me to the chasm, to its dark promise. . . .

She wondered, Is this the darkworld? Will I become a spirit in it, if I just let myself go?

But the chasm promised more. Freedom from the Dungeon. To be reunited with Amanda. Peace.

Come to me, its dark voice whispered.

I will, Annabelle told it. But just let me move. Just give me time to think.

Because there was something wrong about the chasm's promise. How could it deliver her back to the world she'd lost? To her daughter and friends? If it was that simple. . . .

It couldn't be that simple. Nothing ever was.

She swayed at the edge, the darkness swallowing her soul. She wanted to be free—not just of the Dungeon, but of the chasm's dark call, as well. To be free of the fear that paralyzed her, making her body betray her.

Just let me go, she told the darkness. Give me time to figure out what's going on. . . .

Then Shriek literally took matters into her own hands. She caught Annabelle with her lower arms, hugging her close to her chest, and set off at a run along the narrow pathway, using her upper arms for balance.

Sound finally escaped Annabelle's swollen throat—a raw, piercing scream tore from her lips—and finally, she could move. She struggled in Shriek's grip. The movement threatened to unbalance the alien, plunging them both into the chasm. Without missing a step, Shriek withdrew a hair spike with her upper right arm and thrust it into Annabelle's arm.

The thornlike spike broke her skin. As its potent chemical content entered Annabelle's body, mixing with her blood system and bringing relief in the form of unconsciousness, she went limp in the alien's arms. Shriek flicked the spike away into the chasm and continued to run.

Behind her, Sidi and Tomàs followed at a trot. They were a good hundred yards down the narrow path, the chasm dropping sharply on either side, when the first of the silver-suited Quanians stepped through the gateway. Leveling his weapon, he fired. The red laser beam crackled in the air beside Sidi's head, coming so close that it burned some of his dark hair.

He knew, without a doubt, that the next shot would hit one of them.

The skin between the blades of his back prickled in anticipation. He chanced a glance back, saw the man aiming his weapon more carefully, and braced himself for the impact. But a second man stepped through at that moment, laying his hand on the first man's arm. The first man lowered his weapon.

The two of them looked at the escaping party, arms folded now across their chests.

Why weren't they firing? Sidi thought.

Then the answer came to him. There had to be something worse awaiting the party farther down this narrow ribbon of a path. Something that so assured the Quanians of their fate that there was no need for them to chase after the trespassers or shoot them down. They would simply stand guard to see that none of the party attempted to retreat.

Giving them a last glance, he hurried on after the others. The phosphorescent glow continued to light their surroundings. For as far as he could see, the path simply bore on ahead of them, with no destination in sight.

Finally, they had to rest. They sat straddling the path, legs dangling on either side of it, the dark of the chasm licking at the soles of their feet. Shriek continued to hold Annabelle close with her lower arms, resting the human's weight on her knees now. The alien had turned so that she sat facing the other two.

Seeing Annabelle's limp form in her arms, Sidi knew a moment's panic. Had she been hit by one of the Quanians' weapons?

"What happened to her, Shriek?" he asked.

It was necessary to inject Being Annabelle with a tranquilizer, the arachnid replied. *Otherwise, she would have tumbled us both from the path.*

"But is she . . . ?"

She will be fine, Shriek assured him. *She is merely sleeping. The effect of the tranquilizer will wear off soon.*

Sidi's relief was almost physical.

They rested for a good fifteen minutes, before Shriek rose to her feet again.

Time to go on, she said.

Hefting Annabelle easily, she regarded the pair of them. Tomàs and Sidi arose to stand with her, and then the three of them began to trudge on once more, following the narrow path.

They were hours crossing the cavern. Annabelle was just beginning to stir as the path led them onto another ledge. The cavern face had another opening here, but it wasn't set off by the same shimmering glow as the one in Quan had been. The phosphorescence remained with them as they entered the tunnel. Well inside it, Shriek lowered herself into a sitting position. She propped Annabelle up, keeping a firm grip on her until Annabelle could sit up by herself.

"Oh, my head," Annabelle said.

She blinked slowly, trying to place her surroundings. The last thing she remembered had been the call of the chasm. She'd been about to step over the edge, into its darkness, when. . . .

"You saved my life," she told Shriek.

I'm sorry I could give you no warning, Shriek replied.

"Well, you're not going to hear me complaining. You did the right thing."

Annabelle looked around. They were in a tunnel. She sat beside Shriek. Close by, Tomàs and Sidi sat as well, gazes fixed on her. But it was what lay beyond them that called up a sense of vertigo in her. She could just see the end of the tunnel, the chasm beyond it.

She shivered and turned her head quickly. "Now I know what undying thanks are," she told Shriek. "All I've got—they're yours."

The alien gave Annabelle one of her odd, lopsided looks that passed for a grin on her curious features. *They are accepted, Being Annabelle,* she said.

Annabelle looked at the other two. "Any idea where we are?"

"We crossed the cavern," Sidi said simply. "Other than that, you know as much as we do."

"But the Quanians . . . ?"

"They seemed happy to just let us go."

Annabelle frowned. "As though there was something in here that would take care of us?" she asked, thinking aloud. "Or maybe they were just happy to see the back of us."

"Considering most of the people we've met down here," Sidi said, "I doubt their thoughts were charitable."

"In other words, expect the worst."

Sidi nodded. "Who knows? Maybe we'll get a pleasant surprise."

"Right. Like a bullet with our names on it."

She rose to her feet, one hand against the wall for support, and concentrated on her body. Her headache was fading, but the pain in her leg was rising up to take its place. Otherwise, she felt pretty much in one piece.

She looked at her companions. "So I guess we go on," she said.

The tunnel wasn't long. After a few turns that—thankfully, as far as Annabelle was concerned—put the cavern, with its chasm, well behind them, it opened up into a new cave. Here there was less of the phosphorescence, making the light dimmer, except in one corner, where there was a hole in the floor from which a bright, honey-gold glow issued. Other than the hole and the tunnel through which they'd just come, there was no other way in or out of the cavern.

They made a thorough search of the walls before they finally gathered around the hole. Looking down into it, the yellow glow was very bright. Sparkles floated in it, like dust motes set on fire. There was no way to tell what it was, or where it led, but there was a ladder set into the rocks leading down into it.

Annabelle stepped back from the edge.

"Chew one of Chobba's byrr leaves," Sidi said.

Strangely enough, Annabelle got no sense of real depth from the hole. Her breathing remained normal, her chest muscles loose. The trace of unreasonable fear that flickered at the back of her mind was only her memory of the chasm and its seductive voice.

"It's not that," Annabelle said. "I just don't like the way we don't have any choice about where we go. It's like, we either go down there, or we go back. If the Quanians are guarding the gateway back there, that means we can't go out. So we either head down this ladder, or . . . ."

She left the remainder of her thought unspoken, but it lay heavy inside her. Or we go back to the chasm.

She looked at her companions. Had any of them heard its voice? The promises it had made? What if she'd blown her one chance of getting home again by not listening to it? If Amanda was gone forever. . . .

"Or what?" Tomàs asked.

Annabelle shrugged. "Or nothing. We stay here, which is not a good game plan, right?"

Tomàs nodded. Beside him, Sidi regarded her thoughtfully.

"The pouch," he began.

"I really don't think I'm gonna need a chew of the old byrr," she told him.

Right now, she wanted to be attentive, not relaxed.

"But," Sidi began.

Annabelle shook her head. "Nope. C'mon, kids. Last one in's a dirty duck."

Without waiting for a response, she stepped over to the hole and lowered her feet down to the first rung. She hesitated a moment then, waiting for the fear to grab her, but everything remained normal. She was a little tense, but no more than she expected to be, heading into the unknown. Taking a couple of slow breaths, she started down.

Once her head was below the lip of the hole, she couldn't see anymore and had to go only by feel. The honey-gold glow was so bright, dancing sparkles flickering in her sight, that she ended up closing her eyes. And even then, the glow was a bright redness through her closed lids. The air began to feel thicker, although it didn't affect her breathing. It was just . . . really like honey, she thought, the sparks like speckles of crystal in an otherwise clear liquid. Moving down was like descending into water that one could breathe.

She felt for the next rung with her foot, going carefully as she put her weight on her bad leg. Settled on that rung, she lowered herself to the next.

The glow continued to get brighter, but there was no heat, and the air continued to thicken. She was aware of the others following her, by the vibration of their movement through the metal rungs of the ladder.

"Everybody okay up there?" she called. She almost expected to see bubbles form as she spoke.

"*Muito bem*," Tomàs replied. "No problems."

Sidi and Shriek called back, as well, their voices a little more distant.

Descending the ladder, Annabelle found herself thinking of entirely inappropriate things. Like a recent gig of the Crackbelles, before the blue glow took her away, when they were interviewed backstage by a writer from *Rolling Stone*. Instead of letting the journalist interview them, they kept firing questions at him, driving him crazy. Asking him what it was like working for the *Stone*. Had he ever done a piece on The Wailing Men—Jimmy Dancer's latest band? Had he ever met Hunter S. Thompson?

Hunter S. Thompson.

I should've been taking notes, she thought. If I ever get outta here, I could sell it to the *Stone*. "Fear and Loathing in Bizarroland." Things not weird enough for you, Hunter? You should try this place.

Her foot, reaching down for the next rung, came up empty.

Wait a minute, she thought.

She lowered herself a bit more, foot carefully feeling about to see if there was merely a rung missing, but that was it. End of the line. From here on out, you're on your own.

"The ladder just ended," she called up.

"Are you on the ground?" Sidi asked.

"Nope. At least, not so's I can tell."

Tomàs sighed heavily above her. "Then, back we go," he said.

"I don't think so," Annabelle said.

"Annabelle, don't!" Sidi cried.

"Look, what've we got to lose? We go back up, we get a choice between the chasm and the Quanians. This thing's gotta go somewhere, right?"

"This is *estúpido*," Tomàs told her.

And he was right, Annabelle thought.

But when you stopped to think about it, everything was totally screwed up. This might be suicide, but at least there was no darkness down there, calling up to her with its silky voice. No way she could face the chasm again. Not a chance. Besides, the air felt so thick she figured she'd just end up floating.

Wouldn't she?

"Annabelle!" Sidi cried.

"I'm gone," Annabelle called back.

Then she let go.

Chapter 25

With three of the enormous snake creatures coming at them from as many directions, Clive was at a loss as to which way to lead his small party. No matter which direction he chose, it would be leading them toward one of the creatures. There was no safety for them anywhere in the maze. There wasn't any in the whole bloody Dungeon, when you came right down to it, he thought.

"Sah," Smythe said. "We have to get moving."

Clive nodded. "I agree—only, which way do we go? I'm open to suggestions."

"Away," Finnbogg said.

Clive regarded the dwarf's hopeful features and gave him a brief, vague smile. Away. Yes. Very good, Finn, he thought. But away to where? No matter which direction they chose, one of the creatures was waiting for them. And if they remained in one spot long enough, all three of the monsters would arrive, to find the party dawdling here while he tried to come to a decision.

Use your head, Folliot, he told himself.

Then, to his annoyance, he found himself trying to think of what Neville would do in a situation like this. Not that his twin was likely to ever get himself in such a situation in the first place. Oh, no. Not Neville. He was too clever by far—always in control, never without an answer to any problem.

And considering how things had been for them so far, Clive wouldn't have been surprised to find that Neville had orchestrated this little surprise for them, as well.

Your brother sends his regards, the man pretending to be Neville had said.

Yes, it was all part of some complicated game Neville was playing. What Clive couldn't decided was if Neville was playing the game with his own twin as his opponent, or if he played with someone else, making Clive and his party merely pawns in their game. Or were they higher ranked than that? One of them a king, perhaps? Protected by a bishop, a horseman and a rook?

He tried not to think of the queen, for that would be Annabelle. Her piece removed from the board. Lost or dead. . . .

An elaborate chess game.

Clive knew himself to be a better player than Neville, but it was difficult to make a move when one could only see a few squares of the board at a time. When one only had four pieces left to play, while one's opponent had an endless array of pieces to set upon the board, pieces that appeared in no sensible order, with moves far too random for logical defense.

Such as black moving giant snake to queenside rook five.

Your move, white.

"Whatever you decide," Guafe said, "it had better be decided soon."

Startled out of his reverie, Clive blinked, then nodded. Make a decision. Yes. But every time he reached for a plan of action, he came up empty-handed.

"Can you find us another of those cul-de-sacs?" Smythe asked.

"Probably."

"Then, lead on," Smythe said, "and we'll have on them yet."

It took Clive a moment to find his guiding "moon" in the lofty vault of the cavern above. When he finally spied it, he put its flicker at his right shoulder and led the party off. Their route took them directly toward the second creature that Guafe had spotted.

With a decision made, Clive found his mind clearing. He set the puzzle of Neville and his complicated designs at the back of his mind and concentrated on the task at hand. Some ten minutes after their earlier unplanned stop, he found what Smythe had been looking for. They stood above the dead end, looking down.

"Now what?" he asked.

Smythe didn't answer immediately. He glanced in the direction of the approaching monster, then moved back along the wall. Finally, he knelt down to investigate the stones where he had stopped.

"Can you move one of these?" he asked Guafe.

"Do you mean lift it?" the cyborg replied.

That, Clive thought, was beyond even Guafe's strength.

Smythe shook his head. He had Finnbogg hold the lantern out so that its light was cast on the floor below.

"I just want you to push it down onto that stone there," he said. "Hopefully, it will trip another of the maze's traps."

"What's the point in that?" Clive asked.

"The creatures are blind," Smythe replied, "and they don't appear to have a sense of hearing. By such reckoning, I believe that they're following us either by the vibration of our tread on the stones, or by what they 'hear' of our thoughts."

Remembering the pressure of the creature's mind on his own, Clive nodded slowly.

"Perhaps . . ." he said.

"I know, sah. This reading of minds doesn't rest easily with me, either, but we know it's possible."

Because they had all experienced sharing each other's mind when caught up in Shriek's neural web.

"So," Smythe continued, "I want to trip the trap and bring them run—ah, slithering here. We'll wait, filling our minds with thoughts of panic, and we'll remove our shoes. When the creature's here, we'll creep off, barefoot and silent, keeping our minds empty, until we put enough distance between it and us."

"Do you really think that will work?" Clive asked. It was hard to keep the doubt from his voice.

"All we can do is try."

"And the others?" Clive asked.

"Let's break through the circle they have us in first," Smythe said, "and worry about that later."

Before anyone else could argue, Guafe bent down and put his strength to the stone. It shifted in its setting, then slowly groaned and tipped, falling to the ground with a crash. The four of them looked down, waiting for the trap to be sprung. Dust flew in the air, and the wall shook at the impact, but nothing else happened.

The trap remained unsprung.

"When Guafe led us into that first dead end," Clive said, "we didn't spring a trap."

The nearest of the monstrous snakes was very close now, the other pair closing in.

"Maybe not all traps," Finnbogg offered.

Smythe made no reply.

"Try hitting the next stone," he said, turning to Guafe.

One thing wouldn't be difficult, Clive thought as the cyborg worked at shifting the second stone block, and that was filling his mind with panic.

The second stone hit the floor of the maze. For a long moment there was no response to it, either; then they saw the floor begin to drop. The wall under them started to shift, and they darted onto the next section.

"Shoes and boots off," Smythe said.

As Clive removed his boots, he watched the huge creature approach the sprung trap, its antennae weaving back and forth above its huge, blind eyes. One of the other snakes was only a few corridors away.

"There's more than one of them going to arrive at almost the same time," Clive said.

"Don't talk, sah," Smythe warned him. "Lie doggo and just fill your mind with thoughts of panic. You're trapped, see, and there's no way free."

All too true, Clive thought, but he did as he was told. It was easy to slip into the required sense of panic.

With their walking gear in hand, the stone blocks of the wall cold against their feet, they watched the creatures approach. As the monstrous head of the closest snake came into direct view below them, Smythe rose to his feet. Finger at his lips, he motioned for the others to follow him.

Clive tried to empty his mind, and found that it was easier to fill it with panic than to think of nothing. He tried pretending he was one of the stones that made up the wall underfoot.

He doubted that he was having even marginal success.

They heard the grind of stone as the walls shifted back to allow the creature entrance to where its prey should be trapped. Clive, last in line, glanced back and saw the snake about to enter, when the second closet of the monsters arrived on the scene. Without a moment's preamble, it shot its head forward and bit into the first creature's tail.

Clive paused in his flight. "Hist!" he called ahead.

The others stopped to look back with him.

For all the narrowness of the corridor's confines, the first creature turned with a sinuous sweep of its body, jaws wide as it struck at its attacker. But the second snake had already loosed its grip, its head rising like a cobra's, slowly weaving back and forth, ready to strike.

The first snake's jaws closed only on air. Its attacker immediately lunged forward, its pale, slimy coils wrapping around its victim, who immediately brought its own coils into play.

They began to thrash as each fought for dominance, the walls buckling on either side. Huge blocks crashed down upon them as the walls collapsed, but the creatures merely ignored the rubble, all their attention on each other. Stone dust rose to cloud the air.

"Bloody hell," Smythe said. "They've solved our problem for us."

He bent down and put his boots back on. A moment later, after the others had followed suit, the party set off at a quick trot, Clive in the lead once more.

Using the "moon" to guide him, he had little trouble with the necessary decisions, and they made good time. From far behind them they could still hear the battling snakes, knocking down the walls in their struggle. A series of high-pitched whines came from the battle—so piercing that it hurt their ears. When they paused for a breather, Clive turned to the cyborg.

"Is there any sign of the third one?" he asked.

Guafe shook his head. "I think it has joined the battle."

Sudden silence fell from behind them.

"No time to rest," Smythe said. "Let's keep moving."

Wearily, the party set off again.

Was there no end to this damned maze? Clive wondered. It simply went on and on, wall after wall, corridor following twisting corridor. Their lantern cast an island of light, but what it lit up didn't really change. It was always more of the same, surrounded by the darkness. And then he saw, far ahead, a faint glow. At the same time, Guafe called up from behind him.

"There's another of the creatures on our trail."

Smythe cursed, but Clive pointed out the glow.

"How far back is the monster?" he asked.

"Far enough," Guafe replied. "For now. But it is following the same route we are, and is moving very quickly."

Clive didn't bother to look behind. Instead, he set off at a run for that distant glow. The walls here formed a snarl of corridors—the last attempt of the maze to snare those who got this close to its exit, Clive supposed—but by using his guide, he had no trouble working their way through the complex pattern.

The glow was closer now. But so, by Guafe's reports, was the creature pursuing them. Clive led the party on through a last bewildering series of turns and twists, and finally, the glow was no more than a few walls away—so close he could almost taste it.

"It's almost upon us!" Guafe called.

No, Clive thought. It won't have us—not when we've come this close to escaping it.

For now he could see the source of the light—light spilling from an open doorway. The end of the maze, at least. Perhaps the entrance to the sixth level of the Dungeon, as well? And what lay waiting for them there? Don't even bother to worry about it, he told himself. Let's try to survive the moment first.

They ran the last few yards, and then there was only an open expanse between the lit doorway and themselves. The door itself was set at the top of a short flight of stairs. Its height was just enough for them to get through, small enough to keep the creature out. But there was a twelve-foot drop between the top of the wall and the ground running over to the stairs.

Clive crouched on the wall. Holding on to the top by his hands, he lowered himself over and down, dropping the last few feet. He landed lightly on the balls of his feet. Guafe and Smythe landed on either side of him. Only Finnbogg remained above.

"Come along then, Finn!" he called up to Finnbogg.

"It's too high for Finnbogg to jump," the dwarf replied.

"Jump!" Clive cried. "We'll catch you."

As Finnbogg lowered himself nervously over the edge, the three of them positioned themselves under him to break his fall. And then the head of the monstrous snake appeared around the corner.

"For God's sake, jump!" Clive shouted.

Smythe moved away from them, bringing the rolled-up canvas from his shoulder. Moving quickly, he pulled off the twines binding either end, and shook the cloth open. The snake's enormous head wove back and forth above him, but Smythe kept his gaze firmly fixed on the creature's jaws, refusing to meet its blind gaze.

Finnbogg held on to the top of the wall, then let himself go.

The snake's head darted forward. As its jaws opened to snap at him, Smythe tossed the sheet of canvas into its mouth.

Guafe and Clive caught the dwarf, the cyborg absorbing most of his weight.

The snake snapped its jaws on the cloth, shaking it as a terrier would a rat. The canvas got snarled in its teeth.

"Run for the door!" Smythe cried.

As the other three broke for the stairs, Smythe threw his pry-bar, straight for one of the creature's milky-white eyes. The weapon embedded itself in the enormous orb, and that high-pitched whining they had heard earlier issued from the snake's huge mouth. Hands clapped over his ears, Smythe broke for the doorway as well, hard on the heels of the others.

Guafe was through, then Clive and Finnbogg. The snake whipped its head forward, straight for Smythe where he ran up the stairs, still making that piercing cry of pain. At the last possible moment, Smythe threw himself to one side, and the snake's head battered the stairs, shattering stone. Smythe rolled to his feet, darting for the doorway as it lifted its head for a second strike.

Smythe threw himself through the doorway at the same instant the snake struck at him again. This time, its massive head crashed against the sides of the door. Rocks fell as the doorway widened. Drawing back its head, the snake struck again, and the doorway widened some more, opening onto another tunnel.

The others had caught Smythe as he flung himself forward. On their feet now, they raced down this new tunnel, the bright lights set in its ceiling hurting their eyes. Behind them, the snake continued to pound at the sides of the doorway, knocking pieces of it down with each blow.

The party turned one corner, then another, and came up against a massive door, so similar to the one that the Dramaranians had thrust them through that it might have been its twin. Guafe pounded on it. Behind them, the crash of falling rocks continued.

Again and again the cyborg pounded on the metal panel, the others joining him, and finally, it opened. They almost fell through in their haste to get out of the tunnel, and found themselves in a large, empty room, facing a curious individual.

As the door closed behind them, shutting off most of the high-pitched whine of the snake and the thunder of its pummeling the doorway, they slowly rose to their feet. Their rescuer was a short, tubby individual with a broad, fat face, bald pate, and eyes that gleamed metallically, like Guafe's.

Another mechanical man, Clive thought.

The strange being spoke to them, but the words made no sense.

"I'm sorry, we don't understand," Clive said.

"You are Englishmen?" he said then, in perfect Queen's English.

Clive nodded.

"Then you will be the assassins we were told to expect." The broad face grinned. "The Lords of Thunder will feed well on you tonight."

He pulled an instrument from his belt and aimed it at them, thumbing a lever. A numbness settled over the party and, while they could still see and hear, they could no longer move a muscle.

Chapter 26

You've screwed up bad in your time, Annie B., Annabelle told herself as she let go, but this probably tops them all.

Letting go.

To fall down the shaft, like Alice down the rabbit hole. Except this wasn't a dream from which she was going to wake, as Alice eventually had.

All her muscles clenched into tight knots in anticipation of the coming plummet, but while she descended, floating in the thick, golden air, there was no sense of falling. The descent was as calm as riding an escalator from one floor to the next, as comforting as lying on a warm waterbed, the mattress moving gently underneath.

The sparks that specked the honey glow strobed in her eyes. Each flash burned through her retinas to carry its fire into the recesses of her mind. A Catherine Wheel of memories, sparked, seen, then gone to make room for still more. Each one, here and gone, all in an instant.

Good memories.

The kind smile of a stranger peering down at her as her mother pushed her pram down a crowded city street.

Her first kiss, courtesy of freckled Bob Hughes, in the back of the rubble-strewn lot across from the grade school.

Her second Les Paul—to replace the one stolen as she was bringing it home from the store—that Des helped her strip and paint a canary yellow.

Holding Amanda for the first time, the red, squalling face turned up to hers, features calming as she soothed her.

Hearing about "Gotcha in my Heart," the band's thirdsingle, entering *Billboard's* Top One Hundred—thirty-four with a bullet.

Walking a rain-slick Londan street with Chrissie Nunn and Tripper on their way to the sound check of the first gig of their first European headlining tour.

Lots of first times.

First times were best. Those initial moments that you never forgot. Good memories.

When her feet touched ground and the sparks lost their hold on her mind, the memories fading, she felt a sense of abrupt loss that knifed straight to her heart.

Not yet, she wanted to tell them. Don't go yet. . . .

Her knees started to buckle, a sharp pain rising from her hurt leg, and then she was blinking in the golden glare, one hand pressed against the smooth wall of the shaft for balance. She turned in a slow circle and found the cutaway door that led to—

Where?

More dangers, more pain? She didn't want anything more to do with the Dungeon. She just wanted to float in the golden shaft, remembering the good things of her life. Times past and gone forever now. Better times than what was going to lie waiting for her through that door, of that she was sure. The shaft delivered what the chasm had only promised.

She looked up, but there was no retreat. No ladder rungs leading up into the rich honey glow. No handholds. No way up.

But there were voices. It took her a long moment to focus on them enough to make out what they were saying.

"Annabelle, Annabelle! Can you hear me?"

Slowly, she shook off her reverie. That was Sidi. At least there was something good about her present situation. Sidi and Shriek. Good friends. Maybe even Tomàs as well, seeing how he was turning over a new leaf.

"Annabelle!"

"I hear you," she called back.

"Where are you? Are you all right?"

All right? When she'd just been reminded of all that she'd lost?

"Yeah," she called back. "I guess I'm okay."

Because life just went on, didn't it? Made no difference if you wanted to slow the ride down, or get off, the old ferris wheel just kept on spinning. Up and down. You have a few laughs, some good times, and then you had to go through the times that weren't so good.

Like now.

"It's a real smooth ride," she told her companions. "So c'mon down."

She moved out of the shaft, through the portal, regrets and loss clinging to her like cobwebs.

You never used to be this moody, Annie B., she told herself as she took in their new surroundings.

The place had the feel of a waiting room in a train station or bus depot about it. Nothing was permanent here, everything's just passing through. On the far side of the dimly lit chamber, there was a door set in the wall.

Level six, Annabelle thought humorlessly. Another stopover that we just don't need. Maybe we should've grabbed an express.

Hearing a scuffling sound behind her, she turned to find Tomàs standing in the golden glow, sparks flickering around his dark head. The Portuguese's eyes were shiny with unshed tears.

"You okay?" she asked.

It took Tomàs a moment to focus on her, then he nodded slowly and joined her. He said nothing of what he'd experienced in the shaft, but his losses were written as plainly in his features and stance as Annabelle's own had been.

Well, what *could* you say? Annabelle thought.

It was the same for the others. One following the other, Shriek and Sidi stepped through the portal and crossed to where Annabelle and Tomàs were standing in the broad, empty room, waiting for them.

"Some trip, huh?" Annabelle said after a few moments.

Regrets swam in Sidi's eyes. "In some ways," he said, "that was the worst thing I've experienced in this place."

"Yeah. I know what you mean. We didn't need to be reminded."

She turned to Shriek. The alien's multiple, many-faceted eyes didn't show sorrow in the same way a human's would, but Annabelle knew Shriek had experienced the same kinds of losses that they all had.

"It was hard," Annabelle said to the arachnid, "to have the past, just for a moment, then lose it again."

Shriek nodded. *Very hard,* she agreed.

Her voice, echoing in Annabelle's head, was oddly subdued.

They stood in a quiet group, coming to terms with what they'd experienced in the shaft. Then, finally, Annabelle stirred.

"Guess we should check out what's behind Door Number One," she said, glancing at her companions. "Or do we trade it for what's behind the curtain?"

"Curtain?" Tomàs asked, looking around the empty room.

Annabelle shook her head. "Don't pay any attention to me."

She led the way to the door and tried the handle.

Locked.

Perfect, she thought.

Shall we break in? Shriek asked her.

"Let's try the polite approach first," Annabelle replied.

She raised her hand and knocked sharply on the door. Waiting a few heartbeats, she knocked again. When there was still no response after her third knock, she turned to Shriek and was about to tell her to do her stuff, when she heard the lock being disengaged. She faced the door again as it slowly opened.

A scaled-down model of Chang Guafe stood in the doorway.

Well, he wasn't exactly like Guafe, Annabelle decided, but he was close enough. He was the size of a twelve-year-old, but obviously much older; male, slender, half his body parts made of gleaming metal, both eyes implants. His head was shaved, or he was naturally bald—it was hard to tell which. He wore red trousers and a green shirt. His feet were bare. If his ears had been pointed, she might have put him down as one of Santa's elves undergoing chemotherapy.

When he spoke, his voice had the same hollow ring as Guafe's, and she couldn't understand a word he said.

"Say what?" she asked.

She could almost hear the circuitry humming in his head as he tested her words and began to match them up with what he had stored in his memory.

"You speak English?" he asked finally.

"You bet. What's your name?"

"Binro."

"Okay. I'm Annabelle." One by one she introduced the rest of her company. "Is this the sixth level?"

Binro nodded. "Welcome to the Holy City of Tawn, pilgrims."

"Pilgrims?"

"Surely you have come to view the Oracle of the Lords of Thunder?"

Annabelle blinked, then quickly smiled. "Surely," she said. "What else?"

"Are you Haves or Havenots?"

"Ah. . . ."

Annabelle shot a glance at Sidi and the others, but they were having as much problem following the conversation as she was.

Wonderful.

C'mon, guys, she wanted to say to them. Time for somebody else to lend a hand.

But they made it obvious that she was in command.

Haves or Havenots. It sounded like a trick question. What if they came up with the wrong answer?

"Havenots," she said, deciding that they had less than they should.

Binro beamed. "Then be thrice welcomed, pilgrims."

"We're a little . . . ah . . . vague on protocol," Annabelle said. "What's the deal with this oracle? Can we ask it anything we like?"

"That depends on whether or not your names are chosen in the drawing," Binro replied. "But, you're in luck. There is a lottery tonight. The Lords be willing, you might win a chance to speak to them through the Voice of Their Light."

This was getting too weird again, Annabelle thought. Drawings. Lotteries. What the hell was he talking about?

"Ah . . . what do we do until then?" she asked. "You know, until the lottery's happening?"

"There are always rooms kept in readiness for Havenot pilgrims," Binro assured her. "Come. Follow me."

He ushered them through the door, then carefully locked it behind them. Pocketing the key, he led them down a long hall and up a stairwell. Four stories later, they stepped into another corridor. This one had doors opening from it, all along its length.

It's like a hotel, Annabelle thought. She wondered what sort of payment they'd be expecting.

"Would you like separate rooms?" Binro asked.

Annabelle's first inclination was to go for that, but then she decided that they'd be better off staying together as a group.

"Maybe not," she said. "We're all strangers here and, you know, we'd like to stick together."

"As you wish."

He took them down to the middle of the hallway and opened a door into a large, carpeted room. Bright sunlight came through the windows, making them all blink. There were two double beds, a dresser, mirror, couch, and some easy chairs by the window, and two other doors leading off on one side of the room.

Closet and washroom, Annabelle decided. God, the place was like a Holiday Inn. She wondered if they had a shower.

"Will this be suitable?" Binro asked.

"Oh, yeah. It's great."

"There are clean garments in the closet." He pursed his lips for a moment, taking in Shriek's four arms. "I will have a custom-fitted robe prepared for you, Miss Shriek, which will be delivered in a half-hour."

That will not be necessary, Being Binro, the arachnid said.

Binro chittered in response—speaking in Shriek's native language, Annabelle realized.

Right. The Holy City of Tawn. With an Oracle, expecting pilgrims. All languages accepted here. Stay in our beautiful downtown Hilton while you wait for the results of the lottery.

"Please make yourself at home," Binro added. Then he was gone.

Annabelle slowly closed the door behind him.

"Anybody know what's going on?" she asked.

Sidi and Tomàs shook their heads. Shriek, who had crossed the room to look out the window, called out suddenly, indicating something she saw outside. The others hurried over.

Look, the arachnid said, pointing to a figure that stood on a street corner below.

It took Annabelle a moment to focus on the figure. First, she took in the vast sweep of buildings and streets—it was like being in downtown New York. Tall, gleaming buildings rose high all around them. There was traffic on the streets, both pedestrian and vehicles, though the latter weren't quite right. At least, not for the cities Annabelle was familiar with. They were all either public transports, like old tram cars, or small one- or two-person scooters and what looked like golf carts.

"Jesus," she murmured.

Shriek tugged on her arm, still pointing. Annabelle let her gaze pan down to the figure that had caught the alien's attention.

"Clive!" she cried.

But Sidi shook his head. "No. That's Neville Folliot."

Annabelle started to turn for the door. "We've gotta grab him before he takes off again."

"Too late," Sidi told her. "He's gone now—lost in the crowd. We'll never find him."

"But he's here. . . ."

And Clive wasn't. Jesus. Were they going to spend the rest of their lives careening around this place like pinballs, just catching glimpses of each other, never getting close again? The thought of it depressed her.

"I'm gonna see if they really do have a shower," she said.

Later, refreshed from long showers and the meal that Binro had brought them, they sat around their room, just taking it easy. Except for Shriek, they had all put on the robes that they had found in the closet.

We look like a bunch of acolytes from some weird monastery, Annabelle thought as she sprawled on one of the beds, hands behind her head. God, it felt good to be clean again.

The others had wanted to go exploring, but she refused to budge until her old clothes, which she'd washed when she took her shower, were dry enough to wear. No way she was gonna go running around looking like some Hare Krishna. She had a rep to think of.

In the end they all stayed; none of them wanting to separate. Shriek and Sidi sat by the window, fascinated by the endless parade of people and vehicles below. Tomàs was asleep on the other bed. Bored, Annabelle opened the drawer of the night table beside her bed.

She was used to hotel rooms—and, weird though this one was in terms of *where* it was, it still wasn't all that different from a hundred others she'd stayed in while on tour. She wasn't sure what she was expecting to find in the drawer. Not a Bible. Not here. Though maybe the Tawnian version of one?

Her fingers closed on a book and she drew it out. When she looked at what it was, a cold chill traveled up her spine.

"Oh, shit."

Sidi turned from the window. "What is it, Annabelle?"

Numbly, Annabelle held up her prize. It was Neville Folliot's journal.

Chapter 27

Clive had never felt so helpless as he did at that moment. Whatever the small box that their captor held was, it had somehow managed to freeze all their muscles,' locking them into tight knots so that not one of them could move—not even Guafe, who was composed of at least a third mechanical parts. They couldn't even twitch.

Whistling to himself, their captor unclipped another small box from his belt and spoke into it. Whatever he said was totally incomprehensible.

"Won't be long now," he told them, switching to English. "We'll soon have you transported to a nice little holding cell where I'll free you from your state of stasis."

Why? Clive wanted to ask him. What was all this about?

"You didn't truly believe that you could actually succeed in assassinating the Lords of Thunder, now, did you?" their captor asked, as though reading Clive's mind.

There it was again, Clive thought. The mechanical man thought they were assassins. But all they knew of the Lords of Thunder was their name, nothing more. All they wanted to do was find his brother and leave the Dungeon. If he could only find some way to talk to the man.

"You're not the first to try, of course," their captor continued. "Nor will you be the last, I presume. But no one ever has, or will succeed. It simply isn't possible. The Lords are beyond the hand of death. Still, your kind does provide some amusement for them. I wonder, are you free agents, hoping for spoils, or did the Madonna send you?"

What had the Mother of God to do with any of this? Clive thought. But then he realized that in this place, the name could mean anything. And anybody.

"Ah, here's your transport now," their captor said as a door hissed open in what had appeared to be a blank wall.

A small horseless cart on fat wheels rolled through and came to a stop in front of them. The sound of its engine was a low hum. There were two seats in the front—one occupied by the driver, the other empty—and a cargo area in the back where, presumably, their stiff bodies would be laid.

The driver, while obviously of the same half-human, half-mechanical race as their captor, was otherwise as different from the first man as night was to day. He was thin as a rake, almost cadaverous, bones prominent against the tight fit of his skin, eyes deep-set and ringed with black circles, skin pale. Where the first man had a jolly look about him, the newcomer looked as dour as a Scots churchman.

Because the pair of them were transporting bodies, albeit living ones, Clive promptly christened them Burke and Hare. Burke was the newcomer; Hare the rotund captor who had first snared them.

"Easy now," Hare was saying as they laid Smythe in the back of the cart. "Don't want the goods damaged before the lords have their fun with them, or maybe you'll be taking their place."

Burke muttered something unintelligible in their own tongue.

"It was just a joke," Hare replied. "Of course the Lords would never feed on us. We never meant them any ill."

It was obvious, Clive thought, that Hare continued to speak in English just to make them feel more ill at ease. He wanted them to have to think about what lay ahead.

Clive was the last to be loaded onto the cart. He felt nauseous when it came his turn to be hoisted up and laid down beside the others. His skin crawled at the feel of their hands on him. Unable to move, unable to even speak. To be so helpless. . . . If he'd had a weapon in hand, Clive would gladly have killed the pair of them in cold blood.

"Oh, you're a hater, you are," Hare said, looking down into his face. "Hold that hate to you, assassin. The Lords feed on it."

Laughing, he got into the passenger seat. Burke sat down behind the wheel and the cart moved smoothly off on its fat wheels, through the door and down a long corridor. All Clive could see of their passage was the flicker of the ceiling lights as they went by. He tried counting them, as a means of memorizing the route, but he soon lost track of both the number of lights and the turns that they took.

Finally, after what seemed like an inordinately long journey, through corridors as bafflingly laid out as the maze that they had so recently escaped, the cart came to a halt, and Burke and Hare were hoisting them from the bed of the cart and carrying them into a jail cell. The pair stood Clive and his companions up against one wall, vacated the cell, and locked the door behind them. Not until then did Hare take that small box from his belt once more and aim it at the four.

When he depressed its control button, use of their own muscles returned to Clive and the other three. But their legs buckled under them, and it was all they could do to keep themselves from smacking their heads against the floor.

"Goodbye for now!" Hare called cheerily.

"W-wait. . . ." Clive called.

But Burke had already set the cart in motion, and the pair of them whizzed out of sight.

Slowly, Clive sat up. His muscles felt bruised and sore. His head ached. He was hungry and thirsty, and what little patience he had had completely run its course.

"Damn them all to bloody hell!" he cried.

"Keep it down, would you?"

The voice was familiar, though it didn't belong to any of his companions. Clive turned slowly to face its source, gaze taking in the double set of tiered cots—one pair to either side of the back wall—the water bucket, another for bodily wastes, until he was looking at the man who had spoken.

This was too much.

"You!" he cried. "It's your fault that we're here."

"Me? I've never seen you before in my life."

But if the man wasn't Father Neville of Dramaran—the one who'd stolen the history and name of Clive's twin and abandoned them in the cavern, with its maze and monsters—then he was an identical twin.

Clive rose to his feet and stalked over to the other side of the cell, until he stood against the bars looking into the neighboring one.

"I'm tired of your lies," Clive said.

"I tell you, I've never met you before."

Clive thrust an arm through the bars, and the man backed hastily away, even though Clive couldn't reach far enough into the other cell to hurt him anyway.

"Wait a minute, sah," Smythe said. "Let's give him a listen, first."

"What for? To hear more lies?"

Smythe shook his head. "Look at him. He thinks he's telling the truth. I'll wager that he *has* never seen us before. And besides, how could he have gotten here before us?"

He tugged at Clive's arm, moving him away from the bars as he spoke, and settling him on a lower cot in their own cell.

"The resemblance is uncanny," Guafe remarked. "All the way down to the mole at his wrist."

Smythe nodded. "What's your name?" he asked the man in the other cell.

"Edgar Howlett," he replied. "I came to the Dungeon twelve years ago, from the continent known as North America, on a planet called Earth. The year I was taken was nineteen eighty-three."

Clive, feeling a little calmer now, took in that information. But more importantly, he weighed the man's delivery. Horace was right. Whatever else might be, the man truly believed he was who he said he was.

"And do you have a brother?" Smythe asked.

Howlett shook his head. "Not one," he said. "Now it's my turn for questions. What are your names? Where are you from?"

In the same manner as Howlett had done, they gave him their names, places of origin, and the years of disappearance from their homelands. Finnbogg was the last to speak.

"Ten thousand years?" Howlett said in disbelief. "You've been here that long?"

The dwarf nodded.

"This place has got to be Hell," Howlett said.

In that they were all in agreement, except, of course, Guafe.

"But there is so much to learn here," the cyborg said.

"Screw learning," Howlett told him. "I finished high school. I'm a plumber, okay? What else do I have to know? I just want to get home again—see the wife and kid. Christ, Tommy'll be—what? Eighteen now. I missed seeing him grow up. I . . . aw, what's the point. I figure

I died, you know? Back in Milwaukee. I didn't think I was that bad a guy, but this sure isn't Heaven, so it's got to be Hell."

"We are not dead," Guafe said. "I would know if I had died."

"Christ, look who's talking. The Bionic Man himself."

"I am not sure that I care for the tone of your voice," Guafe said.

Howlett shrugged. "So what're you going to do about it? Call for a guard?"

Guafe stepped up to the bars separating their cells. Getting a firm grip on two, he began to exert pressure on them. Slowly, they started to bend.

Before things got too serious, Smythe crossed to Guafe's side and laid a calming hand on his shoulder.

"There's much we could learn from Mr. Howlett," he said.

Guafe turned, metallic eyes flashing, but Howlett, his own eyes going wide as the bars bent under the cyborg's strength, stood up and held his hands placatingly in front of him.

"Hey, easy now," he said. "You've got me all wrong. I used to love the Bionic Man. It was my favorite show—you know what I'm saying?"

Guafe let his hands fall from the bars. Howlett let out an audible sigh of relief. Then, before anyone else could speak, he turned to Clive.

"You said your last name's Folliot?" he asked.

Clive nodded.

"Any relation to a guy named Neville Folliot?"

Clive's suspicions rose to the fore once more. "He's my twin brother," he said. "How do you know his name?"

"It's also the name *your* twin was calling himself the last time we saw him," Smythe put in.

"I told you," Howlett said. "I don't have any brothers—or sisters. The guy you saw must've been a clone, but I do know Neville Folliot. He's the reason I'm in this jam."

"A clone," Guafe said. "Of course."

"What's a clone?" Smythe asked him.

"Cloning is a form of genetic manipulation whereby an entire exact replica of a being can be grown from just one cell taken from the donor."

"That kind of thing's possible?" Howlett asked.

"Very possible," Guafe replied.

Howlett shook his head. "I only saw it in the movies, you know? I didn't think it was real."

"What did my brother have to do with your present situation?" Clive asked.

"Well, I met him, must have been five or six years or so ago, up on one of the upper levels. We hung around together for a while—came down from the third level, through the fourth and fifth—did you see the dinosaurs on the fifth?—until we finally ended up here. We got snatched by the border patrol, or whatever the hell they're called, and that's when old Neville put the knife to me."

"He attacked you?" Clive asked.

"Naw. He turned rat on me. Told the authorities that I was an agent of the Madonna's—you heard of her?"

"Briefly," Smythe said. "In our time, we refer to the Madonna as the Mother of Christ."

"Yeah? Well, in mine she's a pop singer, sexy as all get-out. But here she's some kind of, I don't know—I think demagogue's the word Neville used to describe her."

"Is she of the Ren, or the Chaffri?" Clive asked.

"No way of telling," Howlett told him. "I never could keep those sides straight. I don't think anyone can. Anyway, this may be something strictly local. There's an awful lot in the Dungeon that the Chaffri and the Ren don't bother getting involved with, even if they are the big bosses."

"What about Green?" Smythe asked.

"Green what?"

"A man named Green. Did Major Folliot—Neville—ever mention him? Is he an ally or a foe? Ren or Chaffri?"

"Never heard of him."

Clive shook his head sadly. Would they never find two pieces of information that fit together?

Howlett continued his tale. "Anyway, Neville told the authorities that I was the Madonna's agent, and not only that, but that she was also sending in a bunch of assassins to kill the Lords, and the way to recognize them was that they'd be speaking English.

"They only half believed him. Kept him in that cell you're in right now up until about a half hour ago—I guess that's when they caught you and found out he was telling the truth. Or, at least, what they perceived as the truth. So they let him go. Or took him away, anyway."

"He was here?" Clive cried. "In this very cell, not half an hour ago?"

"'Fraid so."

"God damn the man. What is he playing at?"

Howlett shook his head. "Damned if I know. I thought we were buddies." He paused, thinking for a moment. "This other guy looked exactly like me?"

"Down to the mole," Smythe said.

"Christ, talk about giving you the creeps."

"What we should also consider," Guafe said, "is the possibility that the Neville Folliot we are chasing is another clone. Who knows how many of them there might be?"

"A clone?" Clive said. "As this man's twin was? This is really possible?"

"In my world it is," Guafe said. "And in this Dungeon. . . ."

He let the sentence trail off, unfinished, as Clive sat back down on the cot and bent over, face pressed into the palms of his hands.

"I feel like I'm going mad," he said.

"First things first," Smythe said. "Let's get out of this place, *then* you can go mad."

"But, Horace. When you think of it . . . two, perhaps dozens of Nevilles running about. . . ."

"I know, sah. It's not a pleasant thought, by any stretch of the imagination. But we still have to escape."

He turned slowly, then his gaze settled on the bars that Guafe had bent between Howlett's cell and their own.

"We need your strength for this," he told the cyborg. "Can you pull the bars far enough apart for Howlett to join us, and then repeat the trick on the ones facing the corridor?"

Guafe nodded. He returned to where he'd first opened a gap between the bars. Gripping them once more, he began to exert pressure on the steel. Slowly, the gap widened until it was just big enough for Howlett to squeeze through. Turning, Guafe stepped over to the bars facing the corridor and repeated the maneuver.

Moments later they were all standing out in the corridor.

"Now what?" Clive said.

"We find your brother, or we find a way out of here," Smythe said. "Whichever comes first."

"I'd like a piece of him," Howlett muttered, but then he realized who he was talking to. "Sorry. I forgot he's your brother. It's just, after the way he screwed me. . . ."

"I sympathize," Clive said. "But if you want a 'piece of him,' as you put it, I'm afraid you'll just have to wait in line."

Chapter 28

"I don't get it," Annabelle said, leafing through Neville Folliot's journal. "What's this doing here?"

Unspoken, but lying there plainly behind her words all the same, was the thought, If the journal's here, then what had happened to Clive and the others? The last time they'd set eyes on this book, it had been in Clive's possession.

Could it be a copy? Shriek asked.

Annabelle shook her head. "I don't think so." She glanced at the others. "You got any ideas, Sidi? Tomàs?"

"Something has happened to the others," Tomàs said.

"*Sim?*"

"Yeah. I got a real bad feeling about this, too." She looked around the room. "I wonder how you buzz room service in this place?"

"Room service?" Sidi asked.

"To talk to Binro, or whoever's in charge. I want to know what this is doing here."

"Perhaps that wouldn't be such a good idea, Annabelle. If the journal is here and something *has* happened to the others, then it stands to reason that our hosts must be involved."

"Right. So let's get outta here."

She swung her feet off the bed and, journal in hand, headed for the door. She gave the knob a twist, but it wouldn't budge.

"Perfect. We're locked in. God, what a bunch of assholes we've turned out to be. Pilgrims, right. Guests. Let's try prisoners on for size."

She turned to Shriek to see if the alien could take down the door.

"Does the journal say anything about Tawn?" Sidi asked.

Good point, Annabelle thought.

Returning to the bed, she sat down and began to flip through the pages. She passed through sections where Clive's sketches filled the blank spaces where once there had been Neville's entries. There was enough there to tell her that Clive and his party had successfully crossed the veldt on the fifth level, and had reached a city there. She didn't want to think about what the portrait of the woman meant. At last, she found a new message.

"Here we go," she said.

As far as they could figure out from Neville's rather cryptic words, Tawn was the focus of an ancient and continuing war between factions led by the Lords of Thunder, on one side, and someone called the Madonna, on the other.

"Jesus," Annabelle said softly as she read further. She looked up at her companions. "What did you see out that window?"

"A large city, much like Calcutta," Sidi said. "Just below our window is a marketplace."

Tomàs shook his head. "No. It is a harbor, filled with ships from many nations."

When the question was put to Shriek, she described some alien cityscape.

And I saw a variation on New York, Annabelle thought.

"There's nothing out there," she said, "according to Neville."

"Nothing?" Sidi asked. He returned to the window. "But it seems so real. . . ."

"They're playing with our heads," Annabelle said. "The whole thing's a scam. Listen to this. 'Trust not in Tawn, even in what your own eyes tell you, for they fill up emptiness with what is familiar. Keep a sphinx's riddle for the Lords of Thunder, lest you be taken for fuels.'"

"The riddle of the sphinx is a question that can't be answered," she explained. "And I don't think I wanna find out firsthand what he means by 'taken for fuels.'"

Annabelle slammed the journal closed.

"We don't need this crap," she said. "Shriek, can you get that door open?"

The arachnid flexed her multiple arms. Advancing on the door, she pressed the palms of her upper arms against it to get a sense of its density.

Bring me a chair, she said.

Annabelle brought one of them over, but before Shriek could use it as a makeshift battering ram, the door opened and Binro was standing there, a smile touching his features. He held a small device in his hand that reminded Annabelle of a remote control for a TV.

"Congratulations," he said. "I took the liberty of entering your names in the lottery as a group, and you have won the privilege of speaking with the Oracle."

"As opposed to being godfood without trying to stump the Oracle?" Annabelle asked.

Binro blinked. "Pardon?"

"Outta the way, pal. We've decided to find new lodgings."

The little man sighed as Annabelle advanced on him. Before either she or Shriek could grab him, he thumbed a button on the device in his hand.

There was nothing to see, and little to feel except for an electric tingle that ran up their nerve ends. But when Annabelle tried to move, she realized that every one of her muscles had been paralyzed. From her companions' lack of movement, she realized that they'd all been hit by an invisible stasis ray.

Oh, beautiful, she thought. The little twerp was a science fiction freak. Except this wasn't the movies. It was the real thing, and they were up the proverbial creek without a paddle.

Fuming, all she could do was watch as Binro called up what looked like a small golf cart to transport the four of them to the Oracle. Its driver was much taller than Binro—a thin, cadaverous individual who made Annabelle think of a junkie. With the driver's help, Binro loaded them onto the flat bed at the back of the cart, then they were carried down a series of long corridors to an elevator.

Binro leaned back to look at Annabelle's frozen face. "There was really no need for things to be so unpleasant," he told her. "This is a great honor for you—speaking with the Oracle, and then meeting the Lords of Thunder."

Screw you, Annabelle thought.

Binro must have read something of her feelings in her eyes for he frowned, then gave a shrug and turned in his seat, leaving her to herself once more.

When I get out of this. . . . Annabelle thought.

The elevator doors slid open, and the cart pulled out into a vast chamber with cathedral ceilings. Binro and his companion unloaded them. When all four of them were lying on the floor, staring up at the vast ceiling, the cart withdrew, back into the elevator. Though she couldn't turn her head to see what they were doing, Annabelle assumed that Binro had thumbed his stasis device again, because she started to feel a new tingle in her nerve ends, and her muscles went slack. She turned just in time to see the door of the elevator slide shut once more.

Her body had that numbed, prickly feeling of an arm or leg that had fallen asleep. It took a few moments for it to wear off enough so that she could sit up and take stock.

"Everybody okay?" she asked.

The stasis ray appeared to have had the worst effect upon Shriek—probably due to her alien musculature—and she was the last to recover. Annabelle helped her to her feet.

"What is this place?" Sidi murmured.

"Home of the gods," Annabelle said. "Can't you tell?"

But for all the lightness of her tone, the place gave her the creeps. The room was enormous—a feeling that was compounded by the immense ceiling that rose some three stories above the floor. There were glass domes set into its curved features, through which a pale, orange-yellow light issued. The floor was the size of half a football field.

Set in the walls, in a long row that ran along two sides of the chamber, were what looked all too much like gigantic sarcophagi. Although they were decorated with glyphs and designs, the motif didn't strike Annabelle as Egyptian so much as heavy metal punk. Lots of ornately detailed figures were carved on the lids of the sarcophagi, their clothing made to represent leather, chains, and studs with lots of sharp-edged objects. Razors. Knives. Swords.

Against the wall facing them was a series of steps that led up to a raised platform. A still figure lay there on a stone slab—corpse-white and huge. Annabelle thought it was another carving, until they got closer and she saw that it was the body of a dead giant. Male.

Alive and on its feet, it would have stood twice her height. The skin was smooth, hair black and fine, spread out in a fan around the head upon the gray stone. The body wore the same kind of leather gear as the carved bas-reliefs on the sarcophagi. Leather skirt, crisscrossed strips of leather across its chest like bandoleers.

Lots of shiny silver studs. Small, sharp blades hung from its ears like earrings—six to each ear, running up from the lobe to the top of the ear. Two more hung from each nostril. More dangled down the length of its arms, the wires piercing the alabaster flesh.

Standing around the stone slab on which it lay, all they could do was stare at the corpse.

"What is it?" Sidi said. His voice, though hushed, seemed loud in the silence.

"The Oracle," Annabelle said.

Her hand lifted to touch the shape of Folliot's journal where it sat in the inner pocket of her jacket. They had to put a question to the Oracle that he couldn't answer—that was the only way out. Because otherwise. . . . Her gaze drifted to the sarcophagi lining the walls.

Were there more corpses in them? And what about the Lords?

Tomàs made a sudden sound. Breath sharply drawn in. Annabelle looked back at the corpse and took a step back. The eyelids had flickered open, cold blue eyes staring up at the ceiling. Annabelle's pulse doubled its tempo.

"WHAT WOULD YOU ASK OF ME?" the corpse asked.

Me, me, me. . . .

Its voice boomed hollowly, echoes resounding through the vast chamber. Annabelle and her party all withdrew from the stone slab. Annabelle reached for Sidi's hand and gripped it tightly.

"PILGRIMS," the corpse repeated. "WHAT WOULD YOU ASK OF ME?"

Me, me, me. . . . the echoes chimed in again.

Oh, Jesus, Annabelle thought. We only get the one question.

"PILGRIMS," the corpse said once more.

Grim, grim, grim. . . .

"Give us a moment!" Annabelle blurted out.

Slowly, the enormous head turned, steely blue gaze fixing on her. Annabelle started to take another step back, but that cold gaze nailed her in place. Her insides began to churn. There was a knot in her stomach, like a hard rock sitting there. A sour taste rose in her throat.

A faint smile touched the corpse's dead lips. "THERE IS NO NEED TO HASTEN," he said.

Ten, ten, ten. . . . the echoes chorused.

"WE HAVE ALL THE TIME IN THE WORLD."

World, world, world. . . .

The voice seemed to come from all around them, the echoing words drifting across each other to become a babble of sound.

Swallowing thickly, Annabelle nodded at the corpse. "R-right," she said. "All the time."

"MYSTERIES AWAIT YOU."

You, you, you. . . .

Knees weak, Annabelle kept retreating. She would have fallen at the top of the stairs, except Sidi was there to help her keep her balance. The small group backed carefully down each step, unable to pull their gazes from the monstrous dead figure.

"PLEASURES YOU CANNOT IMAGINE."

Gin, gin, gin. . . .

I could use a drink about now, Annabelle thought, and almost giggled at the incongruity of the thought.

A drink. Right. What was happening was that she was losing it. Giddy with fright.

Pull yourself together, Annie B., she told herself.

They retreated all the way across the room until they were standing by the elevator again. The corpse's gaze followed them until they paused, then slowly, it turned its head to stare up at the ceiling once more.

Freed of the prison of its gaze, Annabelle sagged against the wall behind her.

"What if it gets up?" she said. "What if it gets up and comes after us?"

"There is no place to hide," Tomàs said.

Sidi nodded. "And no way to escape. We have to put a question to it."

"God." Annabelle rubbed her face. "What kind of question?"

But she knew. An obscure bit of schooling rose bubbling up in her mind. Question and answer time. Final exam. The teacher grinning because he knew she hadn't been studying.

It had to be a riddle. This Oracle was like the Greek sphinx in Thebes, except instead of it posing the riddle, and then devouring those unable to find solutions, it was up to them to come up with a question. And if it gave them an answer, they were godfood.

Oedipus, where are you when you're needed?

"What do we ask?" she repeated.

Her companions shook their heads.

"It's gotta be obscure—maybe something from our own experiences, something it couldn't possibly know about? Like who used to play lead guitar for the Wailing Men before Lee Sands?"

But she didn't think that would cut it.

"The journal said merely a question," Sidi said. "Any question."

"Yeah. And we all really put a lot of trust into what Neville Folliot's got to tell us, don't we?"

"Then ask it that, Annabelle. Where we can find Neville Folliot."

"And when it tells us? Then we're just godfood."

Ask it that question, Shriek said. She gave the Oracle a long, considering look. *I will stop the Oracle.*

Annabelle pointed to the sarcophagi. "Want to bet there's more dead giants in those? Dead giants that can move? I'll bet these are the Lords of Thunder."

Ask the question, Shriek repeated firmly.

Annabelle drew a deep breath. "Sure," she said. "Fine. I mean, what've we got to lose, right?"

Just everything, she thought as she led the way back to the dais on which the Oracle lay.

The immense head turned toward them as they approached. "PILGRIMS," it said. "WHAT WOULD YOU ASK OF ME?"

Me, me, me. . . .

The weight of its gaze made Annabelle's legs feel all watery again. She cleared her throat.

"Uh, we want to know where we can find Neville .Folliot," she said.

"WHICH NEVILLE FOLLIOT?" the Oracle replied.

Ot, ot, ot. . . .

Annabelle and her companions exchanged puzzled looks.

"What do you mean which?" Annabelle finally asked.

"THERE IS MORE THAN ONE."

One, one, one. . . .

Wasn't that just perfect? Annabelle thought. Bad enough just trying to track down one of Clive's twins. Now they find out that the bugger's gone and cloned himself.

"The real one," she said.

Chapter 29

"Do you know how we may exit from this place?" Clive asked Howlett.

"Well, now." Howlett pointed to the left. "That's the direction that they brought you from. And that—" he pointed the opposite way "—is the direction they took your brother."

"Then that is the way we will go," Clive said.

He led off, Smythe beside him, letting the others follow as they would.

"This time we'll have him," Clive said. "He only has an hour or so lead on us. I can almost taste his presence."

"I'd be happier with a weapon in my hand," Smythe said, "for when we flush our captors."

"I'll be happy just to have a grip on Neville's throat."

Smythe nodded. "The humbugger's led us by the nose, all right."

"And do you know what?" Clive said, glancing at his companion. "What will you wager he'll have some convincing tale to make good all he's put us through?"

"If it *was* him," Smythe said. "You heard what Guafe said about these clones."

"Oh, I'll know my brother—don't you worry about that, Horace."

But then he thought about the pretender in Dramaran and Howlett, and how difficult it had been for him to accept that they were not one and the same. Could the replicas be so exact that they *couldn't* be told apart?

"These replicas," he asked Guafe, looking over his shoulder. "Do they all carry the same memories, as well?"

"Unlikely."

"There," Clive said. "You see, Horace? All we'll need to do is put a question or two to our man when we have him, and we'll know soon enough whether or not he's a replica."

They came to a branch in the corridor and paused. Down the one that led to the right they could see more jail cells, which appeared empty from the perspective they had of them. Down the other there was a long expanse of empty hallway, but near its end they spied a number of doors leading off.

"What do you say, Edgar?" Clive asked.

Howlett shrugged. "Your guess is as good as mine."

"Then we'll take the left," Clive said.

They made a grim company as they strode down the hall. Lies and trickery had been all they had met since first entering the Dungeon, and they were all weary to death of being, played the fool.

"It's like Chinese boxes," was how Smythe put it, describing the various levels. "Every time we think the end's in sight, there's another box to open, another puzzle lying in the way."

Well, no more, Clive thought. A man could brook only so much of it. It was time to stand up like a good Englishman and be counted, and by God, he meant to do just that.

When they reached the first closed door, they paused again. Smythe took hold of its knob. At a nod from Clive, he cautiously tested it, then turned it sharply and flung the door open. Clive darted in, with Guafe and Finnbogg on his heels. Howlett remained behind in the hallway.

There was another mechanical man sitting behind a desk in the room. He looked up, startled at their sudden entrance, then reached for one of the black boxes with which Hare had incapacitated them earlier. Clive didn't give him the time to use it.

He crossed the room, one hand closing on the man's fist, the other sweeping the box to the floor. Before the man could break free, Guafe was there, lending Clive his strength. At the pressure of the cyborg's grip on his arm, all the fight went out of their captive.

He spoke rapidly in an unfamiliar language.

"Speak the Queen's English," Clive told him, "or shut your gob."

"Please," the man said quickly, switching to English. "Don't hurt me."

"Brave lot once they lose the upper hand, aren't they?" Clive said, to no one in particular.

Their captive quivered.

"Hold him, would you, Chang, while we search him for weapons."

Though how they were supposed to recognize a weapon in this place was beyond Clive at that moment. With boxes that sent out an invisible ray to steal a man's strength, who knew what else they might have?

They emptied everything out of their captive's pockets and spread it out on the desk, then bound him to his chair. Guafe fetched the black box from where it had fallen.

"Primitive," he remarked, studying it. "But effective."

"Was it damaged?" Smythe asked.

The cyborg pointed it at their captive and thumbed the control. The man went inmobile. When Guafe thumbed the control again, he slumped in his bonds.

"It appears not," Guafe said.

"Look," Finnbogg called.

From a closet he was pulling various bits of gear—things that had obviously been taken from the Tawnians' prisoners, for Smythe recognized his own knife near the top of the pile. Clive smiled when the dwarf held up a saber in a plain leather scabbard. He took it and belted it on.

"That feels better," he said.

He drew out the blade and tested its balance. It was a beautifully crafted weapon, without a blemish in the metal. The balance was perfect.

By now Howlett had entered the room and was bent down beside Finnbogg at the door to the closet. When he stood, he held a modernistic-looking pistol in his hand.

"Now, this is more like it," he said.

"What is it?" Smythe asked.

"This, my friend, is a Smith & Wesson .44 Magnum, one of the world's most powerful handguns, as Dirty Harry'd say."

"And who is he?"

Howlett gave him an odd look. "I forgot. You guys don't know anything about my time. Harry's just a damn straight shooter—played by an actor named Eastwood."

"I . . . see," Smythe said.

Shrugging, Howlett cracked open the magnum's cylinder. He shook out its bullets into the palm of his hand.

"Damn," he muttered, discarding the empty shells. "Only three shots. Do you see any ammo in there, Finn?"

"Finnbogg find this."

He stood back from the closet with a deadly looking mace in his hands, the head spiked with steel flanges, and gave it a couple of short practice swings. As Guafe and Smythe rooted around among the gear for weapons for themselves, Clive returned his attention to their captive.

"What's your name?" he asked.

"M-merdor—if it pleases you."

"Nothing about this place pleases me. What are your duties here?"

"I keep the records of the . . . prisoners," Merdor said. His brow was beaded with sweat.

"And?"

"And catalogue the gear we take from them. That's all—I swear! I have nothing to do with deciding who fuels the lords and who does not."

"Your records," Clive asked. "Are they current?"

"Oh, yes, sir. Completely current."

"Then, show me what you have concerning one Sir Neville Folliot."

"Folliot? He was just released, not an hour ago. The records have already been transferred upstairs."

"And what has become of him?"

"I . . . I'm not really sure," Merdor replied. "I assume he's been set free to go upon his way."

"Damn you!" Clive cried. "Tell me where I can find him."

"But, I don't know—I swear I don't."

Smythe appeared at Clive's side, buckling another saber to his own belt.

"What about the next level?" he asked. "Where is the nearest gateway?"

Merdor blinked. "In the Hall of the Lords of Thunder—where the Oracle sleeps."

"What exactly are these Lords of Thunder?" Guafe asked.

Now Merdor seemed astonished. "They rule this level," he said after a few moments. "They always have, always will."

"Until this Madonna puts the blade to them," Smythe said.

"You would know that better than I," Merdor replied. He sat as straight in his chair as his bonds would let him. "You are her assassins, not I."

"We are not assassins," Clive began, but then thought, Why bother trying to explain? "What is the quickest route to this hall you spoke of?"

Merdor told them without hesitation.

"He seems very pleased with himself," Smythe said. "Perhaps we should take him with us to defuse any . . . surprises that might await us."

"Please—no."

Smythe grinned. "Ah-ha! What did I tell you?"

"It's not that," Merdor said. "I swear you'll have no trouble reaching the hall. It's only when you're inside. . . ."

"Yes?" Clive prompted him.

"Well, it's the lords. They won't be pleased. And what displeases them, they use for fuel."

"You mean eat, don't you?" Howlett said.

Merdor hesitated.

"Speak up, man," Smythe told him.

"Well, in a manner of speaking," Merdor said. "Yes. The Lords do convert the living into fuel for their bodies."

Smythe glanced at Clive, who gave him a nod. Smythe quickly cut their prisoner free, then retied his arms behind his back.

"Lead on," he said.

"Please," Merdor said. "The Lords see no difference between the prisoners we bring them and ourselves. If you want to throw your lives away, I won't stop you—obviously, I *can't* stop you—but but why drag me in with you?"

"Curiosity," Clive said. "We want to see exactly how the Lords 'convert' a man into fuel. Naturally, we're not interested enough in the experiment to use one of our own party for it."

Smythe could feel the man tremble under his hand as he shoved Merdor toward the door. They made him take the lead, Clive and Smythe walking directly behind him. Howlett came next, the magnum thrust into his belt. There had been no extra ammunition for it. Guafe and Finnbogg brought up the rear.

Clive paid attention to the route they took, matching it in his mind with what their captive had told them. So far, there had been no discrepancies. Perhaps Merdor had been telling the truth. But what about this hall where his brother had gone? Would Neville survive his encounter with the Lords? Had he already vanished once more, into the next level?

The sense of time in the Dungeon was obviously very much askew. For Neville, or even his replicas, to have spent anywhere up to five years in places, it seemed that time worked at varying rates for each being trapped in it. One could arrive at the same time as one's companions, become separated, and then a year might pass for you, while only a day or so for them before you met again.

It made no logical sense. But, then again, as they were all so fond of telling each other, nothing here made logical sense.

But there had to be some connecting thread—some reason for it all—no matter how alien it might seem to them. Clive couldn't shake the sense that they had all been specifically chosen to come here—at least all save for Horace, Sidi, and himself, who had merely blundered in while searching for Neville. What was it that connected his brother with Guafe and Shriek and a Portuguese pirate? With Clive's own descendant, Annabelle?

Thinking of her again awoke a pang of sorrow in Clive. He should never have let her—

"My God!" Smythe cried suddenly. "It's him!"

They had come to another branching of the corridors. Down the length of one that led to the left was a small group of Tawnians, with the unmistakable figure of his twin standing among them. One of the Tawnians began to level his black box at them, but Howlett was suddenly pushing between Clive and Smythe.

"Get out of the way!" he shouted.

He had the magnum in his hand, the weapon leveled, left hand gripping his right wrist to absorb the handgun's recoil. When he fired, Clive was sure that his eardrums were going to explode, the sound of the weapon was so loud in the confined space of the corridor. Long after the shot, his ears were still ringing. But down the hall, he saw the Tawnian with the black box lifted from his feet as though a puppeteer had jerked his strings. The Tawnian was flung back against a wall, where he slid to the floor, leaving a red smear on the surface of the wall behind him.

"Don't even think of it," Howlett cried as another of the Tawnians reached for his own black box. "Christ, I've always wanted to use a line like that," he told Clive out of the corner of his mouth.

His gaze never left the group. Besides Clive's brother, there were three other Tawnians, each of them like their earlier captors—part man, part machine. They stood frozen, their gazes shifting from the weapon in Howlett's hand to what it had done to their conpanion. The shock was plain in their features.

With Howlett leading, the party moved down to join the Tawnians. Clive's gaze was riveted to his brother's features, searching each line for its familiarity. There could be no mistaking Neville. This was no replica. He had the stance, the cocky set of Neville's head, the amused look in his eye.

"Well, little brother," Neville said. "For once, you've arrived in time to rescue *me*."

Clive's ears still rang from the handgun's blast, but not so much as they had earlier. He could hear again—enough to know that the man standing before him even had Neville's sardonic manner of speech.

"Careful now," Smythe said softly at Clive's side.

Clive nodded. He would be careful.

"What?" Neville asked. "Nothing to say?"

Easy now, Clive told himself. Don't let him goad you.

Oddly enough, having finally caught up with his twin, he felt strangely let down. The anger that had been brewing inside him like a hot fire was gone. He felt curiously flat—devoid of emotion.

"Disarm them," he said.

His companions approached the Tawnians, careful to make sure that they never stepped between Howlett and the weapon he kept leveled at the three that were still alive. The Tawnians submitted to the search, but when Guafe approached Neville, Clive's twin stepped back, clapping a hand to the hilt of the saber buckled at his belt.

"I think not," he said.

Howlett's weapon moved to cover him, but Clive stepped in the way to face his brother.

"What was the name of Nanny's lapdog?" he asked.

"What?"

"You heard me."

"For God's sake, Clive. We don't have time for games."

"If you're truly my brother, you'll know the answer."

"Clive, *what* are you driving at?"

He doesn't know the answer, Clive thought. God help us, he's so much like Neville he could be his identical twin—more so than I.

"The game's up," Clive told him. "Whoever you are, or think you are, you are not Neville Folliot."

The replica took a few quick steps back, drawing his saber as he did so. But by the time he had it free of its scabbard, Clive's own blade was naked in his hand.

"Get out of the way," Howlett said.

He moved forward again, trying to get a clear shot, but Smythe pulled him back.

"All of you—keep out of this," Clive said, never taking his gaze from the replica's eyes.

Chapter 30

The Oracle gave a smile at Annabelle's question, thinlipped and humorless.

"THE REAL NEVILLE FOLLIOT?" it asked.

Ot, ot, ot. . . .

"THAT IS CHILD'S PLAY."

Play, play, play. . . .

"I EXPECTED BETTER of you."

You, you, you. . . .

As the Oracle arose slowly from its supine position, Annabelle and her companions stepped back from the stone slab once more. The babbling echoes that followed its voice rang back and forth in the room, growing in volume rather than fading. There was a ringing in their ears, and the surface of the floor seemed to tremble underfoot.

Sitting up on the slab, the Oracle towered over them. It lifted an enormous, corpse-pale arm and pointed to the nearest of the sarcophagi.

"THERE IS THE ONE YOU SEEK."

Seek, seek, seek. . . .

"A LORD'S FRESH MEAT."

Meat, meat, meat. . . .

The echoes rebounded until Annabelle had to put her hands over her ears. Lords of Thunder, she thought. They call them that because of their big mouths. But then the moment of black humor drained from her.

The lid of the sarcophagus that the Oracle had indicated was slowly opening, with a rumble of grinding stone. Standing upright inside it was a twin to the enormous shape of the Oracle—just as huge, its skin just as alabaster, its clothing a similar heavy metal punk cut. But the monster wasn't alone in its crypt. Hanging from it was a human figure, dangling from its chest like a marionette with its strings cut. From out of the Lord's mouth a number of tubes protruded that were attached to the man's back.

The Lord was feeding on him.

"N-Neville . . . ?" Annabelle asked, her voice breaking.

She wanted to throw up.

"A SMALL, MOVABLE FEAST," the Oracle said.

East, east, east. . . .

"BUT MY BROTHER FEEDS NOT NEARLY SO WELL AS I WILL."

Will, will, will. . . .

"FOUR CHOICE MORSELS."

Sels, sels, sels. . . .

The Oracle had stood up from its slab now, and was coming toward them. As she turned, staring up at its towering bulk, Annabelle realized how the game was set up. The Lords took turns playing the Oracle, feeding on the hapless victims when they couldn't come up with a decent question.

How in God's name were they supposed to deal with something this size?

Her daughter's features rose in her mind—that expectant look, hope and fear mingled in her eyes.

Are you coming back, mommy?

I promised, didn't I? I'll try, but Christ, Amanda. . . .

You won't forget me, will you?

No way. She was going to make it. They were all gonna make it. There wasn't a chance in hell that she was gonna let any of them end up godfood without going down fighting, first.

"Shriek!" she cried, and pointed toward the dais.

The arachnid pulled free a handful of hair spikes, whipping them at the Oracle in rapid succession, but they didn't slow the monster down at all. So she charged the Oracle, Sidi at her side, as Annabelle ran for the open sarcophagus. With Tomàs's help she pulled the limp form of Neville from the Lord's chest. The tubes made suckerlike popping sounds as they pulled free, leaving ugly, round red welts on Neville's pale skin. But he was still warm to the touch. Still alive.

They dragged him back, away from the sarcophagus. As they did, the Lord's eyes flickered open, the cold iron of its gaze fastening on them. For one long moment Annabelle froze in place.

"YOU DARE?" the monster roared.

Dare, dare, dare. . . .

Maybe she was crazy, Annabelle thought, but yeah, she dared.

She shook her head fiercely and fell back to dragging Neville beyond the monster's grip once more, a new strength fueling her. Tomàs hesitated at her side as the Lord swallowed its feeding tubes and then stepped forth.

On the dais, Shriek barreled into the Oracle, hitting one of its legs with her full weight and alien strength. The monster tottered, started to regain its balance, but then Sidi struck it across the back of the knee on the same leg. The leg gave out, and the two of them hopped out of the way as the creature came crashing down.

One arm batted out, striking Sidi a glancing blow that sent him skidding across the chamber's floor. Shriek lunged for its head, lower arms grabbing hold of its neck, upper ones aiming blows at its eyes. But no sooner had she grabbed hold of the monster than its huge hands gripped her, and feeding tubes came snaking out its mouth to attach themselves to Shriek's torso.

The alien cried out with shock at the pain.

Annabelle turned at the cry. She saw Shriek raining blows on the Oracle, but to no avail. It merely gripped her closer, more feeding tubes coming from its mouth to fasten onto her.

Oh, Jesus. She didn't know what to do—help Neville or Shriek?

There was really no choice. Shriek was her friend. All she knew about Neville was that he'd been leading her on a goose chase ever since she'd first joined up with his twin.

But as she started to drop Neville's arm, she saw Sidi gather himself up from where he'd fallen and charge the Oracle again. The fallen giant swept out his arm, but Sidi jumped nimbly above it and darted forward. He hammered the Oracle straight in its open eye with a fist.

The Oracle bellowed, and the floor literally shook underfoot. It made a grab for Sidi, but the little Indian slid past the Oracle's grasping fingers. He caught hold of two feeding tubes and ripped them from Shriek's back, continuing to pull on them until he had torn them from the Oracle's mouth. The Oracle's cry of pain was now a wet gurgle as blood bubbled up through its lips.

Annabelle concentrated on her own troubles then. She and Tomàs dragged Neville to the center of the room, but the Lord was out of its sarcophagus now and advancing upon them. Annabelle took a stance between Neville and the Lord.

What do I do?

Then she had it. They'd split up, she and Tomàs. Whoever the Lord went after, the other'd move in and try to take it down the way Sidi had, hitting it behind the knee.

She started to turn to Tomàs to tell him, but the Portuguese suddenly pushed her directly into the approaching giant's path and bolted for the elevator doors. Trying to regain her balance, she fell to the floor, using her arms to break her fall.

"You bastard!" Annabelle screamed at Tomàs.

She scrambled to her feet, the monster towering over her, and bolted to one side. The Lord dropped to its knees and swung a meaty fist in her direction. She tried to copy Sidi's move, but she didn't leap high enough, and the monster's arm swept her legs from under her. All that kept her from cracking her head on the floor was the fact that she fell backward, against the Lord's arm. It reached for her with its other hand.

On the dais, Sidi hauled on two more of the tubes, and by then, Shriek was recovered enough to lend her own strength to the task. The Oracle batted at them, but this time Shriek grabbed the large arm with all four hands. Muscles straining, she snapped the bones of his forearm in two.

At the elevator, Tomàs was hammering on the metal door. That sent up echoes that mixed with the general cacophony of the monsters' bellows, creating a kind of thunder that rang against the cathedral ceiling.

Annabelle dodged the Lord's hand. Using the arm she'd fallen on as though it were a pommel horse, she vaulted over it and took to her heels. But the leg she'd hurt previously buckled under her, and she wasn't quick enough to recover.

This time, the Lord's meaty fist ranged out and snagged her. It drew her toward it, the feeding tubes already snaking out of its mouth. Annabelle struggled in its grip, but it held her tight as a vise, its Fingers squeezing the strength out of her.

The first tube slapped against her neck, and the end attached to her skin with a wet, sucking sound.

On the dais, Shriek had a grip on the Oracle's other arm. As it tried to bat her with its head, Sidi launched himself forward, delivering a kick directly under its unhurt eye with such strength that it popped the eye from its socket.

The Oracle screamed. It tried to reach for its eye, but Shriek had too strong a grip on its arm now. She broke that one as well. As the Oracle collapsed on the floor, she and Sidi each grabbed it by an ear and smashed its head against the corner of the stone slab that it had first been lying on.

Once, twice, they battered it against the corner, and then the skull cracked. The Oracle began to convulse, and they both jumped free from the wild jerking of its limbs, running to Annabelle's aid.

Sidi grabbed the feeding tube attached to her neck and ripped it free. As more of the tubes came at the Indian, Shriek got a grip on the Lord's leg with all four arms and toppled him over. The monster fell on its back, Annabelle's weight on its chest. Without its hands free to break its fall, the back of the Lord's head hit the floor with a sharp cracking sound. And then it lay still.

Silence fell across the vast chamber.

Shriek pulled Annabelle free from the monster's chest and helped her stand.

"Oh Jesus, oh Jesus," Annabelle was muttering.

"Everything's fine now, Annabelle," Sidi said.

He stroked her hair as Shriek lowered her to the floor.

"Th-that thing . . . was sucking on me. . . ."

"It's dead now," Sidi told her. "That's all that matters."

Slowly, Annabelle sat up.

Dead.

She looked at the Lord lying stretched out on the floor, then up to the dais, where the Oracle now lay still as well.

They were really dead.

"Christ, we did it," she said.

Sidi nodded and gave her a weary smile. Annabelle's gaze traveled to the far side of the room, where Tomàs was standing very still now, his back against the elevator doors.

"You bastard," she told him. "I'm gonna rip your lungs out and. . . ."

But she didn't finish. Her heart wasn't in it. Scared as she'd been, she found it hard not to understand the Portuguese's panic. So he was a coward. Big deal. Well, so was she. She just hadn't been lucky enough to get free, that was all. And it wasn't like they hadn't already known that he was a weasel, the weasel.

I will kill Tomàs, Shriek said matter-of-factly. Her multiple eyes flashed dangerously as they gazed at him.

Annabelle shook her head. He wasn't worth it.

"No," she said. "Leave him alone."

Slowly, with Sidi's help, she got to her feet.

"What's the story with Neville?" she asked. "Is he still alive?"

Leaning on Sidi's shoulder, she hobbled over to where Clive's twin lay. When she knelt beside him and turned him over, she flinched. There were little round welts all over his skin.

"Jesus, what were they taking outta him, anyway?"

"His life force."

Annabelle started to feel sick all over again.

"I wonder how long they had him in there?"

She reached out a hand to touch Neville's pale cheek, and started when he stirred. His eyelid flickered, and suddenly he was looking a her—right at her—but it was obvious that he wasn't seeing her.

Weakly, he tried to push her away.

"It's okay," she said. "We killed the bugger that had you."

Slowly, his gaze focused on her.

"W-who are you . . . ?"

"Friends of your brother's."

"Clive? He . . . he's here?"

Ah, shit, Annabelle thought. So what do I tell him? We split up, and your brother's probably dead?

"Sort of," she said. "We kinda went our own way a few days ago. Listen, we need some information—like, what the hell's going on around here, anyway? What's with the journal? What's with the mind games you've been playing on our heads?"

"The journal? You found that?"

"Clive did," she said. "And lost it somewhere, and now I've got it. Which gives me the bad feeling that he's dead."

Neville shook his head slowly, wincing at the pain the movement caused him.

"Hey, take it easy," Annabelle told him.

"Clive . . . can't be dead. I would know if he . . . were. . . ."

Right. The bond between twins, and all that stuff. All wired up to a human vacuum cleaner that was sucking up his blood, he was really gonna have had time for that kind of thing.

"Right now," she said, "all we want to know is, how do we get outta this place?"

Neville closed his eyes and lay still.

"Don't fade on me now, Neville." She shook him lightly. "Neville? Damn! He checked out on us."

Sidi leaned closer. "Is he dead?" he asked.

Annabelle shook her head. "He might as well be, for all the good he's gonna do us, but naw, he's just passed out again." She looked from Sidi to Shriek. "So, what are we gonna do?"

At the sound of a step on the floor, she glanced over to see Tomàs nervously approaching them.

"I have been *muito estúpido*," he said. A weak, hopeful smile touched his lips. "I am . . . there was such a fear on me. . . ."

Annabelle nodded. "You panicked," she said. "Plain and simple. It happens."

"I don't see how you can be so forgiving," Sidi said.

He glared at the Portuguese. The look in his eyes was fierce, though not so fierce as Shriek's.

"We're all in this together," Annabelle said. "Don't ask me why I'm not pissed. I mean, I'm the one he left in the lurch, right? But I don't think he was being mean-minded. He just freaked, okay? Like I did when we stepped through that last gateway, and couldn't take the bridge. So let's just drop it."

"*Madre de Dios*," Tomàs said. "I will honor you forever. . . ."

Annabelle waved him quiet. "Give it a rest, would you? I already said it's okay. What we've gotta do now is stop farting around and. . . ."

Her voice trailed off as a rumbling sound filled the vast room. Knowing what she was going to see, not wanting to look, but unable to stop herself, she turned her gaze to the sarcophagi that lined two walls of the chamber. One by one the lids were sliding open to reveal more Lords of Thunder. At least twenty of them. Stirring. Eyes opening, cold gazes fixing on them.

"Oh, shit," Annabelle said.

Chapter 31

He would have satisfaction, Clive thought as he faced the replica of his twin. There had been enough—too much, by God—dilly-dallying about as they were led from one disaster into another, always following the nebulous trail of his brother Neville. He had a grudge to settle with both his twin and whoever was behind this Dungeon. And while the man who stood before him now might not be Neville, nor even one of those responsible for the rule of this damned place, he was still here, close at hand, and Clive meant to have that satisfaction from him.

The saber was a comfortable weight in his hand and he had no doubts as to his own skill with the blade—unfamiliar though this particular weapon might be to his hand. As for the replica, if he followed Neville's lead, he would be relying more on strength and daring in his swordplay than finesse. The latter had always been Clive's particular forte.

The replica looked across his blade at Clive. A sardonic smile touched the corner of his lips.

"What?" he said softly. "Taking up arms against your own brother?"

"You are not my brother," Clive said. "It's that simple."

"I say I am! You are wasting our time."

"On the contrary, it is you who wastes our time."

"You know nothing about this place."

"Exactly," Clive agreed. "Yet I do know that I want satisfaction, and I'll take it out of your hide."

"The Good Lord frowns on fratricide," the replica said.

Clive knew what he was trying to do. If the replica could keep even a bare rumor alive in Clive's mind that this was his own twin with which he would be dueling, that vague indecision would work against him. Not much, but enough to throw off his timing. And against the replica's superior strength, that could be crucial.

"I don't doubt that He also frowns on the replicas that men make of His own creations," Clive said.

"I am not a replica."

"Then answer my question."

"Your question insults me."

Clive shrugged. "Then, have at you!"

He stepped forward, left hand on his hip, blade licking out. The two sabers met with a clash of metal that rang in the hallway. Sparks leapt at the impact. Parrying and thrusting, Clive forced his opponent to back down the hall.

The replica met his every blow with the perfect parry, but such was the impetus of Clive's attack that it allowed the replica no opportunity to mount his own offensive. He was forced to retreat, continually kept on the defensive.

Clive's companions and the captive Tawnians were behind him, so that when he heard a sudden uproar to his rear, he was well-tempted to turn to see what was up, but he knew the replica was waiting for just such a foolish move. So he kept his gaze on his opponent, forcing him into the wider breadth of a joining of corridors. He flinched when he heard the thunderous boom of Howlett's handgun resounding through the hall, but he never turned.

God help them, Clive worried. Now what? But he had no time to think of it.

This crossroads of corridors had given them more room to maneuver, and now the replica took the lead, mounting his own offensive. He feinted, blade darting in toward Clive's left flank. As Clive brought his blade around to block the strike, the replica abruptly changed the line of his attack.

Clive was already committed to his defensive action. He brought his own blade up, enough to catch the main force of the replica's blow in a shower of sparks, but too late to stop his opponent's saber from nicking his shoulder.

"First blood!" the replica cried.

There was a moment's lull during which Clive conserved his energy and said not a word. The wound was nothing. It had missed the muscle, but it was bleeding. Left alone too long, it would weaken him. This had to be finished quickly.

He listened for sound from the corridor that he and his opponent had so recently quit, but the uproar had died down. There was no sound from his companions.

Had the Tawnians overcome them with another of their futuristic devices?

There was no time to turn, no time to think of anything but the battle at hand as the replica got his second wind and launched a new flurry of strikes. Now it was Clive who was put on the defensive, forced to retreat until his back was up against a wall. Their sabers met with a clang, the two blades locking, and suddenly the replica was pushing the false edge of Clive's own blade back against his face.

The replica had the superior strength—as Neville had always had.

"Weakening, little brother?" the replica asked.

"Damn you," Clive muttered as he strained to break the deadlock.

Through sheer force of will, he managed to put a halt to the replica's pressure. Sweat beaded both their brows. The replica's face was so close to Clive's that Clive could see every pore in replica's skin. The resemblance to Neville was frightening, it was that uncanny. It was as though he actually fought Neville—Neville, who invariably beat him, no matter what the game, except perhaps for chess.

But this wasn't chess now. No black and white pieces to be moved on the board. It wasn't a game—it was life or death. Clive could see that plainly in . . . the replica's—his brother's?—eyes.

Suddenly, the replica brought up his knee toward Clive's groin. A true swordsman's sixth sense had warned Clive, however, and he turned just enough to catch the blow on his thigh. Clive's anger at the low blow was enough to fuel him with the strength to slip free of the deadlock. He faced the replica, features flushed.

"Always the gentleman, are you?" he said, forgetting in the heat of the moment that it wasn't his brother that he fought here.

He saw only Neville standing there.

"There are no gentlemen in this place," the replica replied. "There is only winning or losing—nothing else."

The tone of his voice, the spirit of his words, was so like Neville that it left Clive thoroughly confused. God help him, what if this truly was Neville? Neville, who could be so stubborn that all you wanted to do was throttle him, and still he wouldn't change his mind. Neville, who—

The replica grinned at Clive's momentary lapse. He renewed his attack with a bewildering flurry of strokes. It was all Clive could do to parry them. But then he had an opening and he thrust. The point of his saber entered the replica's chest, directly above his heart.

The replica's eyes widened and he faltered. As he stumbled back against a wall, his body pulled free of Clive's blade. Blood flecked his lips. It oozed from the wound to spread across his shirt. Slowly he lowered his own weapon and lifted his left hand to touch the wound. He stared at the blood, then his gaze lifted to meet Clive's shocked features.

"I . . . I never thought you had it in you. . . ." the replica managed.

His saber fell from his hand and clanged to the floor. His head slumped forward and he slid to the ground. And then he was dead.

"My God!" Clive cried, dropping his own weapon. "Neville!"

He no longer knew true from false, replica from original. Not anymore. All he could see was that his brother lay here—dead by Clive's own hand.

"Neville," he said, his voice breaking.

He reached to touch the dead man's cheek, but suddenly Smythe was there at his side.

"Sah!" he cried. "We've no time."

Clive turned slowly to look at Smythe. "I killed my brother. . . .

Smythe shook his head. "You killed a replica of him. God knows, I'm hard put to tell the difference myself, but you saw the man, sah. He couldn't answer the simple question you put to him."

"Couldn't? Or wouldn't?"

For that would be very like Neville, Clive thought. Lord help him. How could he face their father now?

Smythe laid a hand on his shoulder. "We've no time for this, sah."

Clive gave him a blank look, the shock of his deed still just settling in. Neville dead. By his hand.

"Some more of the buggers attacked us while you were fighting," Smythe went on. "Howlett took out one and Guafe used their own stasis ray back on them, but one of them had time to fire a projectile weapon and kill Howlett."

"There's no end to the killing," Clive said dully.

"Not if we stay, there isn't."

Smythe hoisted Clive to his feet. He bent and retrieved Clive's saber, cleaning it on the replica's shirt and replacing it in Clive's scabbard. Picking up the replica's blade as well, he steered Clive toward the vehicle they had commandeered.

"There are more of the buggers coming," Smythe said. "We have to go now."

"But, Neville. . . ."

Finnbogg helped Smythe tug Clive up onto the back of the cart. Guafe was behind the wheel. As soon as the cyborg saw that they were all aboard, he started up the cart and they shot down the corridor.

"That wasn't Neville," Smythe told Clive.

"But how can we *know* that?"

"We'll find the real Neville," Smythe told him. "He's here, somewhere in this Dungeon, and we won't rest until we find him."

But Clive only shook his head. Somehow, it didn't matter. Replica or not, it was still as though he'd killed his own brother. They had had their differences, God knew, but surely he never meant Neville that much ill?

It was true that Neville had led them a merry chase through the various levels of the Dungeon, but Clive had always expected that when they finally caught up with his twin, there would be a reasonable explanation for it all. He'd be angry—who wouldn't?—but it would blow over, because they were still brothers, in the end. Twins. Surely to God that still stood for something?

But he'd killed that man wearing Neville's face so easily. And what if it *had* been Neville . . . ?

Lord, but his head hurt to think of it all.

Smythe left him sitting beside Finnbogg, the dwarf seeing to Clive's hurt shoulder, while the sergeant climbed into the seat beside Guafe.

"Do we have a destination in mind?" he asked.

"I assumed we would continue to this Oracle Chamber, as we had initially planned," the cyborg replied.

Smythe nodded. "That's logical enough. What do you think of what just happened?"

Guafe shot him a sidelong glance, the look in his metallic eyes unreadable. "What is there to think?"

"*Was* that Sir Neville?"

"I really wouldn't know," Guafe replied.

"We turn here," Smythe said as they came upon a distinctive mural that Merdor had described to them back in his office.

"I know that," Guafe replied. "Here," he added, passing over the stasis ray control device.

"What is this for?"

But then there was no need for the cyborg to explain as they rounded the corner, the cart taking it on only two wheels, and they were aimed straight for another group of Tawnians. Smythe thumbed the device's control and the Tawnians froze in place. Guafe slowed the cart down so that Smythe could lean forward and push the rigid bodies out of the way without having to plow through them.

"Handy little toy," Smythe remarked as they entered the last corridor before they would reach the elevator taking them down to the Oracle's Chamber.

"It is more than a toy," Guafe said, "but not by a great deal. Judging by its size, it can't hold enough of a charge to immobilize a truly large creature."

"Like the brontosaurs?"

Guafe nodded. "They would be entirely out of the question. Even something twice the size of a man—it would slow down more than completely immobilize."

"Then, let's pray we meet nothing larger than men."

"Prayer is only superstition," Guafe said.

Smythe shrugged. They had reached the elevator now. He got down from the cart and pushed the control button beside its closed doors. As the doors slid open, he hopped back into the cart, looking back at Clive as Guafe drove the cart inside.

"Feeling any better?" Smythe asked.

Clive nodded, but the haunted look in his eyes belied his response.

As the elevator took them down, Clive sat up straighter, preparing himself for the next disaster that the Dungeon had to throw at them.

Chapter 32

There were twenty-two sarcophagi in the chamber. One belonged to the slain Oracle, and it remained shut. The one from which they'd rescued Neville was also empty. That left twenty stone lids grating open. Twenty Lords of Thunder stepping out from their coffins, like the walking dead in a Romero flick.

We really don't need this shit, Annabelle thought.

"BLASPHEMERS!" one of the Lords bellowed.

Ers, ers, ers. . . .

Other Lords took up the cry, until the chamber rang with the thunder of their furious voices.

"FOR THIS YOU WILL DIE!"

Die, die, die. . . .

Oh? Annabelle thought. Like you were gonna let us go before?

Shriek ran to the slain Lord and ripped free the bandoleers around its chest. She swung the leather bands experimentally, getting a feel for them. With the sharp blades that were stitched to the leather, they would make a better weapon than her hair spikes, which had already proved ineffective.

"That's not gonna be enough!" Annabelle cried, having to shout as loud as she could to be heard over the thundering voices of the Lords.

"What else can we do?" Sidi asked.

He started for the dais to rip the Oracle's bandoleers free as well, but he was too late. Two Lords had already blocked the route. Their movement made the curtain behind the dais flutter, and Annabelle caught a glimpse of what looked like wood, before the curtain fell back to cover it.

An exit, maybe? A way out? Unfortunately, they weren't going to be able to try it, as there were now five of the Lords between the dais and themselves.

The small party retreated, Sidi and Annabelle dragging Neville's limp form with them, until they had their backs almost up against the elevator doors. There was nowhere else to go.

Tomàs, as though atoning for his earlier cowardice, took up a stance a few yards in front of Annabelle, so that the Lords would have to attack him first. Shriek swung her bandoleers, waiting for the nearest of the monsters to come in range. Sidi stood at Annabelle's side, hands clenched into fists beside either thigh.

"Well, kids," Annabelle said, swallowing dryly. "It's been real nice knowing you."

"Perhaps we can make a break for the dais," Sidi said.

"You saw it, too?" she asked. "What looked like a door?"

Sidi nodded. "Some of us might make it."

Not bloody likely, Annabelle thought. But what did they have to lose?

"Okay," she said. "You and Shriek take the right—Tomàs and I'll go left."

But then she heard the elevator doors open behind her.

"Take 'em!" she cried.

She turned to meet the new threat, then darted aside as one of the Tawnian golf carts came whipping out of the elevator. It took her a long, shocked moment to recognize the cart's riders, then she gave a whoop of delight.

"Hoo-ha! The cavalry's here. Go get 'em, boys!"

Smythe leaned forward, holding out one of the Tawnians' stasis devices. He aimed it in an arc, sweeping the room. The Lords came to abrupt halts, then slowly began to lurch forward again, moving as though they were a film in slow motion.

"I told you," Chang Guafe said to Smythe.

Annabelle could have kissed the cyborg, never mind his know-it-all attitude.

"Where is the gateway?" Smythe asked her.

"There's one in here?" she replied. When he nodded, she pointed to the dais. "Then, it's gotta be behind that curtain."

She and Sidi began to hoist Neville's body onto the cart. A very pale Clive was there, with Finnbogg to help them.

"Hey, Clive-o—how's it going?"

"Who is this?" he said as he pulled the limp body on board.

"Your brother. Who did you think? Errol Flynn?"

"He's not a replica?"

Annabelle nodded. "I get the picture. Naw, the Oracle says he's the real thing."

Clive touched the pale cheek of his twin. "Thank Christ."

"Will the rest of you get on?" Smythe shouted.

Annabelle, Tomàs, and Sidi climbed into the back. Shriek stood on the front of the cart, whirling the bandoleers as the slow-motion giants approached. By weaving back and forth through them, and thanks to the Lords' now-slowed reflexes, they reached the foot of the steps leading up the dais without anyone being hurt.

"Take the wheel," Guafe told Smythe. "You help me," he added to Shriek.

The Lords were turning, slowly, slowly, but approaching them all the same. While Smythe got the cart moving, Shriek and Guafe helped it climb the steps by pushing it along, literally lifting the vehicle at times. Annabelle jumped off at the top and ran for the curtain, ripping it aside.

There was a door there, big enough to take the cart. But the door had a padlock on it. Shriek and Guafe each took a side of the large shackle and tore it apart. They pushed open the door to reveal another corridor, ceiling lit and running off into the distance.

"Okay, kids," Annabelle cried. "Let's go for it!"

Smythe drove the cart through. Shriek and Guafe pulled the immense door closed behind them. A cross-beam lay to one side of the corridor, and they hoisted it up, fitting it into place to bar the door from their side. They heard the slow hammer of the Lords' fists on the wood, but the door held.

"I don't believe it," Annabelle said, leaning back against the side of the cart's bed. "It's like a miracle. Not only did we all survive, but we're back together again."

"This is really my brother?" Clive said.

Annabelle nodded. She gave Smythe a questioning look. Clive looked right out of it, as far as she was concerned.

"Major Clive fought an exact replica of Sir Neville," Smythe said. "Fought and killed him. It was an . . . unsettling experience."

"I guess," Annabelle said. "I'm not feeling so settled myself."

She turned to Sidi and put her arms around him, hugging him close.

"I can't believe we made it," she said.

Sidi stroked her hair. "Only this far, Annabelle."

"Sure. Rain on my parade."

She felt a weird tension in the air then, and looked over to find Clive watching her with a pained expression. Right, she thought. Fraternizing with the hired help, and a native, to boot.

"Don't you even thinking of saying anything," she told him, holding Sidi closer.

Chapter 33

With all that they had just gone through—their escape, killing Neville's replica, the monstrous Lords, finding Neville—Clive's mental state was in an uproar. Seeing Annabelle embracing the Indian was just too much.

"Annabelle—" he began, but Smythe gripped his shoulder, stopping him.

It was his hurt shoulder. The pain cut through him like a piercing fire. He turned, struck numb at this further betrayal, but Smythe was already letting go of his shoulder.

"Good Lord," Smythe said. "I forgot your wound, sah."

"Damn my wound. I—"

Smythe shook his head before Clive could continue. "Be happy they're safe," he said, "and that we're all together again. Companions in a bad situation, it's true, but together."

Finnbogg nodded. "We have found your brother, if not mine," he said. "Now we have a chance to escape. Together."

Clive frowned. "But. . . ."

"What they're saying, Clive-o," Annabelle told him, "is it's none of your business what I do or anybody else does, just so long as it doesn't screw up the party's chances as a whole."

"Fighting each other is *estúpido*," Tomàs agreed.

Slowly, the red flush left Clive's features. "You're correct," he said finally. "It's none of my business."

"Besides, it's not what you think," Annabelle said.

Clive touched his brother's brow and stroked the pale skin. For all his weakend state, Neville had never looked better, so far as Clive was concerned. He looked around at his companions, letting their presence sink like a balm through his troubled heart.

"I'm sorry," he said. "Truly I am."

Annabelle disengaged her arm from around Sidi's waist and leaned forward to give Clive a kiss. "Good seeing you again, ancestor."

"It's good to see you again as well . . . all of you."

Annabelle reached out and scratched Finnbogg's head. "Even you, Finn."

"Annie not mad at Finnbogg anymore?"

"Annie not mad," she said with a sigh. "I couldn't give up a friend like you. I'm too glad to see you again."

Annabelle settled back in her seat. "All right. So let's get this show on the road. We've got places to go, people to meet, stories to tell, like—" she drew Neville's journal from the inner pocket for her jacket and handed it to Clive "—what this was doing waiting for us in Tawn."

"How did you get this?"

"Better yet, how did *you* lose it?"

As Guafe got the cart moving once more, they began to exchange their tales. It was crowded on the back of the vehicle, but with Guafe, Smythe, and Tomàs squeezed into the front, there was room for everyone.

The corridor led them on. They left behind the thunder of the Lords, still hammering on the door, and all the dangers they'd survived so far. Ahead waited the next level of the Dungeon and, when Neville woke again, finally some answers. There would be more trials, of that they were all sure, but they would at least be together to face them.

For now, that was enough.

Selections

From the Sketchbook of Major Clive Folliot

The following drawings are from Major Clive Folliot's private sketchbook, which was mysteriously left on the doorstep of *The London Illustrated Recorder and Dispatch,* the newspaper that provided financing for his expedition. There was no explanation accompanying the parcel, save for an enigmatic inscription in the hand of Major Folliot himself.

Our travels have led us through yet another level of the mysterious Dungeon. As our party temporarily split, I have recorded these images from memory and from Annabelle's recollections. How strange these images must appear to you, if you see them at all!

Now Annabelle's and my party have been reunited, and my brother has been found. May we escape this prison with godspeed and return to England alive!

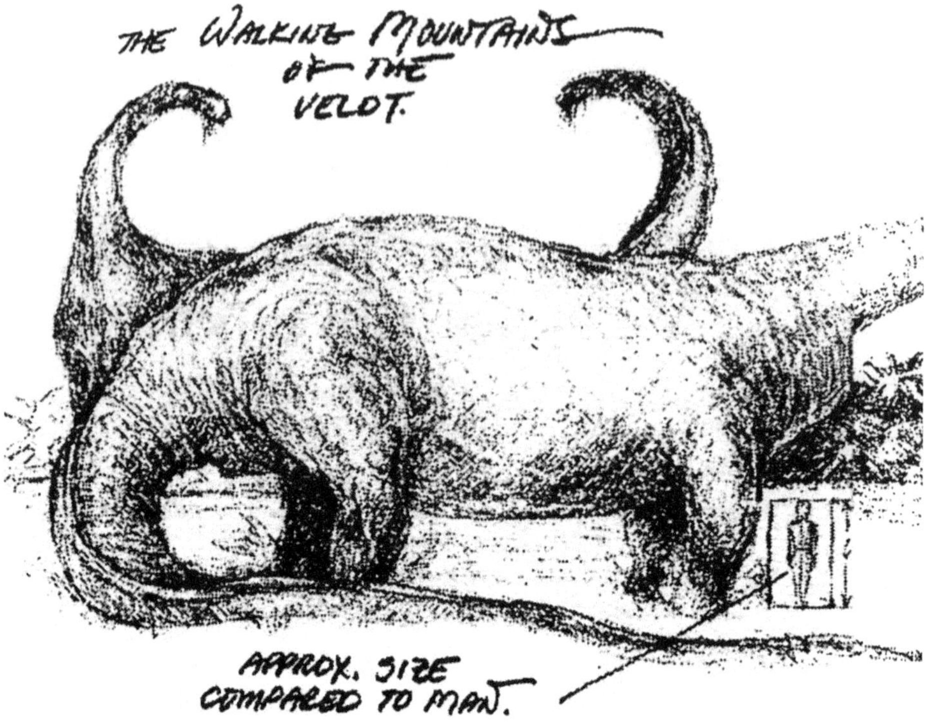

THE WALKING MOUNTAINS OF THE VELOT.

APPROX. SIZE COMPARED TO MAN.

THE RUINED CITY of DRAMARAN.

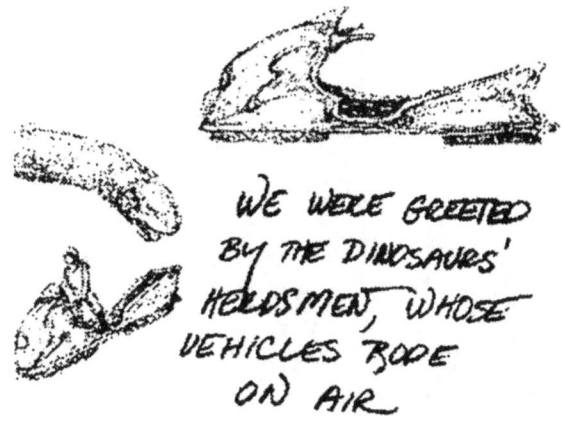

WE WERE GREETED
BY THE DINOSAURS'
HERDSMEN, WHOSE
VEHICLES RODE
ON AIR

KEOTI VECHLO —
FIRST SCOUT OF
THE DRAMARANIAN
DYNASTY AND OUR
WORTHY GUIDE.

FROM LIFE.

(FROM ANNABELLE'S DISCRIPTIONS)

A LANDSHARK PRIEST
BEARING THE SKULLS
OF THE ROGHA,
THE APE-PEOPLE.

LUKE DREW, THE NEWFOUNDLANDER, WHOM ANNABELLE'S PARTY ENCOUNTERED IN THE TREETOPS OF THE ROGHA.

REENA — FETISH CHIEF OF THE ROGHA, WARNS ANNABELLE OF HER FATE IN THE DUNGEON.

CAVE CREATURES WE BATTLED AND SLAUGHTERED BY THE THOUSANDS IN THE MAZE BELOW DRAMARAN.

'AS RECOUNTED BY ANNABELLE)
THE VILLAGE OF
QUAN AND THE GLOWING
STANDING
STONE.

THIS STONE
PROVED TO BE YET
ANOTHER
GATEWAY.

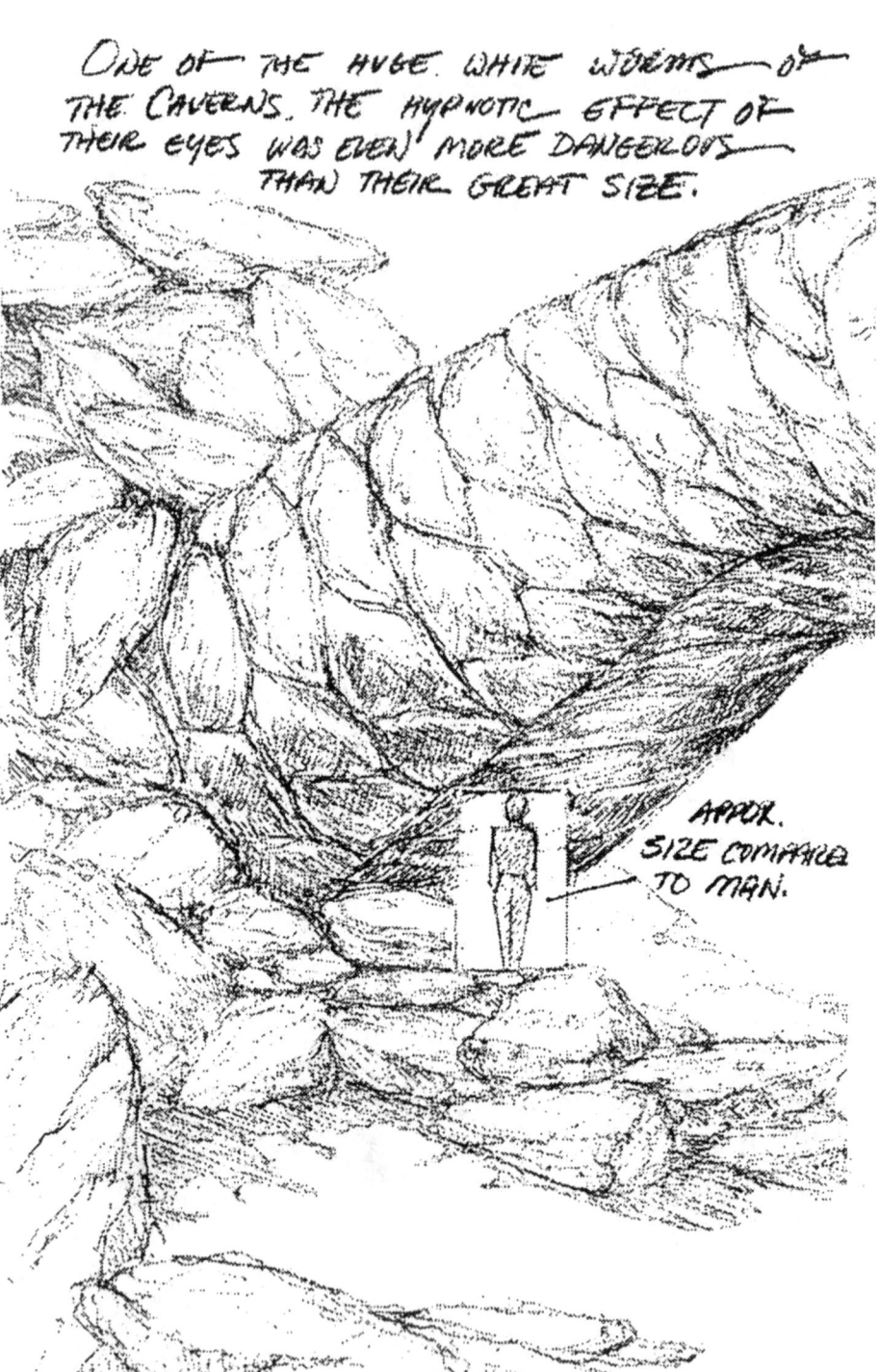

ONE OF THE HUGE WHITE WORMS OF THE CAVERNS. THE HYPNOTIC EFFECT OF THEIR EYES WAS EVEN MORE DANGEROUS THAN THEIR GREAT SIZE.

APPOX. SIZE COMPARED TO MAN.

BINRO —
THE CYBORG/BOY
WHO LED ANNABELLE'S
PARTY INTO TOWN.

(FROM ANNABELLE)

THE ORACLE ON
A SARCOPHAGUS.
NOTE THE PIERCED FLESH!

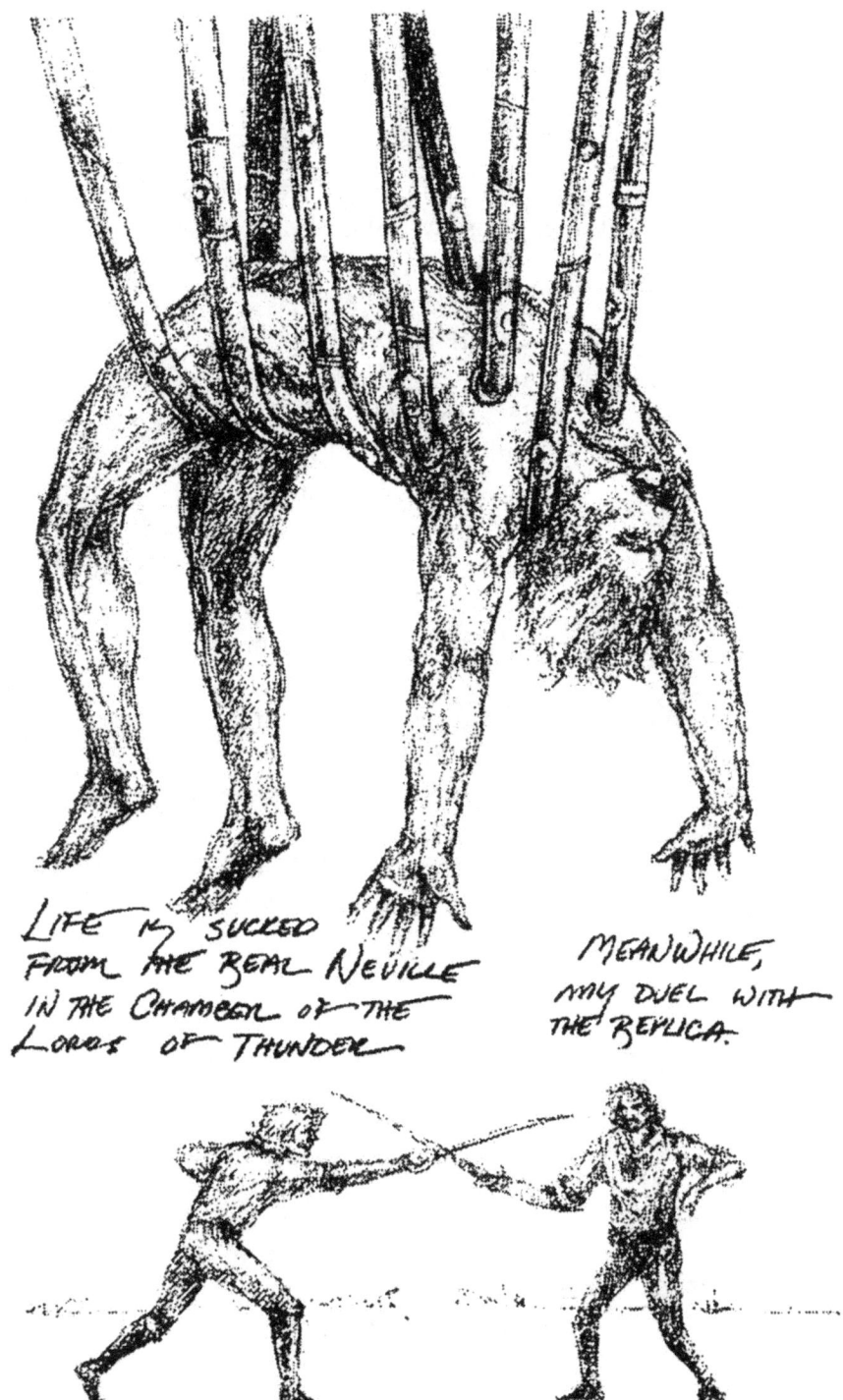

LIFE IS SUCKED FROM THE REAL NEVILLE IN THE CHAMBER OF THE LORDS OF THUNDER

MEANWHILE, MY DUEL WITH THE REPLICA.

For sales, editorial information, subsidiary rights information
or a catalog, please write or phone or e-mail

iBooks
Manhanset House
Dering Harbor, New York 11965-0342
Sales: 1-800-68-BRICK
Tel: 212-427-7139
www.ibooksinc.com
bricktower@aol.com

www.IngramContent.com

For sales in the UK and Europe please contact our distributor,
Gazelle Book Services
Falcon House, Queens Square
Lancaster, LA1 1RN, UK
Tel: (01524) 68765 Fax: (01524) 63232
stef@gazellebooks.co.uk

www.ingramcontent.com/pod-product-compliance
Lightning Source LLC
Chambersburg PA
CBHW071827020726
47502CB00004B/1268